JUST THE TIPSY

AUDREY VAUGHN

Copyright © 2025 by Audrey Vaughn

All rights reserved.

No part of this publication may be reproduced, distributed, or transmitted in any form or by any means, including photocopying, recording, or other electronic or mechanical methods, without the prior written permission of the publisher, except as permitted by U.S. copyright law. For permission requests, contact audrey@audreyvaughnbooks.com

The story, all names, characters, and incidents portrayed in this production are fictitious. No identification with actual persons (living or deceased), places, buildings, and products is intended or should be inferred.

Book Cover by Mayhem Cover Creations

❋ Created with Vellum

CONTENT WARNING

This book is a lighthearted read, but it does contain some discussion of body image and body size. Please feel free to skip this book if you'd prefer to avoid those topics entirely.

ONE
BIANCA

"YOU CAN ALWAYS STAY with us, sweetie. Anytime," Mom says. Her smooth, alto voice fills my car and tugs at my heart. "You don't have to go all the way over to some random town to get away."

"I know." I swallow and pause as the GPS tells me to pull off the interstate. "But I'll be fine."

Mom doesn't speak for a few beats, letting my doubts creep in.

Yeah, fleeing from LA to Jepsen, Tennessee, a town I've never been to, is easily the most impulsive thing I've ever done. But things just happened to click into place — I needed somewhere to lay low after my relationship very publicly exploded. My great aunt passed away and left her house in Jepsen (and dog) to me.

Have I seen this house? In a shitty picture, yeah. Have I ever had a dog (or even a pet in general)? No. But if I had to choose between staying in a random small town for a little while and staying in LA to be harassed by my shitty ex, his legion of fans, and the press, I'm choosing the former.

Even if I'm doing something like this completely on my own for the first time. Or anything big on my own, really.

"Why not go to New York to stay with Kaitlyn?" Mom asks. "You two are already working on the spa, aren't you?"

"I know, but New York would probably be as bad as LA. Plus she and her husband just got married so I don't want to crash," I say. "And we can work on the spa over Zoom. It's not a big deal."

Mom lets out a sound of acknowledgment and I brace myself for her opinions on the spa my best friend and I are working on opening. It'll finally get me out of modeling and being an "influencer," but the fact that I turned down my parents' help with it is killing them.

Thankfully her opinions don't come. Not that she'd have anything new to say.

My GPS tells me to make another turn down a long, tree-lined road. At least it's pretty.

"I'll let you drive since it sounds like you're getting close," Mom says with a sigh. "But just let me know, okay? You can always move home since it's nice and private. Our security system is top notch."

"Thanks, Mom." My dad wouldn't allow anything less. Just because he's behind the scenes and Mom's music career peaked twenty years ago doesn't mean he's not protective. "Love you."

"Love you too."

She hangs up and I come to a stop at a light. I'm about ten minutes away from Jepsen and there's *nothing* out here besides a bunch of trees and fields. A gas station with a Burger King attached doesn't count. At least there's a sign saying that there's stuff out there in the direction I need to go and not just more trees.

I turn toward Jepsen, my stomach twisting in knots. My great aunt Gloria and I weren't particularly close and I hadn't seen her in person since I was a teenager, so I have no idea what to even expect. She lived there for years and years, but what if I'm the only Black (or even brown) person there now that she's passed? I've never had to deal with that before.

I've been the only or one of the few Black people in a space a lot throughout my life — my private schools, an alarming number of runway shows — but there's that and then there's a whole town.

With two more turns, the landscape starts to change. A few subdivisions of cookie-cutter brick houses appear, then a few buildings. Finally, I reach downtown (or what I assume to be downtown) Jepsen. It's cute, at least — not a suburban hellscape of strip malls like some of the spots I drove through on the way from the airport. The businesses and buildings have character, like they've been around for decades and lovingly kept up.

I turn again toward the veterinary clinic, my hands sweating all over again. All I know about the dog I also inherited is that her name is Sadie and she's been living with the veterinarian since my great aunt passed. I like dogs and all, but how do you care for one?

The veterinary clinic is in a standalone building somewhat close to downtown. Another building is under construction next to it with a big sign that says *Future Home of Jepsen Animal Shelter* with the logos of several businesses that are sponsoring the shelter underneath. The most prominent one is for Stryker Liquors. I'm supposed to be meeting with a Dr. Stryker. He's probably related, right? Who knows how these towns work.

I park in the small front lot and head inside.

Right when I step in, I'm greeted by a young Latina woman wearing scrubs, her hair tied back in a bouncy ponytail. A tiny bit of tension leaves my body — at least I'm not the only brown person in a fifty mile radius. Her name tag says *Marisol* with a cute dog sticker next to it.

"Hey there! How can I help you?" she asks with a big smile.

"I'm here to pick up a dog. Sadie? She's been living with Dr. Stryker, but he knows I'm coming today," I say.

Marisol's vibe shifts to something more reserved. Shit. Either this Dr. Stryker is such an asshole that just bringing him up kills her mood or I accidentally bitchfaced her. Probably the latter, but I genuinely can't help it. My face is just like this. It worked for modeling — I just had to have my normal expression going down the runway and people ate it up. But in a small Southern town I doubt it'll win me any favors.

"Okay, great! I'll let him know you're here — he's just finishing up with a patient now," Marisol says. "You can have a seat."

I sit down on one of the few chairs in the waiting room, across from an older woman with a black and white cat in a carrier, along with a small dog wearing a vest that says, "Shy and nervous! Do not pet!"

Honestly, same. Do they make the vest in human sizes, too?

A middle-aged man who looks to be waiting for his pet adjacent to where she's sitting smiles at me, catching my attention. I blink back at him.

"Are you Miss Gloria's niece?" the man asks.

"Yes?" I raise an eyebrow.

"Ah, I thought so." His smile stays on his face. "I knew Dr. Stryker was caring for her dog after she passed away, but I didn't realize her family had come into town. Sorry for your loss. She was a sweet lady. We always saw each other around town."

"Thank you."

This town must be really small for this guy to know all of that. The guilt of only keeping in touch with her on the phone around Christmas or her birthday starts creeping in again. This stranger probably knows more about her than I do.

"Her dog is a good dog too," he says. "Very sweet. Used to be with Gloria all the time."

I just nod. I forgot how to have small talk like a normal person. It's not like people in LA or any of the other cities I regularly go to are itching to talk. In New York if a stranger started talking to me, I'd assume the worst.

But this man seems like he genuinely cares.

A few moments later, a warm, masculine laugh floats from the hallway, followed by the sound of a dog scrambling on the tile floor. Eventually a dog with a cone around his neck appears first, followed by the man who laughed.

As cute as the dog is, my eyes go straight to the man. He's tall and broad-shouldered, with a thick muscular build. The kind of body that's naturally strong-looking. His dark hair is slightly curly, falling into his forehead.

I've seen a lot of hot men, to the point where I'm desensitized to them. But this man is breaking right through and hitting a nerve I didn't know was exposed.

The man who was sitting without a pet hops up and reaches out for the dog, who can't decide whether to pay attention to the man or her owner.

"She did really well," the man in scrubs says, squatting down to the dog's level. The dog tries to lick his face, but she can't reach with the cone.

He scratches the dog's backside as he gives the owner instructions, getting whipped with her tail. If I were a dog, I'd be wary of a nurse or a vet, but this dog seems to love him. He gives the dog a few more pets before the dog and owner head out.

He finally notices me gawking at him and blinks, like he's a little stunned. My whole body heats up like I've never made a man stop and stare at me. Then again, I usually don't feel just as stunned looking back at the man, though.

"Hi, are you Bianca?" he asks. I nod and he gives me a polite smile, his cheeks flushed. "I'm Waylon — Dr. Stryker. I'm guessing you're here for Sadie."

"Yeah, hi." I stand up. He's a lot younger than I expected, maybe four or five years older than me.

"Great — let me run to the back and get her. Then we can chat about her care."

He disappears, then soon rounds the corner with a small, fluffy dog in his hands and some papers under his arm.

"Let's go in here," he says, nodding to an empty exam room.

He lets me go first, then steps inside and shuts the door. Being in this small room with him makes me realize just how tall he is. I'm 5'11" and he's several inches taller than me — maybe 6'4" or 6'5".

I never feel self-conscious around men, unless they're responsible for booking me for a show or a campaign, but now I'm way too aware of everything about myself. Especially my expression. If I plaster on a smile, I look like I want to commit murder. But if I default to my regular expression, he'll probably think I hate him for no reason.

Usually I don't particularly care if men like me, but with him, I do.

"This is Sadie," Waylon says, putting her on the table.

Sadie is adorable — a Pomeranian, with cute little fox-like features. Her tawny brown fur is trimmed a little shorter than what I've seen Pomeranians with in the past.

My hands start to sweat for literally no reason. What is Sadie going to do? Bite me for fun? I put a finger out and she eagerly sniffs it, her tail wagging.

"Hi, Sadie," I say, petting her between her ears. Waylon pets her too.

"She's an easy dog," he says. "Really friendly and likes other dogs. You can pretty much bring her wherever you want, as long as she's allowed. I have all her stuff in my trunk."

Sadie turns and I notice her butt is pretty hairless, stopping a little way up her tail and halfway down her legs. "Is she okay? She's missing fur here."

"Yep, she's all good. It's something that happens to a lot of Pomeranians — alopecia X. It doesn't hurt her and it doesn't itch," he says.

"Oh, good," I say, looking at his big hands. He handles her so gently. "It's like she's wearing those things. The cowboy pants?"

I can't believe this man has me forgetting words just because he has sexy hands.

"Chaps," he says with a smile.

"Right, yeah." My face starts to heat up. He has a little dimple in his cheek that's charming me way too much.

"We just have to take care of her skin to make sure it doesn't get too dry and maintain her grooming. Which is where all this comes in." He puts down the folder he had under his arm, which I now see is a bound booklet. "Here's a guide to Sadie that I put together. It's half stuff we give to new dog owners and half stuff I figured out about her in the time she lived with me."

I thumb through it. The first few pages are print-outs and flyers about general dog care, stuff I really need to know. Then it gets into typed notes specific to Sadie — her favorite toys, her favorite people foods (within reason — she loves apples and peanut butter, apparently), where she likes to sleep (literally everywhere). There are even little notes in a neat, masculine hand, like he thought of extra things and just had to add them.

I'm almost annoyed. There's no way a guy is this thoughtful and nice deep down. Unless this town is really a Hallmark movie come to life.

He's probably married anyway, even though he's not wearing a ring. He gives off married guy energy. Married to a wife who can bake without burning the house down, with a bunch of cute dogs and cats. They probably dress up in coordinated Christmas pajamas for an annual photo.

"This is really helpful, thanks," I say, closing the booklet. "I don't know much about raising a dog."

"Yeah, the estate lawyer mentioned you hadn't." He gently rubs Sadie's forehead with one finger and she closes her eyes. "But if you had to choose a dog for your first one, she'd be perfect. I've really enjoyed having her live with me for the past few weeks."

Sadie looks up at me, sniffing my stomach and hands. Her tail hasn't stopped wagging the whole time she's been in here.

"And if you have any questions, we're neighbors," he adds. "My yard backs up to yours. And Sadie likes to play with my dog Duke and my brother's dog, Murphy."

"You live with your brother?" So he's probably not married? Why do I even care? I need to pull myself together before I even think of dating. I have a whole bag filled with sex toys to keep me satisfied. I had to lean on them even when I was in a relationship, at least after my ex fell asleep.

"Yeah, it's a duplex. I'm on one side and he lives on the other with his fiancé," Waylon says.

I just nod. So, no wife. Okay, I really shouldn't care if he's married or not. Men are off the table. Even though my relationship with Kyler was fizzling before it imploded, I need some time to figure myself out.

Then again, what's wrong with a little bit of fantasizing? I really don't know why he's doing it for me so much, but he's a nice change from all the guys I've dated in the past.

"Let me walk you through a few specifics since there's a lot there," Waylon says.

He walks me through a few specifics of Sadie's care, like her grooming and her walk schedule. Eventually he has to move on to the next patients and he brings me outside to put Sadie's things in my car.

I parked next to his dark blue SUV, and he pops the trunk. It's full of luggage, which he transfers into my car, squeezing it next to my bags.

"So that's it." He runs a hand through his hair. His biceps are ridiculously impressive, even with that small movement. "You can call or text me whenever you want. Or whenever you need, I mean."

His cheeks flush pink, which makes stupid butterflies appear in my stomach. Can this man stop being so appealing?

"Sounds good." I pet Sadie's side.

"She'll have her booster shots next month, by the way. The office will give you a call to schedule it," he says.

"She'll be there with her assless chaps on," I say with a smile, gently squeezing his bicep as I pass by him to get to my car door.

Oh my *god,* what does that even mean? Even saying, "she'll be there with bells on" would be goofy enough. But I had to go and make a stupid joke? Fucking kill me. I've always been the one pursued versus the pursuer, but I'm not *this* awful at flirting.

This man needs to be stopped. No man has ever scrambled my brain like this before just by having great biceps. Is he bench pressing St. Bernards in between patients? Then again, looking at him and his slightly dazed expression, I've gotten to him too.

"Chaps," Waylon says.

"Sorry?"

"They're just chaps." Waylon's face gets more and more

pink, like he wishes he could stop talking. "Chaps are already assless by default since people usually wear them with pants. So it's just chaps. I don't...know why I felt the need to say that."

"Oh."

The silence between us could not be more deafening. It's like we're in one of those rooms that absorbs all sounds and drives the people inside insane because all they can hear is their blood coursing through their veins.

I think both of us want to die. Why can't the universe have mercy and take a swipe at both of us?

"Uh, gotta go," Waylon says. "Bye."

"Bye."

I get Sadie buckled into her car harness and hop into the driver's seat, taking a deep breath to try to diffuse the unpleasant embarrassment rushing through my veins. Once I pull it together, I put the address for the house into my GPS.

The house isn't too far from town, which is nice, and all of the houses are somewhat far apart, but not so far that I'd feel too isolated. The front yard is huge and overgrown, with some out of control plants along the front porch of the house. All in all, it's cuter than I thought it would be. I can see Waylon's house behind it too, a bit closer than my neighbors on the left and right.

Once I park in the driveway, I hop out of the car and grab Sadie so we can go inside. Now that I'm up close, I can see that the house isn't in great shape. The steps up to the front porch creak and a lot of planks are out of place. Inside isn't much better — it's clean, but it's clear that it's been a while since anyone's fixed anything or updated it.

Well, shit. My first thought was to lay low here for a bit, then sell it, but how can I sell a house that's falling apart?

I put Sadie down and sigh. I guess I have a lot of time to figure it out.

TWO
WAYLON

I MANSPLAINED CHAPS.

I mansplained chaps to the most beautiful woman I've ever seen.

I want to walk behind the clinic, into the woods, die of embarrassment there, and let nature reclaim my body, but I have work to do.

The only thing that can distract me from my embarrassing unforced error is my mom coming in with one of the dogs for a checkup. Only it's not a fun distraction because I have a gut feeling on how this visit is going to go, and I don't like it.

One of my family's dogs, Lady, almost tackles me the moment I walk into the exam room. I can't help but grin. My family has had Labrador retrievers my entire life, and the breed is even the mascot of our family's bourbon brand, Big Bubba Bourbon. I'll always have a soft spot for them, and for Lady.

"Hey, pretty girl," I coo, kneeling down and scratching

all of her favorite spots. She goes nuts, tail whipping back and forth as she tries to give me kisses. My mom clears her throat. "Hey, Mom."

"Hi, honey." My mom is dressed in tailored pants and a blouse. She probably had a meeting with the board of the new animal shelter next door, which Stryker Liquors is donating heavily to. "How are you?"

"Not bad." I sit cross-legged on the ground, as I usually do with larger dogs, and she puts her nose into my neck. "How are you?"

"Good. There's just so much planning with Wes and Rose's engagement and the wedding and the family reunion and the last touches on the shelter." Mom sighs, her high-heel clicking on the floor. I know that sigh — it's asking for me to ask about it.

My twin brother, Wes, just proposed to his girlfriend Rose about a week ago, and it's been the best thing to happen to Mom in years. They've already chosen a date only three and a half months from now since the venue they like has a last-minute opening. Wes is the first one of the four of her sons — me, Wes, Ash, and John David — to get married, which has been her dream since we were all old enough to get into serious relationships.

She always assumed I'd be the first one. I did too. Now an engagement (and relationships in general, to be honest) are the last thing I want.

"Have you been giving Lady her vitamins?" I ask, running my hands down Lady's sides to check for any weird lumps or bumps. "Her fur is looking good."

"Mmhm." Mom examines her nails. "A lot of these events will require a date."

Here we go. In record time, too. I peek inside Lady's ears. Healthy but a little dirty, but she's always hated having them touched. She shakes her head after I peek inside each one.

"Will they?" I ask. Wes and Rose have barely been engaged long enough to have many serious plans, but I guarantee they won't have a stuffy wedding where everyone needs a plus one.

Nope, that's all Mom. I'm sure Rose and Wes could talk her out of it, but I don't put it past Mom to pretend that a plus-one rule exists.

"I'd say so." Mom shrugs and tucks some of her dark hair behind her ear. "Wouldn't you want to bring someone special?"

"Mom." If today were less of a mess, I'd have more patience. But the fact that she's already going down this road within three minutes is pushing me to the end of my rope. "Please. Can we just have Lady's appointment and move on? And not talk about my dating life?"

"I'm just saying! It's top of mind." Mom shrugs, as if we haven't had this very same discussion countless times. "And it's been almost two years, sweetheart."

The way Mom's voice softens when she talks about how long it's been since I've dated makes me a tiny bit guilty for just a second. A very, very brief second.

Yes, it's been a year and a half since my short-lived engagement imploded, but I don't think there's enough time for me to want to date again. To be honest, Catherine was my only serious relationship and we've known each other since fourth grade. We didn't start dating until college.

Then our relationship fell apart the first time by senior

year because she wanted to "explore and experiment." Five years passed and I took her back because I thought that she'd actually changed.

Yeah, she didn't change.

But despite knowing that, Mom doesn't get why I don't want to get married and pop out a bunch of kids right this second. In her eyes, I'm young, fairly good-looking, and have a good career — I should have my pick of all the women in town, who she frequently sets me up on horribly awkward dates with.

And to her, me dating someone would push me up to the level of perfection she's always driven me to. The level that until somewhat recently, I've always hit.

I think the only way I'd be free of this issue is if I start dating someone. And since she won't let it go…

Maybe I can wait it out. But Mom is relentless. It's almost admirable.

I turn my attention to Lady again, checking her eyes and hips for any issues.

"Lady looks great," I say instead of addressing what Mom said. "But her weight is a little bit high. As long as you get her more exercise and avoid people food, we should be able to get it under control before it affects her hips."

"She doesn't eat that much people food." Mom looks offended for a second, but I stare at her. "Okay, fine, she's been having a lot of pup cups lately."

When she says pup cups, Lady whips around like she's looking for one, hitting me in the face with her wagging tail. I raise an eyebrow at Mom.

"I know, I know. I'll lay off them." Mom sighs, tapping around on her phone.

"Good. Let me give her her boosters, then you'll be good to go." I hop up and grab the tray of shots that the vet tech brought in for me before I came in.

Lady knows and trusts me, so she stays still while I give her shots. I dispose of the needles and stand up.

"By the way," Mom says as she stands. "Do you remember my friend Michelle? Her daughter—"

"No," I say before she can even finish her sentence.

"You haven't even seen her!" Mom shows me her phone. "She's pretty."

She's okay, but Bianca pops into my head. I don't think any woman is going to hold a candle to her.

Her perfect features. Her soft-looking tawny brown skin. Her tall frame with just the right amount of curves to it.

Sure, she gave off an icy vibe, but first appearances aren't everything. She might just be shy.

I'm not sure how much we'll see each other as neighbors, but I want to see more of her. From a distance, because I don't think I can ever speak to her again without wanting to die.

My face heats again. I have no idea what happened. I was doing just fine the whole time even though looking at her perfect, gorgeous face was making my heart practically vibrate in my chest. Having some things to say — things I'm confident in — helped me.

But then she touched my arm. And my brain short-circuited.

A touch to my damn *arm*. If she touched me anywhere else, I don't know what would happen.

"She's fine, but I'm not interested." I clip on Lady's leash and open the door. Yeah, I'm being a bit rude, but I'm exhausted. "Marisol will check you out."

"Maybe y'all can meet each other," Mom says, like I didn't speak at all. She takes Lady's leash. "She's invited to Wes and Rose's engagement party."

"When is that again?" I ask.

"In two weeks," Mom says, exasperated that I didn't remember this completely unnecessary event. Do Rose and Wes even want this? "Check the family Google calendar."

"Okay, fine." I sigh and run my hand through my hair. "See you then."

"See you then." She gives me a kiss on the cheek.

I'm really happy for Wes and Rose. I really am. Especially because they've been into each other for a long time, not that they admitted it until a year and a half ago. But him getting engaged has thrown gasoline on the fire of Mom trying to get me to date.

I head into the back again, feeling like I just finished an hour-long surgery rather than a fifteen minute booster shot appointment.

OVER THE NEXT week and a half, the engagement party grows from a thing that I forgot was on my calendar to something I can't escape. Our family text chain is all about it — the food, the guests, the music — and for whatever reason, Mom needs all of our opinions.

The guest list that seems to include every single person in a ten-mile radius of Jepsen. If the engagement party is this draining, then I don't even want to think about the wedding.

Two days before the event, I get home a bit early and hear my dog, Duke, and Wes's dog, Murphy, playing in the backyard. By the time I've changed out of my scrubs and showered, both dogs are tuckered out, stretched out on the grass gnawing on opposite ends of a stick. Wes is sitting on the back patio, legs stretched out in front of him.

"Wow, you're home early," Wes says, checking the time on his phone.

"For once." I sit down in the seat next to him and sigh. "Thanks for letting Duke out."

"No problem."

Duke realizes I'm here and hops up, trotting up the stairs to greet me. He puts his paws in my lap so I can pull his front legs up on my shoulders. I rub his back and let him snuffle my neck for a bit, like we're hugging. I'm not sure when we started doing this, but getting a hug from him every day, especially after a long day, is just as comforting for me as it is for him.

"Work's busy?" Wes asks.

"Yeah." I say, letting Duke back down. "I haven't even gone to trivia."

"Damn, no trivia?" Wes raises an eyebrow. My best friends, Jeremiah, his twin sister, Jada, and I are reigning trivia champs at the bar our family also owns, The Copper Moon. We're way too into it and I almost never miss it. Wes is the bar's manager, but he usually doesn't stay for the whole shift for trivia.

"Nope." My phone buzzes and I see another text from Mom. "Why does Mom need all of us to weigh in on everything?"

"Yeah, tell me about it." Wes leans back in his seat. "But

Mom's eating this shit up and aside from weighing in every once in a while, we haven't had to do all that much. It's not too bad."

"I guess." I scratch Duke's back leg where he can never quite reach. "She's been bugging me about a date, though. She keeps saying it's been nearly two years, but she doesn't get it."

I stare off at Bianca's house, not really focusing on anything in particular. I see her pass by a window for a brief second and my heart skips a beat.

"I know," he says, his voice quiet. "I don't think she could."

He, along with Jeremiah and Jada, weathered the storm of me being a fucking wreck after the second breakup with Catherine. They're the only three people I trusted with it all. Even now the rush of shame and self-loathing pops up in my chest, but I can stuff it down.

"I need to head to work, but go have a beer or something and mute your notifications." He stands up and stretches, and finally, Murphy does the same before trotting up the steps. "Maybe Mom'll get the hint and stop blasting you with texts."

We both stare at each other for a beat and burst out laughing at the same time. But when Wes and Murphy head inside, my smile fades.

I can tell my mom no, and I have plenty of times. But some things she just can't let go. Should I bring someone just to keep her off my back? With all the people who are coming, we'd probably only say hello to each other and have a short conversation before someone else takes her attention.

I stay outside for a few more minutes until I feel overly antsy.

"Want to go for a walk, buddy?" I ask Duke.

He's half lab, half husky, and the husky part of him gives him an alarming amount of energy. He's always down for a walk or a run.

I clip his leash on and guide him to the path that runs along our property and Bianca's, toward an easy path into the woods. As we pass, I can't help but glance up at Bianca's house again. I mostly spoke to Miss Gloria when she brought Sadie into the clinic or when she needed help with something around the house.

The house looks a bit worse for wear, now that I'm looking at it up close, and there's a tree in the small space between our fences whose roots are going to screw up both of our fences if we don't take care of it.

The house is just a few steps behind me when the unmistakable sound of a bloodcurdling scream echoes from inside Bianca's house. Duke and I sprint up her front porch steps without a second thought and I bang on the front door.

"Bianca?" I call out. "Bianca?"

I don't hear her respond, but I hear her whimper. I rush around to the back side of the house and try the door handle, pushing my way inside.

THREE
BIANCA

I HEAR Waylon burst into the kitchen, but I can't take my eyes off the wall to look at him directly.

"You okay?" he asks. I hear the gentle taps of his dog's paws on the tile floors too.

"Can you help me get this spider out of the kitchen because I don't want to take my eyes off of it and if it runs away I'm going to spend the whole night wondering if it's in my bed and then I'll burn this whole house down if I even *think* it's there," I say in one breath.

I need to take in another breath but I'm scared that if I breathe, the spider will move. It doesn't make any sense but a spider being that huge and inside my house doesn't make sense either. It's the size of my palm, easily. And it's just *there*. Aren't spiders supposed to be outside? Or making webs or something?

"Yeah, that's a big one," Waylon says with a chuckle, as if we're not inches away from some sort of mutant escapee from a lab. At least he's not judging me whatsoever for practically pissing myself. "Do you have a bowl and some thin cardboard?"

"Bowls are in the cabinet in that corner." I point without taking my eyes off the spider. "And maybe there's some thin cardboard in the recycling? It's in the corner too, in the bin."

He rustles around behind me and appears with the bowl and cardboard. I let him step in front of me and capture it like it's no big deal, taking it out back. He walks deep into the yard and lets it out in the grass.

The tension finally leaves my body and I can finally sag against the doorframe with a sigh.

Waylon's dog is looking up at me expectantly, tail wagging. He's cute and has an intelligent gleam in his eyes, with blonde-ish fur and ears pointed up like he's ready to listen.

"Hi," I say. His tail wags harder and he noses my hand, lifting it so I can pet his head. I scratch him between his ears and check his tag. "Hi, Duke."

"Okay, spider's way off in the backyard," Waylon says when he comes inside.

"Thank you." I run both hands over my face. God, this day is already a mess.

"It's no problem." His brow furrows. "Also not to cause more panic, but this smells a bit like hot rubber?"

He takes two long strides and he's standing at the pot on my stove. And before I can stop him, he pulls off the lid.

"Wait!" I say, even though he's already looking inside.

Inside, at the brand new silicone dildos I'm sterilizing. One of which is hot pink with a suction cup on the bottom, and the other of which is shaped like a dragon's (theoretical) dick, just because I was curious and had two glasses of wine in my system when I was shopping.

He blinks and slowly slides the lid back on, his cheeks flushing.

Once again — can the universe just take me out? A gamma ray blast. An asteroid. Literally anything to save me from the depths of my mortification.

"That's not soup," he finally says. "Sorry."

"It's fine. Just…pretend you didn't see all that," I say. I click the burner off since they're probably sterile by now.

"We just leveled out the cringe scales in the universe," Waylon says after the longest pause of my life. I lift an eyebrow and he adds, "I incited the assless chaps incident because my mouth wouldn't stop running. And now you have this. So, we're even. I guess."

The logic's a little iffy because we both made things cringey, but it's better than nothing. I smile. "You mean chaps?"

He grins. "Right, chaps."

I guess we did balance the cringe scales in the universe because the tension in the air starts to disappear.

Sadie finally wakes up from her deep nap on her bed in the living room and walks in with a yawn. Like she's right on time.

"I thought you could fight a spider," I say to her as she sniffs Duke, her tail wagging. "Or at least bark at it."

"Sadie would fight a moose but not a spider," Waylon says. "The bigger the opponent, the more interested she is. Though that spider was about half her size."

"So maybe we'll have better luck with an axe murderer," I say with a snort. "Thank you for helping."

"Yeah, it's no problem. I heard you screaming and..." He shrugs.

I finally let myself take Waylon in. I've only seen him in scrubs, but now he's in a blue t-shirt and black joggers, which fit him to perfection. My hand remembers that light squeeze to his bicep and how muscular he felt too. Where else does he feel that good?

His eyes skim over me too, riding the line between polite and heated. I was going to workout before taking my new toys for a spin, so I'm in next to nothing — a workout unitard that rides up high on my thighs and cuts low in the back.

I like the way he looks at me too much. Especially now that the cringe scales of the universe have been recalibrated.

"It's a good thing you didn't squish the spider," he says, tucking a hand into his pocket. "Sometimes those spiders are pregnant and a bunch of their babies come out if you squish them."

My eyes widen, and he quickly adds, "But they're not too common. You probably would have been fine."

"It would be just my luck to have a whole bunch of them in the house." I sigh. "Do you want something to drink? I mostly have seltzer. Regular and hard seltzer. And a bunch of non-dairy milk. I can't have dairy, so sorry if you wanted a tall glass of milk for some reason."

Apparently, my mouth and my brain aren't quite in sync when it comes to speaking to Waylon. Who the hell would ask for a glass of milk in this scenario?

"Regular seltzer would be great, thanks." He leans against the wall and Sadie walks up to him, her mostly hairless butt wagging back and forth. "Is this house giving you a lot of trouble?"

"Yeah." I grab two seltzers. All my motivation to workout is gone. "I moved here kind of fast so I haven't really had the chance to catalog it all. But a lot of stuff needs fixing and I don't have a single handy bone in my body."

"Oh, and there's the problem with that tree that's growing between our fences," he says, scooping Sadie up with one hand. "It's not that big of a problem right now but it will be in a few months when it gets rainy. I'm happy to help with that since the fences can be a bit of a project."

"You don't have to do all that." I open a seltzer and hand it to him. "I'm sure you're busy."

"It affects us both, so I don't mind. And I'm a whole lot cheaper," he says, taking a sip of seltzer. "I can even fix a few things in here too if you need it. I'm right there."

I bite my bottom lip. I'm not hurting for cash at the moment, but I'd love to save as much as possible for moving to New York and investing in the spa without need to do some dumb influencer posts that I hate doing just for money.

"You really wouldn't mind that much?" I ask.

"No, it's fine. Like I said, it affects both of us and it can be a bit of a hassle to deal with," he says. Sadie licks the side of his can and he holds it out of her way.

"Okay, but I'd have to do something for you in return," I say. "I wish I knew what."

"Unless you want to come to this family barbecue for my brother's engagement with me, I don't know either," he says.

He seems like he's half-joking, but still, I say, "Sure, if you need someone to come."

He blinks. "You're serious?"

"Yeah, why not?" I shrug. "Sounds easy enough."

"That would be a massive help." He puts Sadie down

and she trots over to me. "My mom's a little obsessed with setting me up with someone. We wouldn't have to pretend to be serious, but we could at least hold her back a little bit. At least until I think of something else to do for the next event."

"A stopgap," I add.

"Exactly." He pauses, rubbing the back of his neck. "You really don't have to if you're not comfortable."

"Nah, it's fine. I've been a fake date before," I say. My PR team had set me up on some to distract the press from whatever scandal was happening — on my end or my fake date's. "Sometimes just being seen with someone once is enough to get whatever narrative you want out there."

"Thank you. Seriously." At least twenty pounds of weight seems to lift off his shoulders. "I can text you the details if you give me your number."

We exchange numbers and he texts me the time and location of the party. Is this a terrible idea? How bad could a barbecue be?

He heads out with Duke after giving the kitchen one more check for mutant spiders, leaving me and Sadie alone. She follows me into the living room, where I've set up my mat for my workout, and steps back into her fluffy pink bed.

Right as I turn on my video, my phone rings. It's an unknown number with an LA area code, so I hesitate. It might be a loose end from back in LA. Or it might be the last person I want to hear from.

"Hello?"

"Baby," my ex, Kyler says. "Don't hang up!"

I don't speak for a few seconds. He's been calling me ever since I dumped him and left LA, all from different numbers. It's like the world's worst game of whack-a-mole.

Kyler isn't threatening — he's just annoying. And in the two and a half years we were together, a lot of our lives mixed, including our apartment. I'm still paying rent since the lease ends in two months and I don't want to deal with the logistical mess of trying to pull out of the lease now.

Hopefully he has something of value to actually say, like we got out of the lease early or he wanted to pay a bill. Or a million of the other administrative bullshit that I'll inevitably have to handle because I did all of that while we were dating.

I hold in a sigh.

"Why shouldn't I hang up?" I put him on speakerphone and toss my phone on the mat. "What do you want?"

"Just hear me out."

"What else could you possibly say?" I fold myself forward and grip my feet. "Is this about something important, or no? Like the lease or the bills."

"I just miss you, babe," he says. God, he sounds so pathetic.

I swallow and sit back up. He probably misses my connections. Was he ever into me at all, or did he just want a connection to my dad? If my dad produced an album for him, the odds of it being a bigger hit than any of his past albums were pretty damn high. And my dad didn't produce albums for just anyone.

But his son-in-law? Yeah, he'd probably do it.

The fact that Kyler decided to "ask my dad for my hand in marriage" and pitch an album idea at the same time was such a red flag that my dad called me right after.

At least Kyler didn't full-on propose. But he did drop every hint like it was a ball of lead — telling me to get my nails done, planning a vacation himself (which he always left to me), telling me to pack certain things. Good thing I saw his texts to some girl he told me not to worry about before we left.

He put in a thousand times more effort into those texts than he did with our relationship.

I'm not sure what I was expecting, though — nearly all my relationships, platonic or romantic, end up just like that.

"Bianca?" he says. "You still there?"

"What?" I bark. "Again, is there anything important — as in our apartment or bills or cars — that you need to tell me about?"

"Are you seeing someone else?" he asks. "Is that why you're so stubborn about this?"

I squeeze the bridge of my nose and resist the urge to scream. Sadie's ears prick up, like she's thinking, *is this asshole for real right now?*

"It wouldn't make a difference if I was or wasn't," I say. "I'm not coming back."

"So, you are seeing someone," he says, leaping to conclusions. Of course. "Who is he?"

"Bye, Kyler," I say.

"B—"

I hang up on him and flop back on my mat with a heavy sigh. I'm not going to date anyone for the foreseeable future. Being burned by him and by all the friends who have chosen his side is more than enough reason to take time to sort myself out. Alone.

FOUR
BIANCA

WAYLON SAID this engagement party was casual, but how do I even do casual? Like Jepsen casual?

I looked at what everyone else was wearing at the grocery store the other day, and I just don't have clothes like that. No flannel. My denim looks too new. My blouses are too snug or too fashionably loose.

"Okay, Sadie. Which outfit?" I ask her, tossing two different options on the bed in front of her. She does a cute little head tilt before yawning and stretching.

An unexpected benefit of a dog: I can talk to her and not feel nuts for talking to myself. So far she's been just as easy as Waylon said she'd be.

I waffle between two dresses, then pull out some shorts and an off-the-shoulder blouse. Maybe shorts will work more? My phone pings and it's a text from Waylon, saying he'll be here in five minutes. I throw on the shorts and blouse, double checking that I didn't mess up my hair and makeup, then grab Sadie.

I step outside right as Waylon steps out of his car. My stomach flips up into my chest. He's wearing a green button-down shirt with the sleeves rolled up, showing off his muscled forearms, and shorts. I've never paid a lot of attention to men's legs before, but his thighs and calves are thick and muscled too.

"Hey, you look beautiful," he says with a soft, polite smile. But his eyes travel up and down my body, a little heat in them.

"Thank you." The way he says it hits differently than it does from everyone else. "You look nice too."

Now that I'm not ogling him, I let out a tense breath. We actually look like we're going to the same place, which takes a mountain of stress off of my shoulders. I always hated it when Kyler would be wearing sweats and a t-shirt — both designer, but still — when I'd be wearing a dress. It made me feel like I was trying too hard for no reason when in reality, I was just dressed for the occasion.

"You ready to go?" He opens the passenger side door for me. It could come across is ridiculously corny, but it feels sweet from him.

"Yep. Thank you." I slide into the front seat and immediately feel something damp on my shoulder — a dog's nose. Duke is in the backseat, buckled in with his harness, and wags his tail when I look at him. I pet him between his ears.

Waylon slides behind the wheel and starts the car again, a podcast coming through the speakers. He pauses it before I can hear what it's about.

"There'll be a ton of dogs, by the way," Waylon says.

"Your family are animal people too?" I give Duke one more pet.

"Oh yeah." Waylon backs out of the driveway with ease. "They're definitely the reason why I love animals so much. We always had at least two dogs — they have two right now. Speaking of, how's Sadie so far?"

"Good. I think?" I pet her inside the bag. "She follows me everywhere and takes a lot of naps, so I bought her a few more beds."

"Yeah, she loves a good nap. Sleeps pretty deeply too," he says. "When she lived with me, I had to wake her up to go for walks, and even then, she'd be a little annoyed that I wasn't carrying her the whole way."

I take a peek at his hands on the wheel and try to ignore how good his forearms look as he controls the car. We've only been on the road for about a minute but I can tell he's a good driver. Or at least a way better driver than Kyler, who drove like he was intentionally trying to be an asshole.

Waylon just seems like a nice, rule-following type of guy. *Seems.* But hey, I'd prefer him seeming some kind of way with a superficial relationship like we'll have.

"That kind of reminds me that I don't know anything about you and we're supposed to be...on a date? A one time date?" I ask. "I just know you're the town veterinarian and you like dogs."

"Right. And all I know is..." He trails off. "You're from California. And you're Miss Gloria's great niece."

"Yeah. I'm from LA," I say. "Lived there my whole life. Up until now, of course.'

"What do you do for work?" He gently slows to a stop at a sign.

"I'm a model and influencer." I don't mean to sound like I'm saying I have to fight babies for a living, but it comes across that way. My distaste for modeling has only grown since I basically quit six months ago. I barely wanted to be an "influencer" but social media and modeling go hand in hand these days.

"You are?" He doesn't look particularly surprised.

"Yeah. I'm trying to get out of it, to be honest. My friend and I want to open a spa so we're working on that." I fidget with my bag. "But for now I'm just laying low. Dealing with the house and taking a break."

I can't keep the wariness out of my voice and I hope he doesn't pry. I'd rather not rehash my whole messy relationship and the reasons why I'm here to a near stranger.

"What do you want our story to be?" He asks. "Like how we met?"

"I guess through the estate lawyer would make sense. Maybe we've been talking and just hit it off." I shrug and look out the window. "The simpler the story, the more believable it'll be."

"Yeah, agreed. And to be honest, people might not even ask."

His parents' house isn't much further. We turn down a private side road, which is lined with trees, and eventually end up in an open clearing. The massive, sprawling ranch-style house is gorgeous, with a big garden and yard in the front. All my Googling told me his family had to be well-off, but they're more well-off than I even thought.

"We're still good on everything we discussed?" He asks as he parks in front of a massive six car garage.

"Yep, all good." My heart is about to pound out of my chest, though.

"Don't get out yet," he says, putting a hand on my shoulder. "There are about to be a ton of dogs out here. Hang onto Sadie so she doesn't get trampled."

Like they were on cue, two dogs, both Labrador retrievers, come rushing out of the front door and down the path, making Duke start to howl out the window. Waylon hops out of the car and rushes over to let Duke out. Duke flings himself out of the car and howls at the sky again like a little wolf.

"Does he do that a lot?" I ask after stepping out. The other two dogs sniff me, excited, then go back to sniffing Waylon.

"Yeah, he's chatty," he says. "Also, if you hear a woman screaming outside your house, don't worry - it's him."

I blink, waiting for him to say he's kidding, but he doesn't.

"That sounds like something someone with a murder basement would say," I say with a smirk.

"I know, I know." He laughs and starts petting the two dogs who ran outside. "But I swear, I'm not making it up. If he's being particularly saucy, he'll just start yelling. And it happens to sound like a woman."

"Uh-huh." I look him up and down. "I wouldn't have guessed you were the murder dungeon type."

He grins. "I've upgraded from a murder basement from a murder dungeon? Sounds fancier."

"Waylon!" A woman calls from the front porch, pulling our attention away. "What are you doing down there?"

My heart leaps into my chest. That has to be his mom. Even from this distance, I can see the resemblance between the two of them — tall, with dark hair.

Waylon glances at me, tension around his eyes. His mom

showing up right away feels like jumping straight into the boss battle in a video game when I need the tutorial.

"Be there in a second," Waylon calls out. "I mentioned I was bringing someone, but she doesn't know the details."

I nod. Should he have mentioned the details?

He finishes petting the dogs and shoos them to go in front of us. The dogs rush up the stairs to where Waylon's mom is waiting, a warm smile on her face.

She's extremely beautiful, exactly what I'd think of if someone told me to imagine a slightly older southern belle. Nothing about her is out of place – not her professionally colored hair, her classic makeup, or her nice-but-casual dress.

"And who is this?" she asks, opening her arms to me for a hug.

I'm not a hug person at all, especially with strangers, but rejecting her hug would be the worst way to start this off. I hug her — awkwardly — and she pulls back, her hands on my shoulders.

"This is Bianca," Waylon says. "Bianca, this is my mom."

"You can call me Delia." She beams — Waylon has her smile. "I'm so happy that Waylon is finally dating again. And such a beautiful girl, too."

I open my mouth to say that we aren't really a serious thing, but she looks so thrilled that I keep my mouth shut. We can clarify things later.

"Come in. Let me get you a drink," she says, opening the door for me.

The inside of the home is tasteful, but almost to the point where it's too manicured. Every bit of decor coordinates in a purposefully rustic kind of way. Each room flows into the other, with a huge kitchen on the far back. Beyond that is their huge back yard, where most of the party seems to be.

"What would you like to drink?" Delia asks, opening the fridge once we get to the kitchen. "We have a little bit of everything. A moonshine cocktail? Rose and Wes created these canned ones and they're selling like hotcakes."

"Sure, I'll try one." I've never had moonshine in my life, but I might as well try it today. Doesn't this stuff blind people, though?

"I'll have one too." Waylon rests his hand on my back.

Delia opens up the cans and pours each of them into a glass. It just looks like iced tea to me, and when I taste it, it's like lightly boozy tea with lemonade.

"This is really good," I say, hopefully not sounding too surprised. I thought it was going to be like drinking battery acid.

"Isn't it?" Delia leans her hip against the counter, looking between me and Waylon. "Do you live in Crescent Hill? I've never seen you before."

I vaguely remember signs for Crescent Hill University on the drive over.

"No, I just moved here. My great aunt Gloria passed —"

"Oh, you're Miss Gloria's great-niece," she says, putting her hand to her chest. "I'm so sorry for your loss, honey."

"Thank you." I take a larger swig of my drink than I probably should.

"So you've moved into her house?" Delia asks. "Is that how you two met? Through arranging things with Sadie?"

"Yep." Waylon slides his hand up my back to squeeze my shoulder. Tingles erupt up my back along the path his hand took. "We're going to head outside, actually."

"I'll walk with you. Come this way," Delia says, waving us away from the sliding glass door and toward a little hall. "We're trying to keep the dogs out of the kitchen. They'll rush this door if we open it."

"Wait, Mom..." Waylon hesitates.

"Here's our family photo wall," Delia says as we round the corner.

The long hallway is absolutely plastered in photos — family photos, individual photos, paintings of labradors.

"It's more or less in chronological order," she says, slowing down and blocking us from going out the door. "Look at how adorable Waylon was."

"Mom, please," Waylon says, his cheeks red. "This is Bianca's first time here."

"There's no reason to be ashamed of your accomplishments." Delia shrugs as if Waylon didn't say anything at all.

I look at the wall because Delia is looking at me expectantly.

At first there are wedding photos of Delia and Mr. Stryker. The wedding fashion is aggressively of the era, but she still looks stunning. I can see where Waylon got his strong build and the rest of his height, now that I've seen his dad.

Over the years, his two older brothers are born, then eventually, Waylon and Wes. Once Waylon hits kindergarten, it's like a parade of achievements. Delia must have saved every single award he's ever gotten, and there are a *ton*. They crowd out his brothers' achievements by far.

Academic awards. Recognition for volunteering. Ribbons for winning some animal husbandry competitions, whatever that is. Football trophies. Everything from when he was little all the way through veterinary school.

Holy shit. Is he good at everything? Thank god this is just a single date or everyone would question why a guy like him would be with a low-tier model who was an average student at best.

"C'mon," Waylon says, taking my hand and guiding me past his mother. "We're going to say hi to people, Mom."

Someone calls Delia's name down the hall and she looks over her shoulder.

"Okay, fine." His mom finally moves. "It was so lovely to meet you, Bianca. I hope we can get together again soon."

"Nice meeting you too," I say.

Waylon pulls me outside onto the huge back patio, tension leaving his shoulders but his cheeks still flushed.

"Sorry," he murmurs. "I didn't think she'd whip out the photo wall right away."

I have so many questions now — like how did he have the time to do all of that, and why does his mom have a whole ass shrine to him, basically, when he has three other brothers — but I can sense his discomfort and stay quiet.

The party outside is in full swing already, with a few grills going on one side and some seating and tables peppered throughout. Dogs are hanging around too, some laying down with their humans and others playing in empty spots.

"Waylon!" a woman yells, her voice traveling way over the sound of the crowd. "C'mere!"

I spot the source of the voice — a black woman wearing a super cute printed jumpsuit and cat-eye glasses, who's waving at us. Next to her is a black man who seems to be just as tall and muscular as Waylon, who nods, then looks at me in confusion.

"Those are my best friends, Jada and Jeremiah," Waylon says in my ear.

I nod, taking another long drink of my drink. The warmth of a buzz is starting to spread through my veins, thank god. I need something to loosen me up.

"Jada, everyone at this party heard you," Waylon says with a smile when we get to the table. "No need to point at us like we've committed a crime."

"It's loud out here!" Jada protests, adjusting her glasses. "What if you didn't hear me?"

"Has there ever been a moment when I haven't heard you? Ever? Since third grade?" he teases. Jada's eyes narrow, but she smiles too. "Exactly."

"Excuse my sister. She's only semi-feral," Jeremiah says to me.

"Rude, I'm mostly domesticated. Like a house cat." Jada tucks some of her locs behind her ear. They're cut right at her shoulders and are dyed pink at the ends.

"Aren't semi-feral and mostly domesticated kind of the same thing?" Jeremiah asks, taking a sip of his drink.

"Whatever, it doesn't matter." Jada turns to smile at Bianca and extends her hand. "Sorry, I swear I'm an actual human with actual human manners. I'm Jada, that's my twin brother Jeremiah, and Waylon didn't say a damn thing about him bringing a *date*."

She seems amused, thankfully, and not overly suspicious.

"Nice to meet you. Both of you. I'm Bianca."

"Bianca." Jada studies me, tilting her head to the side a

little, like she's trying to figure me out. "So, where'd you and Waylon meet? And when?"

"We met arranging things for Sadie a few weeks back." I move my bag so Sadie will pop out, but she's still napping. "She's asleep."

"Sadie is pretty much always asleep. She's the chillest Pomeranian on the planet," Jada says. "Anyway, so are you and Waylon...?"

I kind of appreciate how straight to the point she is, even though I need to look to Waylon to answer the question in the best way.

"It's casual," he says, resting a hand on my lower back again. It's warm and grounds me from flying off into an anxiety spiral.

Jada and Jeremiah look at him, then each other, seemingly speaking in an unspoken language. It's a little unnerving, but I'd prefer to be in the dark about whatever they're thinking.

"We're just surprised," Jeremiah says. "But not in a bad way."

"Oh." I nod because I don't know what to say to that. Plus, I can feel Jeremiah's skepticism already. Unlike his sister, he's much less cheerful.

But Jada already looks like she's moved on. She and Waylon quickly catch up — she's getting her PhD, though I don't know in what, and her and Jeremiah's family run a historic hotel where she gives tours. Jeremiah is a high school math teacher, which sounds hellish, and the school's football coach.

I try to file every little detail away just in case. I'm keeping quiet in the conversation but I don't want everyone to think that I'm zoned out. Every once in a while, a dog wanders up to Waylon, tail wagging, and he pets them before they move on. It's like a processional where they're all getting a little blessing from the dog pope. Is this man like Snow White, just summoning dogs?

Soon Waylon brightens a little more when a pit bull mix comes trotting up to him.

"Hey, Murphy," Waylon says, squatting down and putting his forehead to the dog's big blocky head. He glances up and nods in greeting at someone behind me.

"Hey." I follow Waylon's gaze and spot who I'm guessing is Wes, based on the photo wall. They're fraternal twins, so I can see the brotherly resemblance without them looking the exact same.

Behind him, holding his hand, is who I assume is Rose — a petite black woman with long braids and a nose ring. She gives off cool girl energy, genuinely cool girl energy and not the manufactured stuff so many people try to create on Instagram. Like she knows where the good bars and restaurants that aren't overrun with people are.

Everyone greets each other before Waylon introduces me to Wes and Rose. Wes's eyebrows shoot up for a second, but he smiles and shakes my hand.

"This is pretty damn new, isn't it?" Wes asks, not taking his eyes off Waylon's.

"Yeah." I hope my hands aren't too sweaty. I shake Rose's hand too.

"Things just sort of clicked," Waylon adds.

Rose and Wes don't push it — they just invite us all over to eat with them.

The party has a ton of guests, and there's more than

enough food for everyone to take home leftovers in a sectioned off area of the yard. The dogs that followed us stand outside of the barrier, looking forlorn that they aren't allowed to eat all the human food.

"Since this was kind of last minute, I was only able to find out what stuff is dairy free versus having something made for you. And I wasn't sure if you were just dairy free or if you were vegan, so I asked about both," Waylon says. "There are a few options, but not a ton when it comes to desserts or anything."

I only briefly mentioned I can't eat dairy to him, but he thought to mention it to whoever arranged all this food? Kyler literally never remembered, even though we had a lot of moments where I accidentally had dairy and broke out in horrible cystic acne that took weeks to clear up.

He always remembered to point *that* out, though. As if it wasn't painful and actively bad for my career. He had to go and say shit like "well, it's not like it'll kill you."

"Thank you. That's really thoughtful," I say. "And I'm just dairy free. It's not an allergy but eating it isn't good for me."

"Oh, good, because there's exactly one vegan option," he says with a sigh of relief. "If you like barbecue, then you're set."

I've never had it, but saying that out loud when there are at least five different types of barbecued meat spread out in front of me, buffet style, feels blasphemous.

We fill up our plates and find a table with everyone else. The food is outrageously good — smoky and juicy and flavorful meat, plus a ton of good sides I can safely eat. Once everyone gets the edge off their appetite, an easy flow of conversation comes back.

Thankfully, Jada and Wes are chatty in a way I like, so I don't have to talk that much and make things awkward. And as far as I know, they don't think I'm some awful ice queen.

I let out a breath. *It's okay.* Everyone is nice. No one is sitting down and interrogating me or Waylon either.

But I can't help but notice how everyone who walks past us looks at us, like we're making a fuss even though we're just sitting there. Their eyes even follow us when we get up and go get more of the moonshine iced tea.

I guess Waylon having a date is more of a big deal than he was letting on.

But why do people care this much? Maybe he's just popular, which I can easily see too. People keep saying hi. Still. It makes sense for his mom to care about who he's with, but for half the town to care? Weird.

Being in a small town is really fucking odd in a lot of ways.

"And there's Waylon's girlfriend," Delia says, beaming as she passes by us with a whole fleet of women who look like they might be related to her. "Hi, hun."

I wave because what else can I do? I resist the urge to look at Waylon. They keep moving, though, like we're a dull exhibit at the zoo, and head to the table where we were just eating.

"I'll correct her later," Waylon says to me, his voice low.

My phone buzzes in my purse yet again, waking Sadie. She pops her head out of my bag like *what the fuck is it this time?*

I quickly check the message. Kyler. Of course. From a

different number, once again hyper-fixating on whether I'm seeing someone. It's getting creepy.

But things suddenly click into place in my head. How did I not think of this before?

"Wait, no," I say, my voice low even though no one is around us. "This is perfect. We should keep this fake relationship going. My ex is blowing up my phone, asking me if I'm seeing anyone. If you play my boyfriend on Instagram, he'll stop calling me. Probably."

Kyler probably wouldn't push further if I had evidence I was dating someone.

"Is he harassing you?" Waylon asks, frowning deeply.

"He's harmless." I wave as if I'm dismissing Kyler the way I wish I could. "Just a little creepy and a *lot* annoying, like a bug. But even after a while, you want to kill a fly, you know?"

He slowly nods, apprehensive. A flare of panic at the idea of him saying no lights up in me even though this idea has only been in my head for less than a minute.

"We don't even have to show your face - just your back or your side or something," I add. "And I moderate comments, so people won't be too awful. Well, mostly."

Kyler's fans would be awful to any woman he dated, but they were particularly shitty to me. They thought I was "too bitchy" for him, mostly, which only fueled (completely unsubstantiated) tabloid fodder that I wasn't nice.

But Kyler is a C-list celebrity at best, mostly known to his fans and people who like his flavor of pop music, so it could be a whole lot worse.

"Plus you mentioned those other events you need dates

for. Like Rose and Wes's wedding. You wouldn't have to find another excuse," I add.

He glances around, pensive.

"Okay, let's do it," Waylon says after a long pause. "But you'll have to let me fix up the rest of your house or something to even this exchange out."

"Seriously?" I grab his shoulder and scan his face to see if he's kidding. "Thank you. You have no idea how much you're helping me."

"It's no problem." He shrugs. "Plus, I don't think we can put this whole dating thing back in the bag anyway."

FIVE
WAYLON

WE *REALLY* CAN'T PUT this fake relationship back in the bag.

I deeply underestimated how much people would give a shit about my dating life. My mom, I expected. She looks so thrilled even across the party. But my friends? My relatives? People I know from way back in high school? All of them have been gawking at us the whole time.

Maybe it's also because Bianca is new in town and absurdly beautiful. Not a lot of brand new people drop into Jepsen.

"Okay. I should tell you about myself then." She sighs softly, her stunning bright smile fading. "At least a little more."

"Go for it." I put my hand on her lower back and guide her to a set of seats somewhat far away from everyone else.

She starts to sit, but finds the chair is rickety as hell.

"Here, take my seat," I say, starting to stand up.

She motions for me to sit down. "Should I sit on your lap? If we were dating for real, I'd probably do that."

"Sure." The idea of her pressed up against my body, her ass dangerously close to my cock, makes sweat bloom under my arms.

But she's right - it would look couple-y.

I make space for her on my lap and she sits down, close enough to me so that we don't look awkward. And unfortunately, her ass is just inches away from a place my body wants it to be, but my brain doesn't.

After she adjusts, she leans against me a little bit. She smells so fucking good. What lotion or perfume or shampoo could she possibly be using, and can I get it by the gallon?

"So, my mom is Miss G, who had that song Fire like fifteen or so years ago," she finally says.

The name sounds familiar, but I can't think of what it sounds like.

"You'd know it if you heard it," she fills in, tugging at her shorts. They expose a lot of her long legs and it's been hard to keep my eyes away from them. "And my dad is a music producer. There's no way you haven't heard a song he's produced."

"Okay...?" I'm not sure where she's going with this. But I'm surprised her parents are famous. She's pretty normal, considering the circumstances.

"Throw in the famous-ish parents, my modeling, and my musician ex, and there are more eyes on me than normal," she says, pulling Sadie out of her bag by our feet. "And a lot of those folks don't have the nicest things to say about me online."

I frown. "What do you mean?"

She swallows, scratching Sadie between her ears. The dog's little tail wags. "Basically, I have a reputation as being a bit of an ice queen. Kind of bitchy, really, even though I think the latter is more of a result of my ex's fanbase. At least I think so."

"Who's your ex?" I ask. I hate that I even care.

She rolls her eyes. "Kyler. If you aren't a young woman who likes a particular kind of pop music, you probably haven't heard of him."

"You're right about that," I say. I've literally never heard of him in my life, which pleases me more than it should. "And what about him? Your reputation shouldn't affect this situation."

"But..." She blinks, looking at me like I'm crazy. "You're you."

This time I'm the one looking at her like she's nuts. "What is that supposed to mean?"

Her eyes soften a little bit. To be honest, there's a little truth to the ice queen image, but only if you aren't looking at her closely. Even just knowing her a little bit, I can pluck out the deeper emotions underneath. She seems more shy than icy, the kind of person who warms up once you get to know her more.

"You're so *good*. So clean cut," she says. "You've been the best at a ton of stuff and save animals for a living, for fuck's sake. I walk down runways in clothes no one would reasonably wear in public. Or in next to nothing. At least I used to."

I consider her words. "But who cares if you were a model?"

"The point is that my image and your image are complete opposites," she says with a sigh. "Kyler and I aren't *that* famous but I wanted to give you a heads up before we get too deep."

She's not entirely wrong. We do sound like opposites. But how much could her reputation — assuming people put together the pieces of where she came from — really affect mine?

"It's a short relationship," I say. "Like until after the wedding. I'm sure any damage that's done — if it is — will be fixable. The town has known me a lot longer than they've known you."

She considers my words as Sadie gets up and makes a turn in her lap. Sadie already looks so comfortable with her. I firmly believe that dogs can sense people with good hearts. Bianca has to be one of them.

"Okay, true. I just wanted to give you a heads up so you weren't thrown off entirely. Odds are it won't be a problem."

She didn't have to tell me all of this, but she did. And while I appreciate the honesty, a pit starts to form in my stomach. Is this actually a bad idea? It's just a few months — we can fake it for that long before we part ways.

"Hey, can we join you? We got bombarded by people asking us questions about the wedding as if we've been engaged for months instead of maybe three weeks tops," Rose says, approaching with Wes behind her.

"Sure, yeah. Grab a chair though. That one's broken," I say.

Wes grabs one from another cluster not too far away, and settles in it with Rose in his lap. They're comfortably pressed against each other, Wes's arms around Rose.

"They're already harassing you about wedding plans?" I ask. "Not surprised."

"Yep." Wes sighs and pulls Rose closer. "Rose more than me."

"I mean, your mom and cousin had some really good wedding inspiration Instagram accounts to follow," Rose says, pulling out her phone. "Now if only I could just follow them and people I actually want to see stuff from instead of all these ads. And I'm over social media for work, too. Just ads on ads on ads."

"I thought Chrissy was handling social media for us?" Wes asks, looking over Rose's shoulder. Chrissy is our younger cousin and she's not the most responsible person I've ever met.

"She's doing a half-assed job." Rose snorts as she scrolls. "I need a person who actually knows what they're doing. Someone who has actual time to do it."

"I can help," Bianca says, to my surprise. "I mostly have experience with my own social media, but I've helped other models build their followings. I mean, if you need me."

She shifts on my lap, fiddling with her earring. Her curls tickle my cheek with every movement.

"That would be amazing," Rose says. "I mean, the pay wouldn't be crazy high, but my gratitude would be endless."

Bianca looks back at me, gauging my reaction. I nod — if she wants to, why would I stop her?

"Sure, yeah," she says.

"Hold on, let me get your phone number and IG handle before I forget," Rose says, hopping off Wes's lap.

They end up talking for a while, and I peek at Bianca's Instagram over her shoulder while she and Rose talk about it. It looks perfectly curated, exactly as I'd expect.

And she has a whole lot of modeling photos that I'll be

taking a closer look at later. Even though I probably shouldn't.

The conversation slowly morphs from social media bullshit (that thankfully I'm not forced to deal with) to more about whether Wes and Rose will have Murphy in their wedding ceremony.

Like most of the night (aside from Mom's weird attempt to talk me up using the photo wall), it's easy. Bianca's edge of anxiety slowly starts to fade the further the night goes, and she slowly sinks into me, like she can't help it.

I let my hands wander as far as they can while still being polite because apparently, I love torturing myself. She's so soft everywhere, and I feel like her scent is giving me just as much of a buzz as the drinks are.

I always end up a little more drunk than I intend to be at family gatherings, and after another hour, the combo of booze and fatigue starts to hit me, hard.

"Hey," I say, lightly squeezing Bianca's arms.

"Hi." She covers her mouth as she yawns. "Sorry."

"It's fine. I was actually going to ask if you're fine with us crashing here tonight," I say. "It'll take a while for me to sober up and by then it might be too late to drive us back."

"Sure, yeah." She cuddles against me more. Okay, she's also a little tipsy. There's an adorable haze in her eyes that wasn't there before, and it breaks through her deceptively cool exterior.

"See you on Monday, Bianca?" Rose asks.

"Yeah, Monday," Bianca says with a slight smile.

Rose and Wes leave us alone and I give Bianca as much space as I can with her sitting on my lap. I miss her warmth almost immediately. I've always been physically affectionate, but I forgot how much I love casual touch. Especially when she leans into me just a little bit, like she wants my warmth.

"Moonshine is very strong," she says with a hazy smile.

"I can tell you found that out. Want to grab a snack or something before we crash? We'll probably be on the couches but they're comfortable," I say.

"Yeah, I should eat. More." She takes a deep breath. "The food is *so good*. It's been so long since I could eat a ton of bread. Bread is so good."

I smile and guide her toward the house, where some of my family has started to take in leftovers. Am I touching her too much? My hands just naturally wandered up and down her back, gently cupping the back of her neck and playing with the soft little hairs back there. She's been leaning into my touch more and more.

"I'm so glad I'm done with that modeling bullshit," she says. Apparently she's a chatty drunk. "Like, human bodies shouldn't stay exactly the same size? I get bloated. I eat tacos. Are there tacos here?"

"Yeah, probably not nearly as good as the ones in LA though." I peer into the kitchen. "We're more barbecue and southern food types."

"Barbecue is so good too!" Her face lights up and god, she's so pretty like this. "I've never had it until today."

"Never?" I raise both eyebrows.

"Never." She shakes her head. "I like the pulled pork stuff. And the ribs."

"Then let's get some pulled pork. On bread." I grab some small plates and put together some pulled pork sliders.

My mom comes into the room, her hair pinned up. She looks a little worn out but smiles when she sees us.

"Hello, hello! Getting a little snack?" Mom asks.

"Yeah. Can we crash here tonight?" I ask. "I can't drive home."

"Of course! You and Wes's old room is all set up. Just got a new king size bed in there," Mom says, grabbing a plate too.

I freeze for a second before I continue to put some pulled pork on a slider bun. "We're fine with the couches if Wes and Rose want the bedroom."

"No, they're staying in the room above the garage. Much bigger." Mom scoops a huge pile of Nana's peach cobbler onto her plate. "Y'all want any cobbler?"

"No, thanks," Bianca says.

"I'm good too." I wrack my brain for any excuse to try to take the couches instead of the bed, but can't think of any that wouldn't tip Mom off. Shit.

"Okay. You know where the sheets are. And the towels." Mom comes over and kisses me on the cheek, then gives Bianca a hug. "Good night."

"Night."

Thankfully Mom slips away to her and Dad's room, leaving me and Bianca alone in the kitchen.

"I can sleep on the floor," I say softly.

She snags one of the sliders and takes a dainty bite, studying me. I can't quite read her, but eventually she shrugs.

"If you want to fuck up your back, go ahead." She shrugs. "I don't mind splitting the bed."

I blow out a breath through my nose. I can have good self-control. Sharing a bed with a woman who I'd love to fuck in any other circumstance, when we just agreed to a fake relationship. One that's fake for very good reasons.

We finish eating our snack and I guide her to the bedroom. Mom must have slipped in and put some fresh towels and sheets on the corner of the bed. Duke walks straight to the dog bed that's always lived in the corner for any of the family dogs that want to sleep in our room, and flops down. Bianca lets Sadie down and Sadie joins him, squeezing against him.

"This was your room?" Bianca asks, looking around.

"Yeah, Wes and I shared. Mom's redecorated it though, thankfully. It used to be a whole lot nerdier," I say. "Do you want to use the bathroom first?"

"Sure. Can I borrow a t-shirt or something?" She fluffs up her curls.

"Yeah." I go into the drawers and find one of my old ones, then dig around for some shorts. All the ones I have would fall right off her. "I don't have shorts, though."

"It's fine, I don't sleep with pants on." She takes the t-shirt and a washcloth before disappearing to our attached bathroom.

I close my eyes and take a deep breath, trying to redirect the blood from my cock to my brain. Bianca sleeping in just my t-shirt and panties wasn't in my mental fantasy bank, but now it's taken up a permanent spot.

I make the bed and double check that the dogs are fine in their shared bed. Sadie's toasted marshmallow fur blends in with Duke's light brown fur, so they look like one ball of dog. Eventually Bianca comes out, her curls up in a bun on top of her head. If the thought of her in nothing but one of my t-shirts and panties was devastating, seeing her in it is going to fucking kill me before the night is over.

Her height exposes more of her long, smooth legs under

the shirt, and the neckline of it is stretched out just enough to expose a tantalizing bit of collarbone. She's not self-conscious whatsoever, and I'm not sure if it's from her being a little drunk or her modeling making her confident in her body.

She flops onto the bed, face down, and sighs. The hem of the t-shirt flips up, exposing her ass in a tiny pair of pink lace panties. Her ass is so nicely shaped and the way her panties cling to her are like art. I suck in a breath and she tugs the t-shirt over her butt again.

I hustle to the bathroom and splash cold water on my face. The bed is big. I'm pretty tired, honestly. I can keep my cock under control, even though I was having a difficult time keeping it together when she just sat on my lap. After I brush my teeth, I go back out.

"Is it fine if I take off my shirt?" I ask her.

"Mmhm." She rolls over and watches me as I toss my shirt aside. Her eyes scan my chest as I get into bed, trying to stick to my side of it.

I flick off the lamp on my side table, but the light from the moon is just bright enough to cast the room in a slight glow. I can't help but look over at her, and she's facing me.

"Tonight was kinda nice," Bianca says, curling up on her side and facing me. It feels intimate, especially with her guard down like this. Her eyes are filled with sleepy warmth.

"Yeah? You weren't terrified by my mom's shrine to me being an overachiever?" I still can't believe my mom did that. Then again, the only other woman who's come over was Catherine, and she was overachieving alongside me. My accomplishments weren't as big of a deal.

"No. It made this all make sense. The fake relationship

thing." Her expression softens with curiosity. "Is it a lot? Being under that much pressure from her? Or having her and like half the women in town be that invested in your life?"

I swallow, looking up on the ceiling. "Yeah, to be honest. It felt so much easier in high school and even in college because my success was easily measurable — grades and awards. I knew whether I measured up. Now that I'm an adult, it's less cut and dry. I kind of wish I could just...not give a shit about whether I'm seen as successful or not, whether it's work or doing stuff in the community or my relationships."

"Just break free?" she asks.

"Yeah, exactly. Just live life without either my mom constantly in the back of my head or the little voice that tells me it feels good to win." I swallow. "Which feels like I should just be able to ignore. I'm not a kid anymore."

The drinks made that *way* more honest than I wanted to be. But she doesn't judge. She just nods and scans my face.

"Sometimes our brains do shit that doesn't make any sense, no matter how you try to look at it." She fluffs up her pillow. "My brain does it too."

"How?" I ask. I want to know more. To feel more of this — like she's just trying to listen instead of fix. I want to give the same to her.

She shakes her head and closes her eyes. "I guess I've always been under a lot of pressure to follow a path and modeling felt like the best one at the time. Then within that there's a ton of pressure to look a certain way or have a certain number of followers or date certain kinds of people. Which ran me into my shitty ex and kept me with him for two whole years. I wish he'd just leave me the fuck alone."

"You're sure he's not threatening you?" I sit up on one elbow. I saw a few pictures of her ex on her Instagram, but he seemed too meek to harass a woman he'd date. Then again, he did look like a raging douchebag so maybe I'm wrong.

"I'm sure," she says. When I raise an eyebrow, she holds up a hand. "It's fine, really. Complicated. Whatever. But basically, it's been nice being here. I even created some bucket lists so I can actually explore the world beyond my old bubble."

I hate the idea of her ex harassing her, or even reaching out after their breakup, but I don't want to push her too far. So I pivot.

"Bucket lists?" I ask. "Not just one?"

"No, I want to keep them organized." She gives me a little secretive smile. "I have one for dumb, normal person stuff. Like baking things or eating at a restaurant alone. Then semi-normal bucket list stuff like stargazing in a place that's legitimately dark or hiking up a mountain. Then there's the sex one."

I nearly choke on my own spit. "Sex one?"

She laughs, her eyes fluttering shut more out of fatigue than anything else. "God, never mind. It's so dumb. It's not even a bucket list, per se. It's more like a 'I want to learn how to be good at sex and what good sex is' list, but that's kind of too wordy to say."

I blink several times. What do I even say in response to that? Or at least, what do I say that's actually appropriate?

Before I can respond, she chuckles.

"This is weird as hell, but did you know I've gotten railed

better in fanfics written about me and my ex than I have in real life?" she asks. "Everyone thinks he'd be some sweet gentle lover who actually makes me come but in reality, he just pumped it in and called it a day."

My blood is heating, both in arousal and in anger. He couldn't make her come? It sounds like he didn't even try, which is the worst part. I don't understand guys who just fuck women without caring if their partner gets off.

Making a woman get off is one of the best parts of sex. And finding out all the different ways to do it is even more fun.

"Whatever," she mumbles, yawning. "Night."

She's passed out seconds later and I'm left wide awake, trying to ignore all the things I'd want to teach her.

SIX

BIANCA

I'M BARELY over my hangover by Monday, and I'm definitely not over what I think I said to Waylon.

Did I really tell him about my sex bucket list? I was in that hazy area of drunk mixed with extreme fatigue so I can't remember clearly. But I was comfortable for once in a gathering of people I didn't know, so I guess that loosened me up a ton. That and freaking moonshine.

Whatever, I'm never drinking again.

I stand in the shower, trying to get clean with the weak water pressure and trying to keep my thoughts on the first day of this gig and not waking up being spooned by Waylon. He shot away from me when he realized what he was doing, but I was awake enough to feel his huge cock against my ass.

My sexual experience has been both bland and short — just my ex and my ex before that — so my exposure to dicks has been limited. But I know enough to know what I felt.

My hand drifts down between my thighs, but I pull it back up. Getting off to him — or the idea of him — is a slippery slope I shouldn't go down. Banging my fake boyfriend isn't a part of my plan.

As if he would. I know he's attracted to me, but he seems like a rule follower through and through. I doubt he'd want to cross a line with his fake girlfriend.

And if it's never going to happen, I might as well...

No. Still no. And I'd need my vibrator to get off fast before I need to leave, so I wrap up my shower and get dressed. Rose insisted that the office dress code is chill, but I still have no idea what chill means around here. I go for black jeans and a blouse, with flat sandals so I'm not towering over Rose.

I pack up Sadie in the car and follow GPS to the Stryker Liquors office. The offices are on the edge of town in a nondescript standalone office building, only adorned by the Stryker Liquors logo above the door. I park and take a deep breath.

I can do this, even if I said yes when I was a little too socially lubricated. If I'm stuck in the house all day just working on the spa, I'd probably drive myself crazy anyway. I already like Rose, even if I'm a little intimidated by her too. She seems like she knows what she's about and what she wants for the future when I've barely gotten a grip on my next steps.

I head into the office, and it looks like I've stepped back into the nineties with the squiggly carpet pattern and dated furniture. The only slightly updated aspect of the office is the Stryker Liquors logo on the wall above the receptionist.

"Hello, how can I help you?" the woman asks, studying me harder than I'd like her to.

"Hi, I'm here to see Rose? Today is my first day." I hold

onto the strap of my bag, feeling that awful new kid at school energy.

"Sure thing, I'll call her."

The receptionist calls Rose and moments later, she appears down the hall. She's in dark jeans and a t-shirt under a cardigan, her long braids down.

"Hey," she says with a smile. "Thanks for coming in. Seriously."

"Yeah, it's no problem." I shrug, my face hot. Bianca who'd had some moonshine volunteered to do this. What if I can't even help that much?

"We'll start with a little tour."

She leads me around the office, which isn't all that big — there are bathrooms, a small break room, more offices and meeting rooms. As we round back to her office, we spot a chunky chocolate lab in the hallway, waiting outside of a door. His whole body is stretched out, his chin resting on a stuffed toy. His snout is lightly peppered with white, like he's older.

"Hey, Big Bubba. Waiting for John David?" Rose asks in a baby voice. Big Bubba's tail thumps even harder and his tongue lolls out of his mouth as he gets up. He walks over to us, and I let him sniff me.

"This is Big Bubba. He's the 'brand ambassador'," Rose says, rolling her eyes but still clearly amused.

"Brand ambassador?" I raise an eyebrow, looking at the dog. He's all vibes, no thoughts — happy as can be. "Usually that involves some work, no? He's not just the mascot?"

"Mr. Stryker — who, by the way, is always Mr. Stryker, mostly to distinguish him from Wes and Waylon's brother John David — insists on calling him the brand ambassador.

Mostly we just snap photos of him for social media and take him to events."

"Ehn, I guess that's being a brand ambassador in his own way." I pet his big head, then pull my phone out of my bag. "Can I go ahead and take a photo of him?"

"Yeah, go for it."

I kneel down and snap a few photos of Big Bubba. The lighting's not great, but I can fix it in editing.

The door Bubba was waiting in front of opens and Bubba starts doing the cutest little dance. A huge man steps out with a much smaller man, and I immediately recognize the larger man from the photos at Waylon's house — one of his other brothers. John David, I'm assuming. Build-wise, he looks more like Waylon than Wes, thick with muscle. Throw in the dark beard and his serious expression, and I feel like getting out of his way.

The man he's with peels off to go down the hallway, and John David faces us while he pets Big Bubba. He raises an eyebrow at me, like *who the hell are you?* which is a sharp contrast from how hard he's loving on the dog.

"JD, this is Bianca. Our new social media coordinator," Rose says. John David blinks. "Waylon's girlfriend?"

"Girlfriend?" John David's eyebrows shoot up. "Since when?"

"It's pretty new. I just moved here," I say, trying not to fidget.

"You must have missed each other at the engagement party, but she was there," Rose adds.

"Mm." John David stands up and accepts Big Bubba's stuffed toy. "I see. Nice to meet you."

"Likewise."

He walks away without another word, Big Bubba trailing behind him.

"Don't worry, he looks scarier than he actually is," Rose says, squeezing my upper arm.

So he's a fellow 'this is just my face and I don't hate your guts' person. "I understand that completely."

"C'mon, let's go over some stuff for the job. Then we have somewhere to be."

She leads me back to her office, passing a few other people in cubicles. Her office space is small, but cozy, with a half-alive plant and a few knickknacks on it.

She walks me through the basics, like their email system and all of the platforms they're on, along with their general strategy (which isn't really a strategy — it's just posting whenever). The photos they've been posting have been okay, but nothing special. Not a ton of engagement either.

At least it can only go up from here. All those free dinners at trendy restaurants in exchange for Instagram posts will actually come in handy for taking pictures of drinks.

"So, first assignment," Rose says, putting her computer to sleep. "We're going down to the veterinary clinic to take some photos. Stryker Liquors has always sponsored health treatments for animals in foster care as a part of their charity arm, but now they're the biggest sponsor of this new animal shelter they're building. I'm not sure if Waylon has mentioned it or if you know about it."

"Oh, yeah." It's technically not a lie since I've at least seen the building. I tuck my notebook back into my bag.

"Waylon will tell you more about it." She stands up and brushes her braids over her shoulder. "And Delia will be there too to discuss it and do a little promo to get donations and for the booth the shelter will have at the Jepsen Festival — it's basically a carnival that Jepsen holds every year and it's coming up. And we'll need some social media at that event too."

I follow her out to her car and hop into the passenger seat. When she turns on the car, the sound of one of my mom's old songs comes streaming through the speakers.

"You look like her, by the way," Rose says, gesturing to the speakers. "Miss G."

I brace myself — I heavily favor my mom and people freak out a little bit when they hear.

"She's my mom," I say, holding in a sigh.

"For real?" Rose looks at me, wide-eyed. "That's crazy."

"Yeah. She's mostly normal. Or as normal as she can be. She does a lot of stuff behind the scenes with my dad these days. Both of them have always been homebodies anyway so taking on that kind of role suits her." I tug at the ends of my curls, hoping she doesn't dig deeper. People always treat me differently once they know, even though Mom isn't in the public eye as much these days.

"Are you tired of this song, then?" Rose asks with a smile, her finger hovering over the button to the next song.

"Kind of, yeah." I laugh. She switches to the next song. "Thanks. No one's ever asked me that. Usually it ends up being a listening party for all her songs, assuming the other person doesn't have famous parents too."

My whole body relaxes. I knew I felt comfortable with Rose for a reason. It's been a while since people have known and treated me like a regular person.

"Wow, that's crazy." She shakes her head and pulls out of the parking lot. "I guess LA is really different, then. I mean, I lived in New York City for a few years and I can see that happening there too in some circles."

"You did?" I ask. "How did you end up here?"

"I grew up here." She pulls out onto the main road toward town. "Long story, but my shitty ex dumped me and I had to move back here. My dad works at Stryker Liquors in sales and got me a job at the Copper Moon, the bar the Strykers own. I met up with Wes again, a bunch of stuff happened, and now we're engaged."

She and Wes have that "meant to be" vibe that I never believed was real until I met them, so I'm not surprised at the warmth in her voice.

We arrive at the vet clinic a few minutes later — everything is pretty close together in Jepsen — and park in the back. When we head inside, one of the receptionists whisks us into the back area, which is much bigger than I thought it would be based on the size of the building. There's a pen lined with blankets on one side, and an exam table, with counters and cabinets lining the walls. A bunch of wiggly little kittens are in the pen, along with their mother.

Waylon is at the exam table with a vet tech, his back to us. The way his body looks in scrubs should be a crime — all shoulders and strong back and nice butt. Aren't scrubs supposed to be unflattering?

"Rose and Bianca are here for social media stuff," the receptionist says.

Waylon glances over his shoulder with a smile. "Okay, great. Just give us a second."

He finishes up and turns around, a black and white kitten tucked against him, so tiny in his huge hands. He smiles when he sees us, placing the kitten back in the pen with his mother.

"Hey," he says, leaning in and gently kissing me on the cheek. He smells clean, like shampoo. "Where do you guys want to start?"

Rose glances to me and I swallow the lump in my throat. I know how to do this, so I just need to do it. I've done things that are a thousand times scarier. I just want to do a good job.

"Let's just start with some photos of the staff and the kittens," I say. "Then we can maybe do an interview about the fundraising for the new shelter once your mom arrives."

"Works for me." Waylon nods his head toward the kitten pen. "These kittens have a lot of personality."

We follow him and he sits down next to the kitten pen, so we do the same.

"You want to come say hi?" Waylon says in a soft voice to some of the kittens who are waddling around. I snap a few photos of them, right as they meow. "Hi, little buddy."

He scoops up one of the tabby kittens that's come within arm's reach and cradles him to his chest. I snap a few photos of them. Waylon is ridiculously photogenic — which isn't always the case with guys who are hot in person. Him, plus the kittens?

I'm glad Rose made my first assignment easy. Anyone with a pulse will stop and look at these pictures.

"His name is Snickers," Waylon says, letting the kitten climb up his shirt. "And he's going to be up for adoption in the next few weeks. Right now he's living with a foster family along with his siblings."

I make a few notes for captions, then take a few more photos. He introduces a few more kittens — all with candy names — letting them use him as a jungle gym. They're all over him, climbing up his shoulders and sniffing his shoes. His smile is warm and relaxed, even though I'm sure the kittens' little needle claws are digging into his skin.

One of the kittens breaks away from him and starts wobbling over to me. She's brown with little white paws, chunky and adorable.

"That's Reese," he says. "My favorite, but don't tell the others. I usually name my favorites of litters after my favorite things — TV show characters, snacks, candy in this case."

I smile. "Why is she your favorite?"

"She's just ridiculous," he says, right as Reese stumbles and continues on as she was. "And very sweet."

I reach over to pet her tiny head. She squeaks a meow and purrs, butting her head against my fingers so hard that she nearly face-plants.

"She's super cute," I say. "If she's your favorite, why don't you adopt her?"

"Because if I adopted every cat or dog I liked, I'd have ten thousand pets, give or take. And most of the time there's a perfect home for them somewhere." He scoops up Reese. "Someday I'll have a huge house with a big yard for a bunch of dogs and a cat patio for the cats, though."

I can easily imagine that for him, with the perfect wife and perfect house. It bothers me way more than it should.

"You don't want to adopt a cat now? Or you can't?" I ask. "Even if it's not Reese?"

"Nah, Duke and cats don't mix well. If it's small and furry, he'll want to chase it," he says, sliding Reese into the pocket of his scrubs. She curls up and closes her eyes. "Wes's cat Dennis is my cat nephew and I get my cat fix that way.

He chose Wes, though. We don't know where he came from or how he got to the house, but he stood outside his back door and meowed his ass off until Wes let him in. Then he didn't leave."

I snort, snapping a photo of Reese falling asleep in Waylon's pocket.

"He sounds sassy," I say.

"He's most orange cat stereotypes in one cat. Both bold and not super bright." He scoops up an orange kitten and rests him on the ground between us. "He's great. All these cats are great."

He scratches Reese on the top of her head while petting the orange kitten, a soft smile on his face.

I should have realized that seeing him in his element, with cute kittens, would do something to me. But it's doing *a lot* to me. His size in contrast with how gentle he is, the way the kittens are so drawn to him…it's almost too much to handle and honestly? Pretty damn rude for him to be this good-looking.

"Here's their mom, who'll be up for adoption once the kittens are weaned," he says, gesturing to the mom cat, who's laid out, purring inside the pen. "She's about three years old and super sweet. Her foster mom says that she loves to take naps on your lap or in a sunbeam."

"Momma cat?" Mrs. Stryker comes in, wearing jeans and a blue blouse, the same shade as the Stryker Liquor logo. The whole outfit looks incredibly expensive, even though the pieces are casual. "What perfect timing. Hi, hun."

"Hey," Waylon says, gently plucking the kittens off himself. Some complain, but others toddle back over to their mother.

Mrs. Stryker hugs Waylon and kisses him on the cheek first, before she moves onto Rose, then me.

"Hello there," she says to me with a smile, studying me with her hands on my shoulders. I try to keep a reasonable amount of eye contact, but I'm not sure if I do a decent job. "So, what do you need me to say?"

"We wanted to get a little footage of you talking about the plans for the shelter and asking for help fundraising," Rose says. "Bianca's manning the camera."

"Okay." She looks around and gestures toward a seat. "I'll get set up here."

"Let me get the lighting right." I grab the ring light and start to move it around, adjusting it until she's in the best possible light.

"Thank you. I swear, everyone else has made me look as washed out as possible." She crosses one leg over the other, then sits up a bit straighter and adjusts her hair.

"Can you give us a brief bit on the shelter and its goals?" Rose asks. "And how Stryker Liquors is involved?"

"Of course. You can hit record whenever." Delia looks at the camera and fluffs her hair again. I give her a signal to go ahead. "Stryker Liquors has always been involved in helping animals in need. We already donate a percentage of the profits from the sales of Big Bubba Bourbon to our local animal fostering network, and now we're putting those funds toward the Jepsen Animal Shelter. If you'd like to donate to the shelter, which will open in a few months, please visit the link in our bio. Or, visit our booth at the upcoming Jepsen Festival."

She has the smooth, practiced composure of someone who's done a lot of this before. I'm not surprised. Everything about her seems perfect and composed, like she's never had a slip-up in her life.

Rose nods. "That was perfect."

"One take." Delia smiles. "Now what's next?"

Rose looks over her notes. "Can you discuss the Stryker family's involvement in local animal welfare?"

"I'd be happy to." She looks over at Waylon. "Waylon, come talk about it with me."

"I'm not great on camera," he says, even though that's a complete lie. "You're great at it. We'll be done faster if it's just you."

Delia sighs. "Eventually you'll be the face of this shelter, sweetheart. People should get used to seeing you."

"I got great footage of him and the kittens," I say, looking between Waylon and his mother. He's clearly not thrilled at the idea of being on camera anymore. If he doesn't have to be, he shouldn't be. "We'll definitely post that."

"Still." Delia gets another stool and pats it. "Sit down, Waylon. Just a little short interview."

They stare each other down, something silent passing between them that I can't fully decipher. Whatever it is, it's an old conflict that goes beyond just Delia asking him to participate in an interview.

Waylon sighs and rakes his fingers through his hair. "Fine, we can make it fast."

"Thank you, sweetheart." Delia pats his leg. "You can start, hun."

"Alright." Waylon waits until I give him the signal that I'm recording. "Our family has always loved animals, especially dogs. Big Bubba Bourbon was named after a chocolate lab our family had when I was a kid."

"And we've had a few Big Bubbas take up the mantle since," Mrs. Stryker adds.

"Right." Waylon swallows and fidgets with his watch. The relaxed, happy version of him that I saw just a few minutes ago is gone. "We've donated time in addition to the proceeds from the bourbon with sponsoring annual pet adoption fairs and holding the annual gala to raise money for adoptable pets that need extensive medical care. Uh..."

"And you became a veterinarian to help out too," Delia says.

"Well, yeah. Among other reasons."

"Very noble." Delia smiles. "And it's like you're still a part of the company, too."

"Yep." Waylon pauses, jiggling his leg before looking to me. "Okay, that's all I have to say."

"Are you sure? You've barely scratched the surface." Delia frowns.

"We got more than enough material," I add. Hopefully I can convince Delia to put Waylon out of his misery.

"See? I should start doing some prep for tomorrow anyway," he says.

Delia looks disappointed, but she just stands up. "Okay, fine. We can do more later."

Waylon shoots me an exhausted glance and I hope mine radiates sympathy. I'm not the best at being warm but I feel for him. I've seen way too many people pressured into shit by their parents and it never ends well.

"Thanks for coming, Mom," Waylon says.

She lets him kiss her on the cheek, but she's clearly not pleased. Waylon doesn't seem to care all that much about her displeasure, though. His jaw is tight with annoyance. I can't blame him.

"I'm meeting someone for lunch, so I need to go. Rose, I'll email you about the new floral arrangement idea I have," she says. "And good to see you, Bianca."

She leaves and Waylon sighs, leaning against the prep table.

"Thanks for trying to save me," Waylon says once he pulls himself together.

"It's no problem. Felt like you needed a little backup." I want to reach out and touch him, but I hold back.

"I really appreciate it." He lets out a breath, tension rolling out of his shoulders.

Rose putters around, typing away on her phone, but I stand there with Waylon. I let him think for several moments instead of just filling the air to distract him. He doesn't seem to be the type who needs to be distracted when he's dealing with something.

"It's not that I don't care about the cause — I really do. It's just that I don't want to be the center of attention," he says after a few moments. "That's Mom's thing. And she can't seem to hold both those ideas in her head at the same time — that I want to be involved but not do the whole 'perfect figure in town who's at the center of everything' thing, you know?"

"I can tell." I scroll through all the photos of him I took. "But these kitten videos came out really well, if that makes you feel better. I'm sure people will love them and donate."

"Yeah, it does, actually," he says, running a hand through his hair again and studying me, his eyes soft. We're between the exam table and the counter, our bodies inches apart.

He's usually pretty easy to read, but I can't tell what's going on in his head right now. But whatever it is, it's making me tingle from head to toe. Like he's actually understanding where I'm coming from in my attempts to help.

I'm not used to that. People rarely get me this quickly.

"Good," I say with a swallow, looking away from him.

Rose clears her throat and Waylon steps back, avoiding my gaze. His cheeks are flushed.

"We should get back to the office," Rose says.

"Okay." I slip away and start to deconstruct the ring light, my face hot. "See you later, Waylon."

"Yeah, see you. I'll be by tomorrow to look at the house and all that, if that still works for you," he says.

"Right. See you."

He gives me another kiss on the cheek, lingering a little longer than he has to.

SEVEN
WAYLON

EVEN THOUGH WE'RE NEIGHBORS, I still drive over to Bianca's — my trunk is filled with construction materials to start fixing up the fence and her house. It's been a long time since I've done a ton of handy work, but I'm confident I can at least get things started for her.

I feel like I owe Bianca even more now. Mom's pushiness drives me fucking crazy now that I'm an adult who can choose to do whatever he wants. Everyone else in my life doesn't bother to try to stop her — it'd be like trying to stop a train.

But Bianca tried to back me up as gracefully as she could. And that made me not feel like I'm insane for not caving to her every whim, no matter how well-intentioned.

Bianca greets me as I pull up to her garage. I was hoping that she'd be dressed in something that doesn't make me lust after her, but I think I lust after her no matter what she's wearing. Today she's wearing joggers that are slung low on her hips and a matching crop top, her thick curls up in a bun. The deep red shade of her pants looks nice against her skin.

"Ready to tackle this mess?" Bianca asks as I hop out of my car.

"Yep. Just one step at a time." I pop my trunk. "Where did you want to start?'

"With whatever's easiest, I guess? Maybe the fence, maybe something inside?" She shrugs. "I think the bathroom has the most things wrong with it, but I'm not sure if it's best to start with the biggest thing."

I laugh. "Well, let's start with the most annoying thing."

"The master bathroom," she says readily. "The whole thing."

"Then we'll go there." I grab a bunch of my tools and gear that might help with fixing up a bathroom. I can come back later once I see the problems in-depth.

I follow Bianca inside. She's added some more personal touches since I was here last, and even bought Sadie more beds in each room. The dog is passed out on the bed in the living room until she hears us and follows. Her little tail whips back and forth.

"Sadie's doing well?" I ask as I reach down and scratch her between her ears.

"Yeah, she is! We went on a long walk on that trail today and she got tired halfway through." Bianca snorts. "At least she's easy to carry back."

"Yeah, she's done after about fifteen minutes. When I hiked with Duke, I'd carry her instead." We stop at the end of the hall, where the small master bathroom is. There's just enough room for both of us to stand inside, with a tub/shower combo on the far end, the toilet, and the sink.

Every inch of the counter is covered in different creams, lotions, and tools, all organized. The room smells faintly like jasmine, like she's just had a shower.

"Let me pull up the list," she says. "The water pressure sucks, and the tub doesn't fully drain, and these tiles are a mess." She pulls back the curtains and points at the tiles. "And the white stuff between is peeling."

"The caulk." I take a glance at it. It looks like it hasn't been redone since the house was built.

"Yeah. And the toilet runs." She sighs and scoops up Sadie. "And the paint is peeling a bit."

"This isn't that bad of a place to start." I put my bag down on the ground. "If I can't fix the water pressure, you might have to call a plumber. But everything else I think I can handle."

"Oh, good." She lets out a sigh, rubbing one of Sadie's ears. "I guess I'll...leave you to it?"

She looks adorably unsure.

I crack a smile. "You can hang out with me if you want to. You might need to sit in the doorway, though."

"You sure?" She sits down cross-legged, tucking Sadie into her lap.

"Yeah, of course. Otherwise, I'm just going to listen to a podcast or something." The toilet should be easiest, so I start with that.

"What podcast?" She leans against the doorframe.

My face gets hot. "It's kind of dorky."

"No, you?" She says with a soft, teasing smile. I can't help but smile back. "But for real, what is it?"

"A geography podcast." I take the lid off the back tank of the toilet and take a look.

"A geography podcast?" She raises an eyebrow, genuinely curious. "Sorry if this sounds stupid as hell, but hasn't everything been mapped already?"

"Sort of." I lean down and turn off the water to the toilet. "It's more about how geography shapes the cultures and economies of certain places."

"That sounds pretty cool, actually." She adjusts Sadie in her lap. "Way more interesting than the stuff I learned in school."

"School was pretty boring for the most part." I start adjusting a few components inside the toilet tank. "Learning stuff outside of school is much more interesting."

"So you decided to go to college and then to even more school after?" She scratches Sadie under her chin. "You must have been good at it."

"I was." I dig around my bag for a tool. "But a lot of that was just liking the praise I got for getting good grades. I like to win."

That was way more honest than I intended being, but as always, Bianca just nods, pensive, instead of judging.

"Do you think the pressure helped back then?" she asks. "Like you got good grades and had good study habits, which helped you in vet school?"

I sit back on my heels and think about it. "I guess so, yeah. Praise is a drug."

"It's true for most people," she says. "I definitely wouldn't have started modeling if it wasn't for people telling me I should do it. I wish I'd ignored them."

"You didn't like modeling?" I ask, jiggling the toilet handle. "But you were really good at it."

She snort-laughs. It's not the prettiest sound, but I like it coming from her. "I'm so not but thank you. It's just a lot of Photoshop."

I study her face. She really is the most beautiful woman I've ever seen in my life. I can't find a single thing I don't like about her, and I can't think of anyone who wouldn't agree.

"I mean, I'm looking at you now and I've seen some of your photos. You look the way you do in real life."

"Don't be so nice." She waves her hand at me, hiding a little smile. "Seriously."

"Is it nice if it's true?" I shrug and stand up, pressing flush. Thankfully it works. I've only fixed a toilet once back in college.

"It's stupid, but not a lot of guys who look as nice as you are truly nice," she says with a sigh, studying me. She has the longest eyelashes I've ever seen, and they frame her eyes in a way that makes her gaze feel more intense.

"Toilet should be good," I say, because I don't know how to respond yet.

"Okay, for reference, I've had the misfortune of knowing a lot of 'nice guys' who turned out to be dicks," she adds. "But you're not."

Her sincerity strikes a note. She's basically always straightforward, but having her give such an earnest compliment feels really nice.

"Thanks," I say.

I move onto the shower and we sit in comfortable silence. Not having to fill the air with inane chatter is a welcome change. I glance over my shoulder at her and find her looking at me. Maybe at my ass? She glances away, biting her bottom lip.

"What's the deal with the Jepsen Festival?" she finally

asks. "I should probably know since I have to get pics for social media from it."

"It's fun. It's one of my favorite things around here." I peer at her shower head to figure out how it pops off the wall. "It's basically a carnival with a bunch of silly events — a baby pageant and race, a dog pageant, a—"

"A human pageant?" She fills in with a slight smile.

"That too. Miss Teen Jepsen and Miss Jepsen are highly sought after titles." I grin at her. "You get a ribbon and free pie for a year from Gladys."

"Who is Gladys?"

"The pie lady. She usually sells them out of a little place downtown. They're ridiculously good."

"Oh, awesome." She brightens, smiling with her eyes. "Sounds like some good stuff for the bucket lists."

I'm glad my back is to her because my cock hardens at just the idea of her sex bucket list. But at least my memory of it isn't a complete horny hallucination.

Her phone rings and she huffs, silencing it. Then moments later, it rings again.

"Everything alright?" I ask.

"Just my ex, I'm guessing. He's getting slightly better with calling from different numbers so I might pick up." She rolls her eyes but alarm bells start going off in my head.

This is the third time she's mentioned this asshole bugging her, and as casual as she sounds, I don't believe that he's harmless.

"I can install security cameras really easily," I say.

She shakes her head. "It's fine. He's just being annoying. And he'd probably never make it all the way out here."

"Annoying can turn into more. Are you *sure* you're fine?" I ask. "Because I can help."

She bites her bottom lip for a second. "It's fine. He just... it's complicated."

"Mm." I go back to fixing the shower head, making a mental note to get some security cameras anyway if she changes her mind. I don't trust this asshole.

"Basically, he just wants me back because then he'll get back in with my dad and all of his connections in the music industry." She flips over her phone, her expression falling. "He was going to propose and it was basically all for clout."

"Jesus." I step out of the shower so I can test the water pressure. "I'm sure he loved you. Loves you."

The thought of a man getting down on one knee for Bianca just for the connections makes my blood boil. Surely no one's that shallow, but the more she tells me about her life in LA, the more I realize it's extremely different from Jepsen.

"Mm, doubtful." She waves her hand. "Whatever, it's not a huge deal. I just want to move on and take some time for myself. I'm so not about relationships in general right now."

"I feel that." I test the water and the pressure still sucks. "This might be a plumbing issue that I can't really fix. But I can try to fix the other stuff before I try to troubleshoot more."

"Thank you." She tugs at the end of her curls. "So you're a permanent bachelor?"

"Probably." I shrug. "I like my life now with my dog and my friends. I just want to live life without bullshit."

I leave it at that. Just the thought of Catherine puts me in a bad place, making my stomach churn.

"Maybe you should have a bucket list," she says. "Or bucket lists."

"Maybe." I half-smile, getting down on the ground to look under the sink just a few inches. To be honest, since I've been single, I've fallen into a comfortable routine. Trivia nights. Watching football with Jeremiah. Hanging with Wes and Rose. Work. Rinse and repeat. "I'm not sure what I'd put on just one, much less multiple."

"What haven't you done that you want to do?" she asks. "Like the craziest shit you could think of."

My brain goes to the basic stuff, like skydiving or travel, then immediately veers over to all the sex I haven't gotten to have. It's a long list.

The hookups I had between the first time Catherine and I were together and the second were very, very hit or miss, but at least I got some experience beyond the vanilla, missionary-in-the-dark sex that Catherine and I had.

"I don't know. I don't think it'd be stuff you want to hear." I smile at her. Her eyes are wide and curious. My blood rushes south, and I decide to push it a little bit. "But I like your idea of having different ones."

"All three of them?" she asks, shifting so she's sitting on her hip, her thighs pressed together. I've never been much of a leg guy, but hers, even under her sweats, are turning me into one.

"Yeah." I push my hand through my hair, holding her gaze.

"What's something on each of your lists?" she asks, her voice soft.

"For the big, crazy stuff? Maybe climbing a mountain. Not like Everest, but maybe one of the smaller ones in North

America. Regular day to day stuff, I honestly don't know. And the sex list..."

I genuinely haven't thought about this — usually my desires come and go based on how horny I am.

And right now, my dick wants everything about her with a laser focus. I want to feel her lips around my cock. How she feels under my hands without her clothes in the way. See her lose the grip on her control.

"I don't know," I say. "But I'd like to know what's on yours."

For a second I'm afraid I was too honest. But then I swear I see a flush under her brown skin, creeping its way up her neck and to her cheeks. The relative innocence of it makes me want to close the gap between us, but I stay where I am. I only want to make a move if she's down for it.

"Honestly, I just want someone to actually make me come," she says, almost embarrassed. "Without strings attached for something more. And teach me a few things about making it better."

"I can do that. Especially if there aren't strings attached."

"Not even this fake relationship?" She raises an eyebrow. "Didn't we agree that it was all business?"

"It still is. We aren't dating. It would just be me helping you out with your bucket list." I shrug, scanning her face. "And I know for a fact that I can help you check off the first thing."

Her lips press together like she's holding back a smile. "You sound extremely confident."

"I am."

Bianca was right about one thing — I'm a bit of an overachiever. And fucking isn't any different.

"It takes me a long time," she says, swallowing. I see the pulse fluttering at the base of her neck and I want to nip the spot. "To come, I mean."

"I don't see that as a problem." I get closer and make circles just under the hem of her shirt with my thumb. "More time for me to enjoy myself."

She bites her bottom lip, clearly skeptical. But I'm not lying — I get something out of this too. "You're absolutely sure you won't get tired? And that you'll enjoy it?"

"Have a little faith in my stamina. And yes, I'll enjoy it." I cup the back of her neck, and she melts into my touch. "Just let me take care of you. You don't have to think about anything."

She considers it for a second, then says, "Okay."

My blood starts pounding, whooshing in my ears.

"C'mon, let's go somewhere without a freezing tile floor," I say, getting up and helping her to her feet.

She takes my hand and guides me down the hallway to her bedroom. The first thing that strikes me is how nice her room smells, like jasmine and vanilla. Her bed is unmade, with a ridiculous number of throw pillows that have been tossed to the ground. She sits on the bed, fidgeting with her rings.

I sit next to Bianca and I gently massage the back of her neck until the tension leaves her body.

"If you want to stop, just tell me," I say. "And we'll stop right away."

"And leave you in the lurch?" She glances down at where my pants are already slightly tented.

"Yeah, if you're not comfortable." I gently rub a spot behind her ear. "I won't die from blue balls."

I lean in to kiss her jaw as she huffs a quiet laugh, though I'm not sure at what. A kiss on the lips feels a little too emotional for what we're about to do. This is just her bucket list with a little lesson tacked on.

She lets out a soft breath, letting her head fall to the side to give me more exposure to her neck. Her skin is so soft as I skim one hand along her stomach, making her shiver, my hand inching upward toward her breasts.

She's not wearing a bra.

Both of us groan when I brush my thumb across her nipple, which hardens immediately. Her breast fits in my hand just right, and every time I rake my teeth down her neck, she shifts, her thighs pressing together.

"Need more?" I ask, gently grabbing the bottom of her top.

She nods and helps me pull off her shirt. Shit. Her breasts look even better than they feel, perfect teardrops and deep brown nipples.

I press her back to the bed and kiss down her neck until my lips reach one of her breasts. My cock is already aching and I want to rush down to taste her, but I need restraint — to take my time warming her up and feeling her out rather than just going for it like I assume her past hookups have.

I gently lick around her nipple, gauging her reaction. She likes it, but it's not making her back arch or moan.

"Do me a favor, princess, and tell me what you're wanting," I say, licking around her areola.

"Hm?" She glances down at me, clearly surprised. "You want me to...tell you what to do?"

"First lesson - your partner can't read your mind, as much as they want to. But they can read your body." I gently bite down on her nipple and she gasps, her nails digging into my scalp. "I can tell you liked that but I need to know more. I need to know how to make you scream."

"Y-yes," she says, raking her fingers through my hair. "More. Of all that."

I smile against her breast, then bite down on her other nipple, sucking harder. Her sweet little whimpers make my cock strain against my jeans. Finally I let myself slip a hand into her bottoms, my fingers rough against the lace of her panties. She parts her thighs, letting me slip a finger under. Soaked, just as I thought.

"I love how wet you've gotten for me," I say, lifting my head to look at her face. Her beautiful eyes are hazy with lust. "Is your pussy just as tight?"

I work a finger inside of her, just a little, and she clamps down on me. Even tighter than she was before.

"More," she says, wiggling her hips. "Deep."

I push her shorts and panties down and she kicks them off all the way, giving my hand enough space. I slip my middle and ring fingers into her, savoring the way her hips lift with just a slight touch.

"This deep?" I purposefully stop with my fingers halfway to test her and she shakes her head.

"Deeper."

I slip my finger in deeper and crook them up, making her gasp and shiver. With every stroke of my finger, she squeezes me harder, her face warm in the crook of my neck and her thighs clamped around my wrist.

I kiss my way down her body until I settle between her thighs. The scent of her arousal and seeing her wetness this close makes my cock ache.

Her legs slide up, pressing against my shoulders, and I glance up at her. The slight shift in her position feels shy to me, like she's turning away.

"You okay with this?" I ask, sitting back a bit.

"Yeah. Just..." She sighs and lets her head fall back. "I'm just self-conscious even though the idea is hot. My exes didn't really do this. Or at least do it enough to make me feel like they actually wanted to. Like they, um, didn't like the way it looked or tasted or something."

What's wrong with men who don't go down on women when they're probably expecting a blow job each time? And who could resist going down on a woman whose pussy looks this delicious? Slick and pink and ready?

"They missed out." I loop my arms under her thighs and tug her toward me. "Because you look really fucking good, Bianca."

Her exes *really* missed out — she tastes incredible, and when I hit the right spots, she responds right away. Her back arches and she'd kick me if I didn't have her legs pinned back. I follow her short commands — faster, right there, yes — savoring each and every part of her.

Is it taking a while to get her to come? Yeah. But do I care? No. I want to soak in every flutter of her pussy, every scrunch of her nose, every moan and gasp and plead she lets out. If I could keep her here for hours, dizzy with pleasure, I'd love every moment.

"Harder. Really hard," she pants when I start fingering her.

I do as she says, pumping my fingers hard and fast. I stroke her sweet spot each time and she shakes all over, like she's about to fall apart. She's pulling on my hair almost too hard, but I don't stop — she's right there and I need to see her get over the finish line.

And in seconds, she's falling over the edge, hips bucking and her thighs clamping on the sides of my head. I don't stop until she melts into the mattress, her chest heaving.

I wipe my face and sit up, taking her in. She's clearly sated, her body limp and eyes hazy. Eventually she blinks up at me and I smile.

"You alright?" I ask.

"More than alright." Her eyes flicking up and down my body. Her eyes linger on my cock, which is still rock hard.

"Just need a minute?" I run my hand up and down her calf.

"More than a minute."

I let her recover, then she eventually sits up on her elbows.

"Can I suck your cock?" she asks, almost shy in a way that hits just the right buttons for me. "Please? I want to make you feel good, too."

She doesn't have to say please — that look in her eyes is all I need to start undoing my belt. I have no idea how I'm going to last more than five seconds when she's looking at me like this.

A pounding on the front door makes both of us jump, making my cock immediately soften a bit, and Sadie wakes up, barking and whirling around in a circle.

"I can get it," I say, hopping off the bed and making sure my belt isn't halfway undone and my hard-on isn't too conspicuous.

It's someone delivering a package that requires a signature. Great timing. I scribble something vaguely resembling my name and thank him even though my balls feel like they're going to fall off. My phone buzzes in my pocket too with a message from work, too — they need extra hands for a few emergency drop-ins.

"It was a package," I say when I go back into the kitchen, where Bianca has settled. "And I have to head into work for an emergency, actually."

That simmering heat between us cools now that the bubble around us has been popped. Her clothes are on, plus an extra layer of a sweatshirt, almost like nothing happened.

"Oh, thanks. I forgot this was coming today." She puts the box down in front of her.

"Um, yeah." I clear my throat. "So, the Jepsen fest. I'll pick you up?"

"Yeah, that sounds good." She tucks one of her curls behind her ear. "And maybe we can start going down my list. Our lists."

Fuck, I wish I didn't have to leave. But I need to. And maybe the wait will make it even better.

"I'd like that," I say.

EIGHT
BIANCA

I CAN'T GET the memory of Waylon's head between my thighs out of my head the entire night. The thickness of his fingers inside of me, his skilled tongue. The roughness of his voice was what got me the most. It was him, but it was a whole new side of him that I really, really liked.

The next morning, I glance at my toys in my drawer before pushing it closed. I need to get dressed for the Jepsen Festival, not get off to Waylon's deep voice telling me he loves how wet I've gotten.

I turn on the shower, keeping it pretty cold. It doesn't really work.

I'm getting the hang of dressing Jepsen casual, at least of what I already have. I choose a denim mini-skirt and a red scoop-necked tank top tucked in. It's still unreasonably hot, so I go with some comfortable wedge sandals. Pinning my hair up is another must.

I check myself out in the full-length mirror I put up near the door. A rush of insecurity comes up from where I've tried to banish it. All those years of people picking my looks and body apart aren't something that can go away in a few seconds. At least I'm out now so I can start handling all that baggage.

My doorbell rings, making Sadie let out a surprised bark. I scoop her up and answer it — it's Waylon. He looks good in just shorts and a t-shirt, and both are cut just right to show off his muscular frame. His eyes quickly skim up and down my body, lingering on my legs and cleavage for a second before popping up to my face.

I expect it to be awkward after the way things abruptly ended the other day, but it isn't. A little undercurrent of heat is still there, along with the usual friendliness.

"You look great," Waylon says.

"You didn't have to come to the door," I say, trying to ignore the heat in my cheeks. I'm so not used to guys doing polite stuff like this — opening my door, coming to get me instead of just shooting off a text for me to come outside. The whole gentlemanly thing could be so corny, but he's just so damn genuine that I can't be put off by it.

Sadie squirms in my arms, trying to get to Waylon, so I hand her to him while I lock the door.

He just shrugs, petting Sadie between her ears. "Just habit. You ready?"

"Yep."

He gets to the car first and opens the door for me like he did before, putting Sadie in my lap.

Once he's on the driver's side, he pulls out of the driveway and heads toward town. I adjust the fans on the dash to point more toward Sadie, who closes her eyes. Her fur blows around, like she's in a music video.

"Has it been okay in your house with the AC?" he asks, glancing over at Sadie with a slight smile.

"Yeah, I've had the fans going hard. She loves sitting in front of them." I gently rub her forehead, which I've discovered she loves.

"That's cute." He turns onto another road, traffic picking up. "If it gets too hot, just let me know and y'all can come to my place to cool off."

"I might take you up on that." It's a different kind of hot here than in LA — humid and heavy.

We sit in comfortable silence, and I try not to look at his hands. But I can't help it. Why are his hands just gripping the steering wheel enough to make me hot under the collar?

"Can we talk about the bucket list?" Waylon asks. "Just to make sure we're both on the same page."

"Sure, yeah." I swallow. At least he doesn't want to throw it away entirely. My pussy involuntarily clenches at the memory of his fingers inside me, immediately hitting the sweet spot I'd tried to get Kyler to hit for years.

"We're keeping this separate from the fake relationship, right?" He turns onto a different road, where we run into traffic. I can see the Jepsen Festival far ahead. "It's just... friends with benefits with structure?"

I press my lips together, trying not to smile too hard at his description. "Yeah, just that. Nothing serious at all."

"Okay, cool." He rakes a hand through his hair. "Not that I thought you felt otherwise, but...y'know."

"Just wanted to keep things clear. I get it."

"What else is on the list, by the way?" he asks.

"Oh, jeez. It's kind of a running list that changes," I say, even though I know. I'm just too embarrassed to list everything out when I'm stone cold sober in the car. "Phone stuff. Stuff with toys. Other stuff."

"It's cool. You don't have to tell me now if you aren't comfortable," he says, glancing at me with a smile. "Let's keep it a surprise, if that's better? Just let things happen when they happen?"

"Yeah, much better." Thank god he can pick up on what I'm putting down without me needing to flat out say it every time.

We inch toward the Jepsen Festival and finally make it to the parking lot, which is just an empty field. It's packed, with families walking hand-in-hand toward the festivities.

I hop out, clipping Sadie's leash onto her harness so she doesn't have to be warm in her bag. Waylon takes my other hand, threading his fingers through mine. His hands are toasty warm but not so hot that I want to let go.

"Oh wow, this is big," I say once we officially cross into the fairgrounds.

I'm not sure what I was expecting, but it wasn't all of this. Several large tents are to our right, and a bunch of carnival games are to our left. Way down at the far side directly ahead of us are a bunch of food tents and trucks.

"Yeah, it's gotten bigger since I was a kid," he says. "Same rickety rides, though."

"Is that even safe?" I ask.

"Probably not, to be honest." He guides us over to the tents to our right. "Do you want to grab photos for social media first, then take a look at everything else?"

"Sure, that sounds good."

We walk past the tents, which are all setting up for their events or starting them.

"Oh, how cute!" I say, stopping in front of the tent for the baby pageant. Babies are everywhere, many of them dressed in cute costumes. I've always liked the idea of babies, but having one isn't even on my radar right now.

"Wes won this when we were babies," Waylon says with a laugh. "And Rose got second place."

"What about you? You were an adorable baby too." Excessively adorable — a little chubbier than Wes, with big brown eyes and round cheeks.

"I was too fussy." He runs a hand through his hair and laughs. "It's hard to be cute when you're beet red from crying. I got a participation trophy, which my mom probably still has."

"Wow." I start walking again so we can make it to the Stryker Liquors booth. "She kept everything, didn't she?"

"Yeah. At least it was easy to put together my college applications - my mom had a whole record of everything I ever did."

The Stryker Liquor booth is one of the biggest booths, with a line already building up. I snap a photo of the line, including the sign over the booth, and snag a few of the bartenders serving up drinks. Waylon waits patiently as I style a few drinks, snap a few more photos, and post some things to Instagram stories.

The booth for the shelter is next to it, with just two volunteers handing out information on the shelter and how to donate. I grab a few pics of them too.

"Okay, I've gotten everything," I say, handing Waylon one of the drinks and take a sip of one for me. It's not as strong as the drinks I had at Wes and Rose's engagement party, but it's strong enough that I'm going to feel it. "I think I'm going to need some food with this drink."

"Do you want something fried, or something fried?" he asks with a smile. "Or something fried and rolled in sugar?"

"All of it." My stomach growls. "I've never had fair food and I haven't had fried food in god knows how long."

"Then you're in the right place." He threads his fingers through mine again and we walk over to the food.

For a relatively small town, they have a ridiculous number of restaurants and food trucks. They even printed off a mini map of all the available food.

"Where do we even start?" I ask, looking at the map. "I don't know what I want to eat or what's good."

"I know the catfish nuggets are popular every year if you want to start somewhere." He puts a hand on my back and gently guides me out of the flow of foot traffic before people bump into me.

"I've never had catfish, so let's do that. What's it taste like?" I check the map and find the catfish nugget booth.

"Like catfish." He laughs and we start toward the booth. "I honestly don't know how to describe it. It's a white fish. Salty. Crispy. Really damn good."

We reach the booth when the line is short, and in a few moments, we have a paper tray of little golden balls of fish and perfectly cooked fries. We find a standing table and he pushes the food toward me. Sadie lays down at our feet.

He hands me a fork after I snap a picture of the food, his body and hands in the frame.

"Mind if I post this?" I show him the photo and he nods. "Thanks."

"Try it first." Waylon offers me the fork after I'm done posting.

I spear a nugget and lift it to my mouth. It smells good, like fish but not in a bad way. Waylon keeps his eyes on me while I pop it into my mouth.

"Oh, that's really good," I say, holding a hand in front of my mouth so he doesn't see me chewing. "Wow."

"Yeah?" He smiles and snags a nugget for himself. "Does it live up to your dreams?"

"Considering I never even thought of catfish until today, no. But in terms of fried food, absolutely." I snort and take a fry. "The modeling bubble I was in made the world feel weirdly small. I got to eat at some of the best restaurants in the world, but everything was very regimented. I had to keep my body at a very specific size."

I take another nugget, savoring the saltiness and the texture. How did I live without fried food? I like to eat pretty healthy, but in the past, any indulgent foods stressed me out. It meant being pinched and prodded, or the clothes not fitting the way the designer intended.

I dunk two fries into our ketchup and savor those too. I'm glad to leave that part of my life in the past forever. Something so simple as catfish nuggets shouldn't make me feel so free but they do.

"That sounds really hard. I can't imagine it." He shakes his head. "I think that would ruin all the other perks, like the travel to cool places."

"Yeah, it did." I shrug. "But now I can eat whatever and it feels really good. No more worrying if some assistant will tell me she wished she could reshape my ass. To my face."

His eyebrows shoot up. "Someone said that to you?"

"Yeah, not that weird to me. But definitely weird to others."

The disbelief on Waylon's face almost makes me laugh. "I wonder how they can live with such wrong opinions."

Okay, I can't hold back a laugh at that. "Well, thank you."

I've never thought my ass was anything special — if anything, it was an inconvenience for my job — but I'm glad he likes it.

"So you're opening a spa with your best friend after this instead of going back to modeling??" he asks after taking a few fries.

"Yeah," I say quietly, as if saying it louder will somehow curse me. "We're planning on opening it in New York since she already lives there and I like it there."

"That sounds cool. I don't know anything about spas, but I'm sure you know what you're doing."

His complete confidence in me is completely unwarranted, but I appreciate it. So far it's only him and Kaitlyn who have encouraged me. Not that my parents are actively discouraging me, but whenever I bring it up, they want to dive in and help with things I can do myself.

"You're sweet," I say instead of telling him all that.

He shrugs. "Just saying what I think."

The easiness of this — both the conversation and the silence in between — should be throwing up red flags for me. I never, ever get along with people this quickly and easily, aside from Kaitlyn. And the fact that it's Waylon, the guy I have a little sex pact with, feels like I'm walking into the beginning of a problem.

"You want to try something a little sweet?" he asks. "I'm not sure what dairy-free options they have, though."

"We can look."

We go over to a booth a few spots down that has donuts and some vegan options. The crowd has gotten bigger, so the line is winding all the way into the flow of foot traffic.

"Want me to grab a table?" he asks. "I see a free one over there."

"Sure, yeah."

He tells me to just get any donut with chocolate and disappears. I check on the social media posts that I put up, then check an email from Kaitlyn. She's excited to get started, but knows I still need time. But I don't want to leave her waiting for too long.

I take a deep breath and tuck my phone back into my purse. Everything is so open-ended. Now I'm here to fake date Waylon for at least another two months, but after that, it's all unclear. Will I feel more ready to dive into an entirely new life by then?

I step up to the front of the line and order our treats — donuts for him, and a vegan donut for me. The donut is surprisingly good and not crumbly dust. Not too sweet either.

I turn and scan the crowd to find Waylon, but stop dead when I see him. He's talking to a woman and the pure ice between them takes my breath away. Clearly, they know each other, just from how close together they're standing. Or rather, how close the woman is standing to him. Waylon's body language is standoffish. The woman flicks her dark brown hair over her shoulder and crosses her arms over her chest.

I can't read her lips, but whatever she says pisses Waylon off. His eyes narrow and fill with anger, then hurt.

Whoever this woman is, she can get fucked.

I march over, trying to pull myself together so I don't tear her a new butthole from the jump. Instead, I plaster on a smile and lightly squeeze Waylon's bicep.

"Babe, I got the donuts," I say, my voice overly sweet. He can probably tell I'm being over the top, but this woman doesn't know me. "Sorry, who is this?"

The woman looks me up and down in that bitchy mean girl who's going to be fake nice kind of way. I hate her even more now, even though that's extreme. Waylon radiates patience and kindness, so anyone who can smack that out of him must be a shitty person.

"Catherine." She extends her hand and gives me a limp handshake. "And who are you?"

"Bianca," I say. "His girlfriend."

"Girlfriend." Catherine narrows her eyes at me, then at Waylon. "That's new."

"It is." Waylon takes the donuts and puts them on the long picnic table. "Not that it's your business anymore."

She half-rolls her eyes. "We can't magically erase the past."

"But you can ignore it, can't you?" I ask, getting between her and Waylon so I can sit on the bench. She steps back, eyes widening. I didn't touch her, but she looks like she's been slapped. "Super sorry, but we're kind of in the middle of our date. Can't this wait?"

Catherine's cheeks get red as she stares at me, but I don't back down. It helps that I'm several inches taller than her, so just getting a little close to her makes her back up. Waylon's hand rests on my shoulder, his thumb brushing the back of my neck.

"Whatever." She leaves and Waylon's body relaxes behind me.

"Sorry," he mumbles, taking a seat across from me. "She snuck up on me."

He takes a bite of his donut, his mood still low. I eat too, unsure of what to even say.

"Your ex?" I finally say, even though I know the answer.

"Yep." He sighs through his nose and throws back the rest of his drink, his nose wrinkling.

His expression has gone from hurt to blank, which is almost more disturbing. I got the sense that he and his ex didn't end of good terms since he said he wasn't about relationships these days, but they must have ended on *horrid* terms. I can't imagine him being with someone like her. I get that people change, and from what I understand, it's been several years since they've been together.

But even seeing them side by side feels odd. She just seems like a mean person.

I can tell he doesn't want to talk about it, as nosy as I am, so I nudge him with my knee instead of asking him more.

"Do you want to try some of the rides?" I ask.

"Right after eating?" A little ghost of a smile comes back onto his face, and it warms me from the inside out. "Is that a bucket list thing? Getting sick on an ancient fair ride that's probably breaking at least four safety regulations?"

"Okay, maybe not right now." I snort. "But maybe we can play a few games?"

"Yeah, let's do this." He polishes off his donut, and I finish mine.

I might not be the cheerful one between the two of us, but I can try to save the rest of the day.

NINE

BIANCA

WAKING up and being somewhere at the same time every weekday is weirdly soothing. This is a normal life for most people — maybe it's what I should have been doing all along. It doesn't hurt that the social media posts I've made for Stryker Liquors have done pretty well. I don't feel like a complete fraud.

It's just enough to keep me busy while I'm here — work in the day, time to relax, then planning for the spa.

"Morning," I say to Rose when I get into the office the Monday after the Jepsen Festival. My desk is across from hers, and Sadie's bed is placed near the window, so she gets a little sun during the day.

"Morning," Rose says, sounding slightly distracted as she texts furiously. "Sorry, Delia's blowing up my phone about wedding shit."

"Ah." I sit down at my desk and boot it up. "Is everything fine?"

"Yeah." She sighs and puts her phone down. "It's just so

much and she has a whole lot of opinions. Even my own mom is just like, 'do whatever you want' but Delia has a 'vision.' And then throw in stuff for the family reunion and I'm just a little over it all."

"That sounds exhausting."

"It is. And I know she means well, but jeez." Rose starts typing on her computer. "Anyway, whatever. Let's talk about the Jepsen Festival, then some other stuff we have down the road."

"Sure, yeah."

I get settled in and we go over my posts from the festival. Rose tells me about the newest moonshine cocktail they're making and the possible campaign ideas we could put together for social media. Time flies by quickly until we're interrupted by my phone. It's on vibrate, but it vibrates so many times in a row that I have to check it.

"Oh, fuck," I murmur. It's a text from my mom's PR rep, Flo. I let my personal PR rep go before I moved out here, but whatever it is, I'm guessing Mom has me being monitored too.

Flo: *Hi Bianca, please give me a call when you have a chance. It's urgent. Thank you!*

"Everything alright?" Rose asks.

"I have to check. I have to step out for a second, sorry." I get up to leave and Sadie trots behind me.

I scoop her up for emotional support and call Flo back as I leave the building. She picks up on the first ring.

"Hi, Bianca, how are you?" Flo says, her voice calm.

"I'll be better knowing that shit hasn't hit the fan? Maybe?" I pace back and forth.

"It hasn't hit the fan entirely. We can fix this," she says.

"Basically, Kyler has finally announced the split even though a lot of people suspected it based on your Instagram posts. He doesn't paint you in the best light in his announcement."

Of course he didn't. I close my eyes and take a deep breath through my nose. I wrongly assumed that he'd go the 'we still care for each other and please respect our privacy at this time', not...that. His image isn't the type to stir up any controversy on purpose. Or at least I thought so.

"How did he paint me?"

"Mostly in a sad sack kind of way," she says. Her bluntness is a relief — she can see through his nonsense. "That yes, you two broke up a while ago, and that you did the dumping while he was down. He sort of paints it as if you were being irrational and having some sort of quarter life crisis. He definitely leaves the door open for you two to reconcile, though. Almost like he's expecting you to."

"Which will definitely make his fans love me even more," I say, my tone dry.

"Yeah, don't check your Instagram. They're animals out there."

"I have the notifications off."

And I have for years. Dating a singer with a legion of intense fans has meant being bombarded with hate and some truly unhinged threats. I can't imagine how awful they are now that their theories that I'm just as bitchy as I look online have been confirmed.

How did I not see this coming?

"Good, keep them off. Just a moment." She pauses, and I hear her say something to someone else. "Anyway, back to the other problem — are you dating the guy who you've been posting bits and pieces of on Instagram? Because some pictures of him in that town you're in have leaked too."

"Yes..." My heart starts pounding harder than ever. "Have they figured out who he is yet?"

"No. The photos aren't very clear, so they mostly show the back of his head," she says. My heart rate slows a little and I press Sadie to my chest. "But he should know that he might have a target on his back."

I swallow. This was the plan all along and we'd even discussed how many eyes are always on me, but somehow I'd painted it as something abstract in my head — like it wouldn't affect our day-to-day lives and it would just make Kyler back off if he saw hints of Waylon existing on my Instagram. But now it feels very real. I feel dumb as hell for being so naive and assuming Kyler would take the high road.

"He's just a regular person," I say, my voice weak. Sadie licks underneath my chin, like she knows I'm upset.

"That might work in our favor," she says. "Does he have a lot of social media?"

"No. I can tell him to private his Instagram account," I say. His Instagram is mostly dog and nature photos, but it's a big target without moderated comments.

"Give me his name as well so we can get ahead of any issues."

"His name is Waylon Stryker." I heave a sigh. "How big of a story is this?"

"About the same as other stories about you both in the past — not the biggest news, but very big in the circles of your fans and his fans. I just wanted to inform you so we could put out a statement of our own," she says.

"Okay. I have to get back to work, so can we work out the statement over email later?" I ask.

"You're modeling way out there?" I can practically hear her eyebrows shoot up.

"No, I'm doing social media for Waylon's family's company," I say.

Flo pauses. "Wow. Okay. Good for you. Well, I'll go ahead and send you a draft in an hour or two, okay?"

"Okay, thanks."

I hang up and take a few seconds to gather myself before heading back inside.

"Sorry," I murmur to Rose.

"It's fine. Sounded like an emergency," Rose says, frowning. "Are you okay? Because you can totally take a longer break."

"I'm okay, I swear." I adjust Sadie on my lap. "It's just some bullshit I'll deal with after work."

I try to stay focused the rest of the day, but it's hard. My hand itches to check my phone and see what's being said online even though I *know* it's not good for me to do that. By the end of the day, I'm wiped just from being tense all damn day.

Walking Sadie when I get home helps relieve tension, though I wish she wanted to walk longer. But it's enough to calm me down to go over the statement Flo sent over and send it back. I force myself to start texting Waylon about the slight turn the situation has taken, overthinking every detail until I just tell him to call me when he can.

God, what if he hates me for this? I warned him, but I don't know if I warned him enough.

He calls me a few minutes later, and it's a FaceTime call. Did he mean to do this? I answer it either way.

"Hey," he says. He's clearly just gotten out of the shower, and his damp hair and the flush to his cheeks are extra handsome. Plus, he's wearing glasses, which I find inexplicably hot. "What's up?"

"Hey, so, um..." I go to my bedroom and sit down on my bed since it's cooler in there. "There's a bit of a problem that you need to know about. Can you private your Instagram account?"

"Sure, I can after this call?" His brows furrow.

"Okay, good." I sigh. I just need to come out with it. "So, my ex announced our breakup in a way that paints me in a bad light, so the hate mobs are extra bad. And everyone knows you exist, but they kind of knew that before. Someone's snapped a few photos of us around Jepsen."

"Hm." He lays back on his couch, completely nonplussed. "That sucks. Are you okay? Since your ex kind of screwed you over?"

I absently rub my breastbone to calm the flutter in my chest. I'm supposed to be warning him and he's comforting me?

"Are *you* okay with all of this?" I say, leaning back into my pillows also. "I thought that it was going to be a relatively low-key situation, sort of like how I told you at the beginning. But now it feels like Kyler is making this a whole thing."

He runs a hand through his hair. "I mean, I don't really go on social media and my online footprint is pretty small, especially when I private my account. And I doubt that people will go out of their way to come to Jepsen. I guess I'm fine with it. If something happens, then I'll deal with it then. I'd probably bore a media outlet to death before they even finished an article on me."

I snort, curling my legs under myself. "You're way too calm about this."

In a lot of ways, I'm relieved. His calm is keeping me calm, and for the first time today, the knot in my chest loosens up.

"I just know there's not much I can do about it right now." He shrugs. "And people's attention spans are short. We can just focus on the stuff coming up or stuff we actually want to do as a distraction. We could throw in a regular night out if there's anything on your bucket list you want to do but haven't planned yet."

My bucket list. The other two lists have quickly faded into the background, the sex one taking up their places. I bite my bottom lip. Phone sex is one of them — does it count if it's FaceTime? The one time I tried with Kyler, he was confused as to what I was trying to do. Then he figured it out and it was unbelievably awkward.

But as chill as he's being, would he want to do something like this now?

"Where'd your head go?" Waylon asks, his voice soft. A faint smile comes onto his lips, and he rests a hand behind his head. It does great things to his bicep.

"Where did you assume it went?" I ask with a smirk.

His grin widens. "I just didn't want to assume anything. Trying to be polite and all."

The little twang in his words tugs at a part in my heart that it shouldn't. The contrast between him saying he wants to be polite with the ravenous look in his eye makes me ache between my thighs.

"What item on the list were you thinking of?" he asks.

"The phone sex one. Though does FaceTime sex count?" I ask.

"Yeah, I guess," he says. 'It's your list, so you can do what you want."

I study him on my screen. The scruff on his strong jaw, his biceps, those fucking glasses. I want to do everything with him, to be honest. Every last thing on my list, twice over.

"Then let's do FaceTime," I say, biting my bottom lip. "Wait a second, let me get set up."

I put my phone down and grab my small phone tripod. I take a few seconds to set it up and sit on my bed again.

"Fancy," he says. He's moved over to his bedroom, propped up on his pillows, his shirt off.

"I usually do this two-handed," I admit. Now that I'm just sitting there on the bed, self-consciousness washes over me. I've been more or less naked in front of whole crews of people, but being on this bed makes me feel more naked than ever.

"Two-handed how?" he asks, his voice husky.

"My vibrator and a dildo," I say, shifting to sit on my hip. The throbbing between my thighs is already starting to overwhelm me.

"Mm." He holds up a finger and grins. "Let me get a proper set up too."

He puts his phone down and disappears for a few moments. I hear him tell Duke to get out of the room, and I glance over at Sadie, who's napping. Hopefully she doesn't wake up. A second later, the camera shifts and he has both hands free too. His cock is already tenting in his shorts.

"So..." I bite my lip.

"Why don't we start with you taking your shorts off," he says, gently stroking himself through his shorts.

I do as he says, leaving me in just my favorite panties. I have them in every color — lacy and pretty, but comfortable. Waylon nods, taking me in.

"Now what?" I ask. I want him to guide me, half because this is brand new territory and half because I like the way his voice deepens when he gives me commands.

"Get those toys you like."

I lean over to reach my side table and grab my two favorites — a pink wand vibrator and a pink dildo. I've never been able to find a rabbit toy that gives me what I need. I hold them up so he can see them, and he nods in approval.

I go to shimmy off my panties, but he makes a sound.

"Let me see those panties from the back," he says, his hand resting on his cock but not stroking.

I do as he says and get on my knees, showing my ass toward the camera. Despite what that asshole styling assistant said, my ass doesn't need re-shaping.

The quiet *hmm* of pleasure that he lets out makes me look over my shoulder at him. He's hypnotized, his hand gripping the bulge in his shorts.

"Now take them off," he says.

His clear pleasure at seeing my ass boosts my confidence and I make a show of slipping my panties off. I toss them aside, sitting down again. I keep my thighs pressed together, though.

"I want to see you," I say. I've felt his cock against my ass before, but seeing it is different.

He tugs off his shorts, then his boxers, and *oh*. His cock is thick, the kind of thickness I've searched for when buying toys. He grips it at the base, running a thumb up the underside. I want to burn this image of him in my mind forever — stretched out, relaxed, cock hard and body strong-looking.

"Show me what you do with both of those. Nice and slow," he says.

I grab my vibrator first, parting my legs and turning it on the lowest setting. I suck in a breath when I touch it to one lip, sliding it though the wetness that's already pooling at my entrance. My pussy clenches and I let my head fall back onto my pillows.

"Spread your legs more. I need to see how wet you are," he says, his voice intense but low.

I do as he says before I can even think about it, like he's flipped a switch in me. The toy is quiet, so the vibrations against my wetness feel loud in my quiet room.

"Taste yourself." He strokes his cock up and down even faster, his thumb brushing across the tip. "You tasted so fucking good the other day and now I wish I could taste you again."

I dip my fingers into my wetness. I've never tasted myself, but I do it, plunging my fingers into my mouth. The act feels so dirty in the best way.

"So good, princess," he murmurs, sliding his hand over the tip of his cock. "Look how hard you've made me."

I can't keep my eyes off his cock. My pussy clenches, feeling too empty, so I grab my dildo too. I'm wet enough so that it slides right into me. I can't hold back the moan that escapes from me, and the flare of arousal in his eyes makes me want to do it again.

I shift the angle of my body to hit my g-spot. Usually I stick it to the wall with the suction cup at the bottom and push back against it, but this works too.

"Fuck," he says, his abs flexing. A pink flush is making its way up his chest to his face, his glasses askew. "This is torture, not being inside you."

"I wish you were here with me," I say. Even though I'm about to come, I still wish it was him getting me there. His big, warm hands all over my body. The way he talks to me that makes me feel safe but desired.

"Soon," he says, his breath hitching. "You going to come, princess?"

I nod. If I make a sound, I'll break the spell.

"I'll come with you," Waylon says, his breathing heavy. "Let go for me."

I clench around the dildo, savoring the fullness and imagining it was him. The thought of his big body over mine, his beautiful cock inside me, pushes me over the edge. I come with a full body shudder, forcing myself to keep my eyes open to see him. His hand pumps up and down his cock faster and faster until his hips jerk and he comes all over his stomach with a soft groan.

Both of us lay there, breathing hard. I'm lightheaded. My pussy is still pulsing. I feel like I've just knocked something loose in my brain. Waylon looks just as dazed.

"Bucket list item, done," he says with a lazy smile.

"Yeah, definitely," I manage to say, pressing myself up.

"Maybe we can try a few more things soon," he says.

Duke bark-howls in the background and Waylon glances over at him. "I need to go, but talk to you soon?"

"Yeah, soon," I say.

He waves and ends the call. I grab my phone from the tripod. It takes me a long, long time to get the energy to get up and think about anything but Waylon.

TEN
WAYLON

"WHAT WAS THAT?" Jeremiah asks me as I bail out on my last set of squats with a grunt. "You crushed that weight like two days ago."

"I don't know." I yawn. "A little sore and tired, I guess. I still can't believe we used to get up this early in high school and do this almost every day."

We're in the gym he put together in his garage. A few times a week, we work out together before work, and usually I can keep up. But I slept like shit last night because I couldn't stop thinking about Bianca and what we did yesterday. That mix of shy and a little bold she has scratches an itch I didn't know I had.

It's starting to be a problem. Then again, maybe I'm still a little pent up. I've seen just enough to obsess over her. I'm not sure when we'll be able to hook up again — I'm assuming her bucket list has a lot more on it.

"We used to do a lot of shit in high school that makes me tired just thinking about it." Jeremiah takes a swig of his water. "Working out before school, sitting in class all day, going to practice after, then doing homework? While living off beef jerky, energy drinks, and sugar? Sometimes I look at what my students are doing and wonder how they're alive."

"I think I'd die if I tried that today. I still don't know how I made it." I drink some water too and rake a hand over my face.

"Adrenaline and the fear that if you didn't get into the right college you'd instantly die," he says.

I huff a laugh. The pressure we were putting on ourselves and the pressure from our parents — okay, mostly my mom — was so absurd in retrospect. At the end of the day, we both got into our dream school, Crescent Hill University, and we were just fine.

"How are things with Bianca, by the way?" he asks, stretching.

We've known each other since we were in the same class in third grade — I know him well enough that he's asking what he asked, but he's asking about something else underneath.

I raise an eyebrow. "Fine. Good. Why?"

"I've been curious." He motions for me to move, then takes my place when I do, pulling his locs from between the barbell and his back. "She kind of came out of nowhere. One day you were super busy with work, then the next you're bringing this girl to the event."

"It's casual." I spot him while he does another set. "I didn't think I had to make a big announcement."

"I'm not saying that you had to. I'm just wondering how she broke through your defenses." He re-racks the barbell. "I mean, besides the fact that she's literally a model."

"Well, yeah. I only got through our first conversation because I had to talk about Sadie. And after that...I was less than smooth."

"Like what kind of less than smooth?"

"Like..." I take a deep breath. I haven't spoken about this since it happened, and my face is still hot at the memory. "Mansplaining chaps to her the first time we spoke. How all chaps are assless by default, so there was no need to call them 'assless' chaps."

Jeremiah stares at me for several beats before bursting out laughing. Full on, bent at the waist wheezing.

"It wasn't *that* funny," I mumble.

"Bro, *how?*" he asks when he gets ahold of himself. "How did you fuck up so hard?"

"I just got struck stupid." I'm leaving out the fact that her lightly touching my arm is what short-circuited my brain.

"But hey, she still went out with you," he says. "Why not make it serious? You look happy with her."

I nearly blurt out, *I look happy with her?* but I hold back. I do like hanging out with Bianca — she's fairly quiet, but it feels like we're on the same wavelength in a way I can't explain.

Like she picked up on my irritation with my mom at the clinic and actually tried to steer Mom away from her obsession with making me this perfect figure in town who's involved in everything. And she managed to make Catherine genuinely stunned into silence, which is a miracle.

It doesn't hurt that talking to her is just easy. For someone who grew up in an environment where she and everyone else was judged constantly, she isn't judgmental at all.

I don't know what to think, but I didn't think we looked so much like a genuine couple that my best friend would actually say something positive about it.

Guilt fills my chest for lying about the relationship, but a tinge of annoyance is there too. Of all people, Jeremiah should get why I'd keep it casual.

"You know why I wouldn't want to make it serious," I say.

"I know, but it seems like you should get back out there. You guys happened kind of fast and you look happy when you're with her. Why not see if it can be deeper?"

I just shake my head. "Still no. She's not even interested in that right now either."

"I'm just saying." He stretches his shoulder, which has given him trouble since we were seniors and he fucked it up during the homecoming football game. "You two seem like a good match. Invite her to trivia so Jada and I can get to know her more. That's not too serious. And we need your dorky ass to answer the science questions."

I smile. "Okay, fine, I'll invite her."

The rest of the workout goes on without a hitch, and we part ways. After I get home, take Duke for a quick walk, and shower, I head to the clinic.

I fall into the rhythm of the day, calling up owners to tell them how their pets are before seeing a few more for regular checkups. Thankfully nothing goes sideways or throws me off.

But around lunch, I get a text from Mom, asking me if I want to go to Patty's, a lunch spot within walking distance of the clinic — her treat.

Her emphasis on it being her treat gives me pause. Why

is she trying to lure me in? I would have gone even if I had to pay myself. I'm starving, so I say yes.

Around lunch, I head over and spot Mom sitting outside with Lady, who stands up and greets me first. I give the dog butt scratches, then kiss Mom on the cheek. Mom must be running errands or just walking around town, based on how casually she's dressed — nice jeans and a nice blouse. I've never seen her dressed in anything less in public unless she's going to a workout class.

"Hi, honey," Mom says. "I ordered your favorite since I know you don't have a lot of time. They should call it for pickup soon."

"Thanks." I sit down across from her and Lady rests her chin on my feet. "I worked out with Jeremiah earlier so I'm starving."

"How is he?" Mom asks.

I give her the rundown on how he is, then a similar rundown on Jada. She cares a lot about them both, but I can almost feel her buzzing with anticipation to blast me with whatever she wants to say. The walk from our table outside to the pickup counter inside allows me to prepare myself for whatever she's about to ask.

I sit back down, and Mom starts immediately.

"I'd love for Bianca to join a few of the ladies' groups in town," she says. "And maybe she'd be interested in making a few appearances?"

I let out a slow breath. "What do you mean by appearances?"

"You know — just going to an exercise class or two, and the ladies' groups, like I said." Mom examines her nails, which are covered in the same pale pink they've been since I was a kid. "So she can be a part of Jepsen."

What she's left unsaid is that she wants Bianca to be just like her — to be her version of perfect. Outgoing. Involved in every single aspect of town so everyone knows her. Bianca has the look down, or at least she will if my mom manages to wrangle her into whatever outfits she feels are appropriate.

It's just like what Mom is trying to do to me — push me and shape me into something I'm not particularly interested in being anymore.

"What's wrong with what she's doing now?" I ask. "Do you not like her?"

"I like her!" Mom says, almost gasping in horror. "She's so beautiful. A little quiet. But maybe I just need to talk to her more. And you two look so good together."

I take a huge bite of my sandwich to give myself time to gather my thoughts. My mom would probably think I'd look good with a cardboard cutout of a woman, but still. Guilt makes me avert my gaze. The whole fucking point of this thing was to make Mom happy that I was dating someone. Why do I feel weird about it now?

It's a little too late, though, so I shove the guilt down.

"I know, but why do you want her to be any different?" I finally ask.

"Oh, honey." Mom sighs and squeezes my forearm. "She's lovely. She just needs a little push to be perfect."

"Well, why does anyone need to be perfect?" I ask, holding back a sigh.

"Fine, fine, perfect is a stretch." She spears a few chunks of lettuce. "Let's say a push to help her reach her full potential."

I blow out a breath through my nose. Does she not hear what she's saying? 'Full potential' is a loaded term too. It's not bad to think the best of people and their abilities, but I've spent my entire life trying to "live up to my full potential." I nearly burnt out before I started pushing back and I still have a weird relationship with success.

"I can see if she'd be interested in the groups," I say. Hedging is always a bit easier than flat out saying no in this instance. Otherwise, Mom would go around me and start texting Bianca or something.

Mom beams, and that weird mix of guilt and annoyance spreads its way across my chest again. I can't push Mom off forever, but I don't know how much longer I can let her press. Especially if she starts pressing Bianca.

"I hope I'm not disappointed," she says with a smile, making my stomach drop.

As much as I hate all the pressure Mom puts on me, disappointing her is somehow even worse. Like a punch to the gut, no matter what. She's not the type to yell, but seeing her expression crumple, almost in hurt, from me not living up to her expectations is almost worse than if she ripped me a new asshole.

I can't remember a single specific time that my dad chewed me out, though it did happen. But I remember almost every time I've gotten Mom's disappointed talks almost photographically.

"You won't be," I say, more out of habit than anything.

ELEVEN
BIANCA

I'M STILL NOT USED to being able to stay in on the weekend. Every weekend back in LA was a series of going out to clubs or parties. I putter around the house on Saturday, doing nothing in particular, until Sadie needs to go out again. She's a tiny little dog and has a tiny bladder to match.

I grab a baggie and let her outside into the backyard. Rather than just doing her business and trotting away to sniff grass or stare at the sky, she runs toward the fence between my property and Waylon's.

Duke barks on the other side of the fence and Sadie barks back, jumping up and down. She's way too short to make the leap — his fence is probably around six feet tall, while mine is much shorter.

"You want to say hi to Sadie?" I hear Waylon ask. "Come around — I'll open the fence."

I scoop up Sadie, who's been whipped into an excited frenzy, and head over to Waylon's yard, my heart fluttering despite myself. I've thought about our video call sex way more often than I should. But at the same time, I can't even blame myself. It was the hottest thing I'd ever done and somehow, it didn't feel awkward.

I don't have a single regret. And I definitely *have* felt regret after doing things like sending (mostly) nude photos to my exes, which is kind of in the same camp. Probably because those situations felt motivated by pressure to give them what they wanted rather than a desire to turn them on.

And turning Waylon on makes things eighty times hotter for me.

I put Sadie down once we're in and she darts over to Duke, tail wagging. Despite the size difference between them, Duke is gentle with her, sniffing her back.

"Hey," I say to Waylon. He looks delicious in just shorts, a t-shirt, and a baseball hat. No glasses today, but still — I'm a little flustered.

"Hey." He smiles back at me. "How's your day going?"

"Not bad. Just kind of...doing stuff around the house." I shrug, crossing my arms over my chest. I didn't put on a bra, and most of the time I can get away with it. But just standing in his presence has my nipples hardening. "How about you?"

"Same. It was a tiring week." He takes off his hat and rakes his fingers through his hair. "But I was going to take Duke for a short hike, if you want to come? It's more like a walk on an unpaved path rather than a true hike."

"Oh, sure." I haven't had the chance to get a dose of nature out here. "But how long is it? Sadie usually tops out at like twenty minutes walking."

"You got her to walk twenty minutes?" His eyebrows go up. "She usually flopped down on the ground after ten minutes for me."

I glance over at Sadie, who's already sitting down while Duke gnaws on a ball near her. I think Sadie takes naps for at least 80% of the day, shifting from one cozy spot to another cozy spot, usually my lap. Some days I'm a little jealous.

"Yeah, she's not super sporty, sorry," I say.

"It's no problem — I have a solution." He grins. "It's damn goofy, though."

"Okay...?" What could he possibly be thinking of?

"Here, let me get that and get some stuff together, then we can meet back here in ten minutes," he says, his eyes flicking down to my breasts for the briefest moment. The slightest, charming flush of pink appears across his cheeks, as if he didn't tell me my pussy tasted good without a hint of shame just a few days ago. "And you can change if you want to."

I go home and change into something more appropriate for hiking. Or at least what I think is appropriate for hiking — some leggings and a t-shirt, plus sturdy sneakers. And a sports bra, of course.

When I get back to Waylon's yard, he has a bag at his feet and he's putting what looks like another backpack on his chest. Sadie is standing in front of him, watching in rapt attention.

"What's that?" I ask, gesturing to what he's putting on.

He scoops up Sadie and places her into the pack, which has five holes in it. He puts her back to his chest and tucks each of her legs and tail into the holes, securing her inside the pouch. It's a baby carrier for dogs.

"Oh my god." I put my hand to my mouth, unable to stop the grin that spreads across my face. "You're kidding."

"Nope." He grins, rubbing one of Sadie's paws. She looks

so content. "I always wanted to take her on hikes with me and Duke, and I figured this was a good solution. She loves it."

"I can't handle how adorable this is." I dig my phone from my pocket. "Can I take a picture?"

"Sure." He turns his hat backward so his face is more visible, and I snap a photo, from his smile down to where Sadie is. Then I take one that's his whole face. I show him the first photo and he laughs. "I look ridiculous but who cares?"

"You look ridiculous in the best way," I say, looking at the photo.

My phone's camera reel is filled with thousands of photos I'd post online without a second thought. But the one with his whole face, capturing the brightness in his eyes...I want to keep for myself. The pic captures all the things I like about him and that doesn't feel like it should be blasted out there to help us keep up this fake relationship ruse.

But on the other hand, we aren't real and I should push that idea out of my head.

"C'mon, let's go," he says, picking up his backpack.

He clips on Duke's leash and leads me along a path toward the woods that run up to the sides of our properties. Years and years of people walking through the woods created a path, which we walk onto and into the woods. The path becomes more defined once we're further in.

It's gorgeous out here, with tall, old trees and plants everywhere. The day isn't too hot either, with a blue sky up above us. And best of all, it's so peaceful. The sound of our feet against the dirt paths, the chirps of birds, and the breeze through the trees are all I hear.

"It's so nice out here," I finally say, even though the silence between us wasn't uncomfortable.

"Yeah, I love it. It's nice to come out here after I've had a shitty day." He loosens Duke's leash, letting it extend so Duke can explore ahead of us. "There's a lot of cool hiking spots around here, if you want to explore them sometime. Didn't you say something about wanting to see the stars in a really dark place?"

"I think so? I was pretty tipsy that night, which is probably why I even mentioned the sex bucket list in the first place," I admit. "But yeah, I'd love that. There's so much light pollution in LA."

As much as we both clearly enjoyed fooling around, I like this too — just being next to him. I don't get to have these kinds of moments with many people in my life. Peaceful without the need to say something or check my phone.

"Duke, leave it," Waylon says as Duke tries to yank up an enormous fallen branch. Duke looks over his shoulder, tail wagging, then starts to go back to it. *"Leave it."*

Duke trots ahead, nose in the air like he's annoyed. We both chuckle.

"He likes to pull up whole tree limbs," Waylon says. "He'll take out our ankles prancing around with it. He gets very proud of himself."

"I bet." Duke sniffs around, tail whipping back and forth. "Did you always want to be a veterinarian?"

"I think so, yeah," he says. "My family always had dogs, and I was always good with them. Any animals, really. I was the kid who brought home wounded animals and helped them. My school's 4H Club had animal husbandry activities and I interned at the clinic where I work now. It just worked out."

I can easily imagine him as that child, his big brown eyes filled with concern for a baby bird or squirrel.

"It's cool that you actually did it," I say. "A lot of kids are like 'oh, I want to be a vet' or 'oh, I want to be a doctor' and not a lot of them do it."

"Thanks," he says. "To be honest, a lot of it was so I wouldn't have to work at the company. I literally didn't give a shit about it and my dad could tell. It pissed him off for some reason. He always had John David as his protégé and he was always all in, so what did he need me for?"

He looks far off into the distance, gathering his thoughts. I stay quiet to let him think.

"I think he just likes control and power. But once he saw I was all-in on veterinary school, he just kind of...stopped giving a shit about me." He pauses. "That sounds kind of dramatic, but he's just disengaged. Same deal with my brother Ash to a certain point. They fought like crazy back then."

"What does Ash do?"

"He's a musician — he's in a band and has a record deal and everything."

My chest seizes a little, an old reflex. Every single time that someone's a musician or has a relative who's one, I brace myself for them asking me for some kind of connection. Usually I say no, and those friendships fizzle out fast.

But this is different. I take a slow, steady breath to loosen the knots in my chest.

"He left town the day after he graduated high school and has only been back for holidays," he continues. "But even then, sometimes my Dad bitches that Ash never worked for the company. I guess I'll kind of work at the company when the shelter opens. I think Dad will be pleased since the shelter helps the bottom line. Sorry, I'm talking about myself a lot, aren't I?"

"I asked you." I shrug. And it's just nice to hear him talk candidly. He's always warm and friendly but he doesn't let his vulnerability out that much.

"What was the thing you wanted to be when you grew up?" he asks. "An astronaut? A marine biologist? What's up with kids wanting to be marine biologists?"

"I have no idea. I guess it sounds cool but maybe the reality isn't all that exciting." I snort. "I don't know. I figured out I wasn't a good singer pretty early, and while I like music, the whole music production thing isn't my scene. Acting was out of the question too."

"Why were those the only options? Just living where you lived?" he asks. Duke picks up a reasonably sized stick ahead of us, his whole butt wagging with his tail as he shows us. "Great stick, buddy."

"Yeah, entertainment industry stuff was always the first line. Especially with nepotism connections." I watch Duke prance along, very proud of his stick. "But trust me, I saw more than enough people try to launch careers in the industry who were subpar and I didn't want to go that route. At least with modeling it's a little easier to skirt by. Maybe that's why I went into it once I had a glow-up."

"You know what I'm going to say about that." He gives me a slow smile.

"And you know that I'm going to say that there's more to

modeling than how I look." I gently nudge him with my shoulder.

"I still think I'm right," he says. "How old were you when you got into it?"

"Seventeen, so kind of old compared to other models. But before that I had really awful skin. Painful acne, all over," I say. I'm not sure why saying it out loud makes me flush with heat. It's been a while since I've told anyone new. Regardless, it's nothing to be ashamed of. "It took Accutane and a ton of different skin treatments. Even now I'm a little anal about products being simple and safe. Nothing too crazy."

Now my skin is nearly perfect — aside from a few period-related zits once a month and some lingering scars that laser treatments didn't fix, everything is under control. But the emotional scars of it are still inside the back of my brain.

"That's rough," he says softly. "I just had a few zits and I felt so self-conscious. I can't imagine having it bad."

"Yeah, I got bullied for it." I sigh. "Then again, kids find anything to bully each other over."

"Every day I'm surprised at how shitty teenagers can be." He shakes his head. "I can't understand how Jeremiah teaches a bunch of high schoolers math everyday *and* coaches football after."

"I think I'd die. He must have balls of steel."

"Yeah, he's always been like that while somehow being laid back. It's a gift," he says. "Speaking of, do you want to come to trivia with us? Jada and Jeremiah were asking if you want to come."

"Trivia?" I blink and glance up at him. "I'm going to be borderline useless, you know."

"You'll be fine," he says with a smile. "And they just want to get to know you more."

I bite the inside of my cheek. It's probably a good idea to hang out with his friends to sell the fake relationship. But I want them to genuinely like me for some reason.

"Sure, then. It'll help us sell the relationship to your mom if people see us all hanging out," I say.

"Cool, I'll text you the details. It'll be fun," he says, genuine as always. "Anyway, do you want to open a spa because it's skincare?"

"Yeah, exactly. We're thinking of it like a med spa," I say. "Not like, Botox and fillers, but mostly skin treatments for people with scarring or acne. Kind of place where I went when I was a teenager. A place people can go without judgment."

He nods and lets me walk ahead on a narrow part of the trail. "I don't know much about spas, but that sounds like a good idea."

"I still don't really know deep down if I'm going the right direction," I admit. "I study business in my spare time and we're doing what we can remotely, but it's not like I've gone to school for this. Neither has Kaitlyn, but at least she went to college for a bit."

"Plenty of people haven't gone to school, and they've succeeded. The fact that you're trying and doing your research is important," he says. "People who go in with the mindset that they've learned everything are usually the ones who fuck up."

"True." I still shrug. Logically I know he's right, but it's hard to believe it deep down. My life has been both limited and expansive at the same time, stuck in a little bubble without a ton of hardship.

"You don't seem like you believe me," he says. "But you should."

"Quit reading me like a picture book," I say, teasing even though I'm still thrown off by how he can just reach past my usual neutral expression and pull out the truth.

"You're a little hard to read sometimes, but not always," he says. Duke walks back toward us and puts the stick he's been carrying into Waylon's hand before going to get another. "I just have to look a little deeper. And I don't mind doing that."

I stare up at him. What can I even say to that?

I've felt this flip-flop in my chest looking at him before, but it's never taken my breath away. But this time, it does. And for the first time, worry is in the mix too. I can't get too attached to Waylon — he's not a part of my future plans. But I think I'm getting tied to him without even trying.

TWELVE
BIANCA

"DON'T BE NERVOUS," Waylon says as I climb into his SUV. I hold the bottom of my denim mini-skirt, but Waylon's eyes still skim up my legs. The skirt is quickly becoming a staple, and it's only partially because of how he looks at me when I wear it.

"Who said I was nervous?" I ask, an eyebrow lifting.

I *am* actually nervous. He and his friends dominate trivia every week. Y'know who isn't good at trivia? Me. Unless it happens to be about dumb pop culture stuff or certain kinds of music.

"Your face." He smiles at me, and I get that stupid rush of warmth through my whole body that I got on our hike.

I bite my lip to hold back a smile. "Yeah, I'm nervous. We've already met but that was at a big event. Now I can't hide."

"They're pretty much like they were at the party." He half-smiles. "Seriously, you don't need to worry."

I shift in my seat. I've never gotten along with so many

people in such a short amount of time before. And I really care about Waylon's friends liking me for some reason. Even more so than usual. But them liking me doesn't even matter in the long run. So why do I feel like throwing up a little?

"And I'm nervous I'm going to mess up this whole trivia dominance thing you have going on," I add.

"It'll be fine. If anything, we might miss out on a few points." He backs out of my driveway. "Jada and Jeremiah are cool so they won't be super upset if we lose. If we lose, then..."

He can't hide the dread in his eyes at the thought of losing.

"You'll only be devastated for a week?" I laugh. "Until you win again?"

"Okay, yeah, kind of," he says with a grin. "But I want you to come and have fun. Think of it as a bucket list thing."

He's right. And honestly, what would I have done if I were home alone? Watch TV and snuggle with Sadie? I would have done the exact same thing back in LA, minus the dog. I really do need to start working on my other bucket lists. I should use this time in Jepsen to do something new.

We arrive at the Copper Moon and park in the back. Waylon threads his fingers through mine as we enter the bar, which is busy, but not overly packed. He weaves us through the crowd like he already knows where we'll be sitting, and I spot Jeremiah. He's hard to miss — he's Waylon's height, and his locs are in a bun on top of his head.

"What's up?" Jeremiah says, giving Waylon a bro hug. "Good to see you again, Bianca."

"Likewise." I'm not sure what to do with my hands, but

thankfully Waylon squeezes mine again, more out of reassurance than anything.

"Where's Jada?" Waylon asks, sitting down. I slide into the seat next to his.

"Getting a pitcher." Jeremiah leans around, looking toward the bar. "Hopefully not dropping shit everywhere."

"Excuse you," Jada says as she approaches with a pitcher. She's in a violently pink romper, her locs up in two buns. "I'm graceful as fuck."

"Says the person who tripped and threw a mozzarella stick so far across her kitchen that one ended up under the living room couch for weeks." Jeremiah shakes his head.

"Eat shit and die, please and thank you!" Jada puts down the pitcher and glasses, a little bit of drink splashing over the edge. She and Jeremiah exchange a look, her eyes narrowing behind her glasses as if to say *don't say a fucking word.* "Anyway! Bianca! I'm so happy you could come."

I nearly blurt *really?* Not in a sarcastic way, but in genuine surprise. I've never been a person who people are excited to see, and now I have no idea what to say. Maybe she's just being polite. I just smile, the back of my neck heating up.

Thankfully someone comes by with a big bag of food and puts it in the middle of the table, along with a few plates, so I don't have to say anything.

"Thank god, I'm so hungry," Jada says, reaching over the drinks to pull the food out. "And cute nails, by the way."

"Oh, thank you." I look down at my nails. When I was modeling, I wasn't allowed to do anything to my nails in case they had to do them for a shoot. Now that I have the freedom to, I just painted them pink and added a little gem to each one. It's far from professional, but I'm glad I could do it.

Jeremiah pours us each a drink while Jada sets up the food — two types of wings, mozzarella sticks, and fries. My stomach growls.

"Are you excited to beat everyone tonight, Bianca?" Jeremiah asks, putting a wing on his plate. "Waylon said you know a lot about music that's come out in the past thirty years, unlike Jada."

"I know modern stuff!" Jada says, adjusting her vintage-style cat eye glasses. "Just like...the sound of it."

"Which doesn't help us whatsoever when we need the titles." Waylon takes a wing and bites into it. "You singing the song with gibberish lyrics, wildly off key, doesn't get us any points. Bianca will probably know the titles."

"Yeah, you've drastically oversold my music knowledge," I say to Waylon, putting my cleaned chicken bone into the second basket. I've had more wings here than I have in my entire life and I'm not mad about it.

"The three of us have next to none, so you're ahead of us," Waylon says. "I bet you'll know the answers."

"Still — way overselling it," I say.

"We'll survive. *If* we lose," Jada says. "Which we won't, because we're champions at heart."

"BFN Squad, what's up?" A woman in a plaid shirt tied up at the waist and tiny shorts says. "Got a new member of the team?"

"Yep. My girlfriend, Bianca," Waylon says, putting his hand on my knee. It's a little rough and very warm on my bare skin.

"Welcome." The woman hands us a few slips of paper and a pen. "And good luck. These three are really good."

The woman moves on to the next table. Jada slides the slips of paper over to herself and clicks the pen a few times before writing BFN Squad at the top of each slip.

"What does BFN stand for?" I ask.

"Big Fuckin' Nerds." Jeremiah laughs.

"Alright, alright, alright," the woman who gave us the paper slips says into a mic. "If you're here for trivia, get ready. Tonight's a fun one. My name's Greta — holler if you need me, and no, I'm not giving you any answers. For you newbies, here's how it works. We have four rounds, each with a different theme. I'll collect each slip after each round and announce the scores. The first round tonight is *animals and warfare*."

"What?" I look at the three of them. "What does that mean?"

"The categories are kind of broad. You'll see," Jada says, doodling a star on one slip.

"Question one," Greta says. "What animals have been known to wage war? There are a few answers I'll accept for this one."

"Chimps," Waylon says.

"Dolphins, too," Jeremiah adds.

"I'm going with chimps because of that show I saw about the woman with that weird relationship with her chimp," Jada says. "And dolphins are cute, so I refuse to believe they wage war."

"Dolphins are assholes," Jeremiah says.

"Whatever, I reject that reality." She sniffs and writes *chimps* with flair.

Greta repeats the question a few times before moving onto the next ones — they're all questions I don't have a single answer for. They all know exactly what's going on, and if they don't know for sure, they have a ton of possible answers. I'm only able to help on one or two questions because of some random TikToks that ended up on my FYP.

"We're going to take a little break for y'all to get refills or food or whatever. Be back in a bit!" Greta said.

"I'm going to run to the bathroom," Waylon says. "Be right back."

I hold back the urge to cling to him so I don't have to be awkwardly alone. But he slips away, leaving me with his two best friends.

I swallow, swirling ice around in my drink. I can feel their gazes on me.

"So..." Jada leans forward, a little smile on her face. "Now that we have you alone..."

"Pump the brakes, Jay." Jeremiah raises an eyebrow. "We don't need to grill her."

"Nah but we're nosy as hell. Or at least I am." She rests her elbows on the table, then folds her hands so her chin can rest on them. "Can you blame me though? A girl who seems pretty cool actually getting through to Waylon? It's a miracle."

"I'm not cool," I say with a nervous laugh. I'm usually pegged as 'slightly standoffish' or 'cold'.

"Mm, you are. To me, at least. Your whole vibe." Jada waves her hand around. Ironically, I think her whole vibe is cool too — loud and fun in ways I'd never be bold enough to be. Kaitlyn is similar, always going with the attention-grabbing outfits that I love but never choose.

"You're definitely cooler than his ex." Jeremiah's deep brown eyes harden.

"The girl with the brown hair and an attitude?" I ask. Seems like a low bar to be cooler than someone like her, but I don't want to call him out on that.

"Yeah, her. She doesn't even get a name around here anymore." Jada finishes the rest of her drink and tops it off. "Honestly, they shouldn't even be mentioned in the same sentence."

I give Jada a silent *thank you*.

"True." Jeremiah levels me with a serious look. "But we're just getting to know each other."

I shift in my seat. I can sense the intimidating, protective edge in Jeremiah's tone from a mile away and I don't want to bring it out further.

"Relax," Jada says, lightly smacking her brother with the back of her hand. "We got bad vibes from the ex all the time."

"Sorry," Jeremiah murmurs, picking up the pitcher and glancing at me, as if to ask if I'd like more. I nod and push my glass toward him. "Can you blame me for being skeptical? I just don't want Waylon to go through what he went through last time. But I hope you don't think I'm assuming the worst of you."

My heart softens, especially since I can tell how sincere he is about all of it — being protective of Waylon and not wanting to make me feel bad.

"I don't think that. And thanks." I take my topped off drink. "I like that he has friends who truly have his back."

"We always do," Jada says. "And we'll tell him if he's being dumb as hell too. But that's support in its own way."

"Yeah. I know you guys are pretty casual right now, but we're glad to see him dating again," Jeremiah says.

"Especially someone who doesn't make me want to yank my locs out at the root," Jada says, lifting her glass.

My face is burning and thankfully my skin tone is deep enough to hide it. Now I feel like complete shit for basically lying to them. For giving them some shred of hope and excitement for someone who's clearly important to them. What'll happen after Waylon and I "break up"?

Still, I lift my glass and tap it against theirs, the pit in my stomach growing.

"They didn't grill you, did they?" Waylon asks as he slides back into his seat.

"We lightly sautéed her," Jada says.

"It was fine," I add.

"Good." He rests his arm across the back of my seat, lightly touching me.

Greta taps on the mic again to announce the next round and people start heading back to their seats.

"Last round, guys! The next category is called *old and new*. These answers will be a good mix of things from the past and present," Greta says into the mic.

"Isn't that just...everything?" I ask.

"Knowing Greta, maybe." Waylon rests a hand on my knee, almost unconsciously. I love the feel of it and keep my leg in place, even if Jada and Jeremiah know we're just bullshitting.

"Right now, Team Lizard is in the top spot," Greta says. "Followed by Harold's Heroes, and the BFN Squad in second and third."

"We're losing," I say, swallowing.

"Bianca, it's fine, really. And it's not like you've given us any wrong answers. We can pull through at the end," Waylon says.

Fine, he has a point. But I haven't helped either.

"Okay, question one — name at least three artists who have had Billboard Top 100 charting hits across four decades," Greta says.

"Oh! I know this!" I say. I lean in to tell Jada what to write down.

"See, we wouldn't have gotten that at all without you," Waylon says.

"It's just one question." I sip my drink.

"One question can be the difference between winning and losing," Jada says.

I glance around to see how people are taking the question. A lot of people seem confused.

Jada knows the next two questions, and Waylon knows the third. Finally, we're on the last question.

"Last question of the night! What band is responsible for the longest charting album of all time?" Greta asks.

"Wouldn't it be like, the Beatles or something?" Jada asks, looking at me. "They've probably charted for years."

"No, I think it's a band that isn't super obvious. Not like the Beatles," I say. I drum my nails on the table. "I think it's Pink Floyd. Dark Side of the Moon."

"You sure?" Jeremiah asks.

"Yes," I say. Or at least I'm most of the way sure. I don't listen to a lot of them, but I've absorbed enough about them from my dad to feel somewhat sure about my answer.

Jada writes it down and hands the slip off to Greta when she comes around. She takes a while to score the cards and grabs the mic again, clearing her throat into it to get everyone's attention.

"I've tabulated the scores. It's a super close one, but BFN Squad wins by two points. Yet again," Greta says, pointing at us. "Y'all's tab is covered for the night. Congrats."

"Free drinks again!" Jada raises her hand and gives terribly-aimed high-fives to everyone.

We linger for a little longer at the table until Jeremiah says he has to get home and go to bed.

"Are we on for next week?" Jeremiah asks, looking at us both.

"Yeah, if you are," Waylon says to me.

In any other circumstance, I'd feel a bit hesitant making more plans with new people, but for once, I don't. As long as I can shove down my guilt about the fake relationship, I know I'll have a good time.

"Yeah, I'm in," I say.

"We'll be at the family reunion the week after that, though," Waylon says.

"Oof, good luck." Jada slings her enormous purse over her shoulder. "Before I forget, I was going to get my nails done later this week. Want to come, Bianca? The spot in town is tiny but they do a good job."

"Sure, yeah," I say, my chest warming in a way that it hasn't in a while. "I'd like that."

We exchange numbers and finally part ways. When Waylon and I get into his car, I feel light and genuinely happy until that pit of guilt comes back with a vengeance.

THIRTEEN

WAYLON

"HERE'S something else for the bucket list — a little road trip with another person," Bianca says, looking at the GPS map to the resort where the family reunion will be.

"It's a pretty drive too, so it's perfect," I say, starting up the car. Duke lays down and puts his head on the console between us. "Too short for good snacks, though."

"It's never too short for good snacks." Bianca snorts. "You'd deny me road trip snacks because it's only a two-hour drive?"

She pouts, and even though she's joking, my gut says I couldn't deny her anything. But my gut can sometimes lead me a little sideways — just because we had a great time at trivia and we have a shit ton of physical chemistry doesn't mean I should get anything twisted. We're friends who hook up and pretend to be dating. Which is completely normal.

"Fine, we can stop for snacks." I pull out of the driveway. "We can always have them on the way back too."

"Awesome." She starts messing with the music until she turns on a playlist. "This place we're going to is a resort?"

"Yeah. It's not what you're thinking of, though," I say. "It's more like a bunch of cabins and some unsafe water slides that are super fun to go down."

"You have a lot of vaguely unsafe memories of childhood." She reaches between her feet and pets Sadie's head. "The rides at Jepsen Festival. These water slides."

"You don't?"

"Nope. My childhood was wrapped in bubble wrap. Though now that I think back on it, I was in a lot of sketch situations as hard as my parents tried to shield me from them." She winces. "Maybe we can do something to help me relive the part of my childhood that I missed."

"Except you have adult bones that don't pop back as fast as kid bones do." I drum my fingers on the steering wheel. "Unless you want to live on the edge."

"I'll live on the edge. I've never broken a bone before." She shrugs.

"Wouldn't recommend it, but hey, it's your bucket list," I say. "I can set a bone if I have to, at least until a human doctor can show up."

"See? We're all prepared." She gives me one of those little smiles of hers, the ones that make me smile wider.

We drive onto the interstate and stop at a gas station. She goes inside while I top off my gas tank and returns with a big bag.

"I got mini Skittles, which are apparently a thing, chips, Sour Patch Kids..." She rifles through the bag. "I got peanut butter cups too, since you like those. And Cheerwine? The guy working there said it was a regional thing, so I wanted to try it."

"It's good. It's like red Dr. Pepper." I take the peanut butter cups. "And thanks. How'd you know I liked these?"

She gives me a shy glance. "You mentioned you named your favorite kittens after your favorite things at the shelter that day, so I assumed you liked them. With Reese and all."

"Oh." A smile touches my lips and I unwrap the cups. It's been a while since anyone's remembered that kind of thing about me or even put in the effort. "Thank you."

I start the car again and pull back onto the route, popping a peanut butter cup into my mouth.

"So you guys do trivia every week?" she asks, popping open the tube of mini Skittles.

"Yep. Well, except for if there are emergencies at work or something," I say, glancing at her out of the corner of my eye. "Did you have a good time? Did they grill the shit out of you when I stepped away?"

"They asked me questions," she says with a shrug. "They really care about you. It's very sweet and rare to have true friends like that. Probably. I don't even know."

"What do you mean?"

She pours some of the mini Skittles into her mouth and chews for a bit. "I do have — and have had — good friends. Like Kaitlyn, who I'll be opening the spa with. We've been friends since we were freshman in high school, probably because we were both the awkward ones in our class."

"That's basically how Jeremiah and I met," I say. "We were the chubby, nerdy kids and bonded. Then I met Jada later, of course."

"Yeah. The bond of the awkward kids runs deep." She

laughs. "But once I started modeling and doing some influencer deals, I met a whole bunch of people who came and went at the drop of a hat. If I got cast in a campaign and my 'friend' didn't, we weren't friends anymore. If someone even heard a rumor that was negative about me, they were gone. If I passed them in followers on Instagram, I got blocked. It was all kind of fleeting, especially since we were competing against each other in a lot of instances."

"That sounds really shitty," I say.

"It is." She lets out a sigh. "But that's a big reason as to why I want to leave. It's cutthroat and while that works for some people, I'm just not like that. And I definitely don't want it as badly as some other girls. They deserve it way more."

I'm glad she's getting out of it. She's pretty down to earth and nice — she doesn't deserve to be yanked around like that by people.

She takes a sip of the Cheerwine and wrinkles her nose. "What the hell is this?"

"You don't like it?"

"Definitely not." She puts the bottle into my side of the cupholder. "Have at it."

"More for me." I undo the cap with one hand and take a sip. It's been a while since I've had it.

We eat snacks and talk about all the weird signs we see the rest of the drive to the resort. Mom sent out info on where all of us are staying, so I drive us straight to the parking lot closest to our cabin. My family takes over the entire resort for the weekend, so I wave to a few of my cousins who are in a nearby cabin.

"This place is too cute," Bianca says once we walk up to the cabin, Duke trailing behind us. "Is it just for us?"

"Yep. I guess as a couple, we get one." I punch in the key code and push open the door.

Duke rushes in first, sniffing around, and we follow. It's more or less a studio apartment — one big room with a bed and a bathroom on one side, a little couch, a TV, and a kitchenette. It's rustic and cozy. And very private.

I bring the rest of our stuff inside and find Bianca sitting on the bed, taking a picture of Sadie and Duke curled up on an armchair together.

"Do you want to go swim?" I ask. "Wes just texted and said that he and Rose are already down by the water."

"Sure, yeah."

We take turns changing into our swim gear. When she comes out of the bathroom, I suck in a breath. She's in a one-piece, but it's cut high on her legs and dips just low enough to show a tiny bit of cleavage. Somehow having her body not fully exposed by a bikini makes me want to know more about what's underneath.

"Can you help me with sunscreen on my back?" She asks, pulling a bottle out of her bag.

"Sure, yeah." I swallow, making sure my hands aren't too sweaty. Why am I acting as if I haven't literally eaten her out?

I take her sunscreen and cover her back, making sure to cover every inch of exposed skin of her back and shoulders. Her skin is addictively soft. She does me next, covering me well. Her small hands feel nice against my skin, like she's soothing it. Whenever we start on the next item on her bucket list, I hope I can feel more of her.

She slips on a beach cover up and we go out to the manmade lake, the dogs walking along in front of us. We spot Rose and Wes, along with their dog, Murphy, stretched out underneath a tree on a blanket. Rose waves to us first, before Wes realizes we're here and waves too.

"When did y'all get here?" I ask, sitting down. Of course, Murphy, Duke, and Sadie have to greet each other right in the middle of the blanket, managing to hit us all in the face with their tails.

"Not too long ago." Rose leans back on her hands and adjusts her sunglasses.

"We just got here too." I pick up Sadie so Bianca has a place to sit, and she gracefully sinks down, cross-legged.

"You want to make bets on who'll blow up at who first?" Wes asks, scanning our family drifting in the water. "Ten bucks on Aunt Kelly arguing with her husband before dinner. And fifteen on whether Darren and Brett will end up wrestling after dinner."

"Jesus, Wes, we just got here. We can't bet on who's going to fight right now. This is Rose and Bianca's first time here," I say, even though I know that Brett will end up kicking Darren's ass more than once and Aunt Kelly has been on a meditation kick and will hold off until after dinner.

I glance at Bianca, who thankfully looks amused.

"Bro, it's inevitable. Why not have fun with it?" Wes asks. "Rose, are you in?"

"I've never even met your aunt Kelly," Rose says with a snort. "And I haven't spoken with Brett or Darren since high school."

"So you're fine with losing?" Wes gently squeezes Rose's leg.

She narrows her eyes at him. "I know what you're trying to do, babe."

"What? What am I trying to do?" Wes gives her a smile that's all innocence.

"See, this is how he roped me," Rose says to Bianca. "We made one little dumb bet, then another, then another...and here we are."

They grin at each other like lovesick puppies. It would be annoying if I wasn't happy for them both and if they weren't such a good match.

"You want to make another dumb little bet, then?" Wes asks. "C'mon, Rosie. It'll be fun."

"Fine!" Rose sighs. "Um...at least I know Darren and Brett, so I bet they'll wrestle before dinner."

"I'll bet that they wrestle before and after dinner," I say. "And I'm going to have faith in Aunt Kelly's self-control and say they won't argue at all."

Wes writes down our bets in his phone.

"Our family's mostly civilized, by the way," Wes says to Bianca, craning his neck to see around Duke, who's standing in the middle of us all for no good reason. I lightly press on the spot above his tail and he sits. "But the family reunion brings out the worst in a solid chunk of the family."

"I've never been to a family reunion, actually," Bianca says. "I mean, my family gets along, but we aren't super close. My dad's parents passed away before I was born and he's an only child, so my aunt Gloria was the only living family member I was in regular contact with. But my mom has a few sisters and my cousins are all over the place. I don't think many of them would get in a fist fight though, but we've never gotten that heated before."

I mentally tuck that information away. I haven't asked many questions about her family at all, much less her extended family. Then again, who's really going to ask? But also, I still want to know. I'm just even more curious about her in general.

"You know what to do when you see your cousins next," Wes says. "Give them some moonshine and see what happens."

"I'll report back." Bianca laughs, a warm and genuine one.

Jeremiah and Jada are my best friends, but Wes is my twin. If a girl I'm with doesn't click with Wes, then it's probably a sign that we won't last.

Wes hated Catherine once she stopped actively trying to stay on his good side, which apparently took a lot of effort on her end. And even before that, Wes had a weird feeling about her, especially our second time around.

Then again, Wes and Bianca's relationship doesn't matter at the end of the day since none of this is real. As much as I like that Bianca feels comfortable enough to let down her guard a bit.

"Want to go down the water slide?" Wes asks, nodding toward the slide. A few of our younger cousins are on it already, climbing up the stairs to the top.

"The one that Waylon said is pretty unsafe?" She glances at me with a little smirk.

"That's the fun part." Wes stands up and peels off his t-shirt.

"Does everyone in this town have a death wish?" Bianca asks.

"Yep," Rose says, patting Murphy's exposed belly. "I'm staying right here with the dogs."

"I'm going to put you in my lap and go down the slide later." Wes grins at Rose and she playfully rolls her eyes.

"I know where you sleep." Rose says.

"I also know where you sleep." They exchange a look I'd rather not think about too hard.

"Again, does everyone in this town have a death wish? Besides me and Rose?" Bianca takes off her swim coverup, though, and I smile.

"Well, what other thrills are there in Jepsen?" I take off my shirt too. "Besides bonfires in the woods?"

I savor the way that Bianca's eyes flick over my body before checking that Rose has a handle on Duke — Duke loves to leap into the water after me, usually missing and ending up right on top of my head. Murphy will probably bark at the water and run away if it touches him even a little bit. Sadie, as always, is taking a nap.

Bianca, Wes, and I head to the top of the slide. It really hasn't changed all that much, except as an adult, I can see even more safety issues. Both the stairs up to the top and the slide itself are rickety and the guard rails aren't secure. Is the slide even deep enough for us to not go flying over the ledge and into the trees?

"Um, one of you is going to have to go first," Bianca says. "Because this looks like a death trap."

"I'll go." Wes steps up and slides down like it's no big deal. We hear him splash into the lake below moments later, waving his hand. "I didn't die!"

"What a ringing endorsement," Bianca says, her arms crossed over her chest.

"I'll go next," I say. "And I can catch you at the end if you want."

"If I make it all the way down without flying off and breaking my back against a tree," she says. "Go ahead."

I grin and hop on the top of the slide. It feels wobbly as hell under my weight, but it's still fun and fast, shooting me down and into the lake. I swim a little ways out so I'm close enough to catch Bianca, but not so close that she'll crash into me. A few of my family members are floating around in donuts, watching people come out of the slide, so they give us space too.

I motion for her to come on, and she hesitates. For a second I think she's going to back out, but then she sits on the slide and throws herself down it. The ride is short, only a few second, but she makes it, splashing into the water with a squeal. I'm just close enough to grab her.

"Holy shit," she says, letting me hold onto her. "That definitely felt like a death trap."

"But it was fun, wasn't it?" I ask. Her waist feels nice under my hands.

"Okay, yeah, it was," she says, shivering. "Sorry, the water is a little chilly."

She scoots closer to me, like she's trying to absorb my heat. Her breasts brush up against me.

"Is it?" I ask, my voice low as my hands slide down to her hips.

"Yeah." She swallows, looking at my shoulders, then my lips. "Getting warmer, though."

We stay there for a moment, like the simple act of me holding her hips has created a spell over us. The overwhelming urge to pull her even closer almost takes over. Do we have to do this? No. But it feels nice just to touch her without thinking about it much more. The water is dripping off her curls, making her exposed skin glisten in a way that makes me want to lick along her collar bone.

One of my uncles comes shooting out of the bottom of the slide shakes me out of my trance. I loosen my grip.

"I'm going to hop out and warm up," Bianca says, clearing her throat and not looking at me.

"Okay, yeah." I give her more space. "I'm going to...just hang here."

I watch her head back to shore and step out of the water, squeezing water from her curls. Her long, shapely frame looks even better now that she's all wet, her suit clinging to her body in a way it wasn't before.

Someone taps on the back of my head, pulling my eyes away. It's my aunt Nadine on a float.

"Sweetheart, did your um, girlfriend forget the rest of her swimsuit?" Aunt Nadine asks in that annoying 'oh bless her heart' tone. Nadine is one of my mom's four sisters, and is by far my least favorite.

"Nope." I peel my eyes off Bianca. She's not even in a tiny string bikini. It's just a swimsuit that shows some skin. Like a fucking swimsuit in the modern era.

But I hold my tongue. Starting shit with Aunt Nadine usually leads to more bullshit but I get the feeling that she'll keep going.

"We aren't in LA." She tsks.

"You're right. We aren't. And it doesn't matter where we are. She's wearing a swimsuit at the lake."

Aunt Nadine's eyes narrow at my tone. I've kept it light, but I'm probably pushing it.

"We'll see how much she fits in with the family over the trip, then. Why did she move to Jepsen? Isn't she a model? What kind of modeling?"

"Clothes and stuff like that." I don't know what the name of the modeling is but I know she looks good doing it. I've spent a little too much time looking through her Instagram.

I start to swim toward the shore just slowly enough so she won't call me out for being rude.

"Does she do risqué photos?" Nadine follows me, of course.

"Depends on your definition of it," I say. We've drifted close enough to the point where Bianca might be able to hear us. She's standing at the shore, trying to pull a piece of a plant out of her hair.

"Does she want a family and children?" Nadine asks. " What would they think if they knew she did that?"

"What's the point of all these questions?" I ask, my tone sharp. Nadine's eyes widen in surprise — as much as she's annoyed me over the years, I've always been as polite as possible. "Because it doesn't feel like you're asking to actually get to know Bianca. You're asking because you want to start something."

Aunt Nadine blinks. "I don't know what you're talking about, honey."

"I don't want to be rude, but yeah, you do," I say. "And I'm not putting up with it."

Nadine gapes at me. "I'm just trying to —"

I swim toward the shore before she starts spouting off some dumb excuses for the shit she said. Aunt Nadine and I drifted closer to the shore than I thought, so it doesn't take me long to reach Bianca. She's sitting in the sun, where it's noticeably warmer than it was just a little further away. Her expression is the same calm it usually is, but she nibbles on her bottom lip.

"Hey," I say. "Did you overhear any of that?"

"Bits and pieces, but I can kind of sense when people are talking about me." She shrugs, like this is a normal thing. I hate that it is.

"I'm sorry," I say. "She's just kind of like that but I know she'll back off a little now that I've called her out."

"Thank you," she says softly, squeezing my hand. "You didn't have to do anything."

"I had to." I squeeze her hand back. "Even if you're not my actual girlfriend, I'm not letting anyone try to shame you."

She looks at me with a softness in her eyes that I rarely ever see. I want to hold onto the moment for as long as I can, but she looks away.

"Waylon, Waylon, Waylon," she says with a soft sigh, leaning against me a little.

I'm not entirely sure what she means by that, but will I read into it entirely too much? Probably.

And it's going to be a problem.

FOURTEEN
WAYLON

THE REST of the afternoon is pretty much perfect — just enough clouds drift in front of the sun to keep the temperature warm, but not scorching, and we all hang around, having a few drinks and snacks while we talk or float in tubes on the water. It's nice to not need to be anywhere or to feel like I have to do anything.

Soon, we get a text that dinner is ready and head to the dining hall where we'll be eating. Bianca pulls on her swimsuit cover-up, to my chagrin, and takes my hand on the walk over. We sequester the dogs in the gated area behind the building to keep them away from the food.

The food is laid out, buffet style. Thankfully one of my aunts or uncles put out labels about allergens so Bianca won't have any problems. We load up our plates with food and find a free spot.

"This is so good," Bianca says, almost in awe.

"Yeah, we have a lot of good cooks in the family." I take a

bite of macaroni and cheese. It's definitely Nana's recipe. I'm not sure what she does to it, but it tastes better than any mac and cheese I've had anywhere else. She'd never tell me what her secret is if I asked, though.

"If there's anything all of us love, it's food," Mom says, appearing over Wes's shoulder. "Can I sit?"

"Yeah." Wes scoots over a little so Mom can take the last spot at the picnic table.

"Poor pups," Mom says, looking over my shoulder.

I turn to look where she's looking and see Big Bubba standing near the glass door, his nose pressed to it. He looks miserable.

"We can't have a repeat of the ham incident," I say.

"Ham incident?" Bianca asks.

"Ham *incidents*," I say with a laugh. "Because at least once every two years, Big Bubba makes sad eyes at someone during Thanksgiving or Christmas, they let him in, then somehow he eats the whole ham."

"An entire ham?" Bianca turns and looks at Bubba too, and he wags his tail faster. "But how? That's several pounds of meat."

"I honestly don't know. I wish I had the chance to give him a scan just to see how his anatomy works," I say. "I've never known a dog who could just inhale stuff and digest it without much of a problem."

"Speaking of the dogs," Mom says. "We have that board meeting for the shelter soon. It's more of a party, really, since it's Elizabeth's granddaughter's birthday."

I blow a breath out of my nose as subtly as I can so she doesn't latch onto my emotional reaction versus the actual problem. My good mood from today goes flying out the window. Who is Elizabeth? Why should I care about her granddaughter's birthday?

"I don't think I'll go to that," I say. "I'm still not sure if I want to be on the board."

Which is technically not a lie. I'd want to go as long as it was actually focused on getting things done. But this just sounds like a thinly veiled social gathering with a bunch of people I'd never hang out with voluntarily.

Mom sighs and puts her spoon down. "Don't be ridiculous. Bianca, don't you think he would be great on the board?"

Bianca's eyes widen and she glances at me. "Um, I'm sure he'd be great, but only if he wants to. I'm not really sure what it involves."

"It's no big deal," Mom says with a shrug. "Just a few meetings a few times a month for an hour or two. I just think we need a vet on the board."

"Dr. Healey will be on it, won't she?" I take a bite of my biscuit. Dr. Healey is one of the other vets in the practice, who's been there forever.

"But she might retire soon."

"She can be on it until then," I say once I swallow. "Or even better, after. Seems like something she'd enjoy doing in her retirement."

We stare at each other for a few moments. Why did she have to bring Bianca into this to ask her opinion? Probably because she assumed that Bianca would go her way to stay on her good side the way Catherine would have. A sick feeling burrows into my stomach. I love my mom, but this shit drives me crazy.

"It *would* take up quite a bit of your time, and I know

that you're in those early stages of dating. I'm assuming it's fairly serious." Mom looks between us, dabbing her lips with a napkin. "We'll discuss more later."

She's just assuming we're "fairly serious"? At least she's dropping the topic.

"I haven't really had the chance to get to talk to you, Bianca," Mom says, smiling at her. "So you're a model?"

I don't remember telling her that, so she must have been asking around about her. Or worse, she's Googled Bianca and will do a terrible job of hiding it.

"I was." Bianca pushes some potato around on her plate. "I'm taking a break from it now and doing social media for Stryker Liquors."

Mom nods, pleased. "Is that what you'd like to do in the long-term? Social media? Modeling can be so brutal as women age, I bet."

Bianca pauses, her mouth popping open for a second. "Yeah, I think."

"You think?" Mom raises an eyebrow in a way I recognize. She's about to dive into her 'what are your future plans' talk in more detail, which generally ends up badly even when she's just talking to one of my younger cousins.

Mom has probably planned everything in her life down to the day, so she can't fathom the idea of anyone else being different. And that's kind of the problem with her overall.

"She's doing a great job," Rose adds. "It hasn't been long but our engagement is already picking up."

Mom just nods, tearing a little piece off her biscuit. "That's good. So that's your career path? Social media?"

When Mom wants a question answered, she'll ask it in

fifty different ways until she gets what she wants. Bianca just blinks a few times, like she's trying to figure out how to answer.

"I'm not entirely sure, to be honest. But I'm interested in opening a business. A spa," Bianca says. "Someday in the future."

"Oh, a spa in Jepsen would be amazing! There are a few nice ones in the mountains and over in Nashville, but a local spot would save me so much trouble." Mom sips her coffee. "What spot in town were you thinking?"

"It's just an idea at the moment," Bianca says, looking down at her plate. Hopefully Mom doesn't dig much deeper. This spa isn't going to be anywhere near Jepsen but Mom doesn't need to know.

"Ideas need action," Mom says, her smile barely softening her feelings on the topic. "I'd start scouting locations — just to see what's opening and where so you can choose a spot that gets a lot of foot traffic. I'm not sure how much you know about Jepsen's tourism, though. Do you have a business plan? Have you written one before?"

I can feel Wes's eyes on me, silently saying *what the hell?* I give him the same look back.

"Mom, do we need to dig into Bianca's entire future? It's a little..." I nearly say *pushy* but I'm not looking to start something. "A little premature. She said it was just an idea, not that she wanted to open the place tomorrow."

Mom takes a bite, staring at me for several beats. "What's wrong with asking her questions about her future? And making sure that she's taking the right path for Jepsen? It's very different from LA."

The way Mom says it makes it sound like Bianca could never figure out the "intricacies" of Jepsen, as if the population isn't one percent of the size of a single LA neighborhood.

"Bianca is more than capable of starting her own business when the time comes. Grilling her on it right now is pointless," I say, pausing. "Unless you'd like to talk about it, Bianca."

"I don't really have a ton of ideas yet," Bianca says. "I just know it would be more of a spa with treatments for acne, scarring, things like that. And the regular stuff too."

Mom nods, like she's trying to wrap her head around the concept of that kind of place.

"Interesting," Mom finally says.

Bianca presses her knee against mine and lightly squeezes it, in what I'm guessing is a silent thank you for steering us away from the topic.

As soon as we've all eaten, Mom, Wes, and Rose drift off to socialize with other family, leaving Bianca and I alone again.

"Thanks for coming to my rescue on that," Bianca says. "The spa."

"It's no problem. I've been on the other side of that before." I rake a hand through my hair. We're still sitting right next to each other, hip to hip, even though the rest of the table is empty. "It feels like that'll be a recurring theme when talking to her."

"I'm picking up on that." She blows a breath out of her nose. "Are you okay?"

"Me? Yeah," I say. "I can't believe you're the one asking me after that grilling."

She shrugs, her arm brushing against mine. "I can still worry a little."

I lightly squeeze her leg before I can stop myself. Out of anyone I could have chosen as my fake girlfriend, I'm glad I chose someone like her.

FIFTEEN
BIANCA

"YOU WANT TO SHOWER FIRST?" I ask once we get back to our cabin. "I'm going to take longer than you."

"Sure, thank you." He grabs his small pouch of toiletries and heads into the bathroom.

I flop on my back on the bed, resting Sadie next to me. She turns in a circle a few times before laying down with a heavy sigh.

"I know, right?" I say to her. The energy's been sucked right out of me.

Waylon comes out of the bathroom just a few minutes later, and I head in. I take my routine seriously and don't do anything too trendy that'll do more harm than good to my skin. As I expected, Waylon just has a toothbrush, toothpaste, and deodorant on the side of the sink he chose.

I change into my pajamas — a cute silky tank top and matching shorts, which is what I usually wear to bed — and look at myself in the mirror. The shorts are tiny, basically boy shorts, and I'm not going to lock my boobs away in a bra to sleep. Is it too much, though?

As much as I want to get another little lesson and check some stuff off my bucket list, I don't want to seem too needy. But I'm probably overthinking it.

I go back out into the room and find Waylon scrolling on his phone. He's peeled off his shirt and the blankets are low around his hips. The light dusting of dark hair across his chest is something I never thought I'd find hot—I'd never given it a thought in general. And the glasses. The damn glasses. Maybe it's because it makes him look really Clark Kent-ish, or maybe it's the way the dark green frames look nice with his chocolate brown eyes.

"Everything good?" Waylon asks, glancing up at me.

"Y-yeah." I swallow. "Um, do you want to do more bucket list stuff?"

A smile spreads across his face and puts his phone on the side table. "Yes."

"Sorry, I'm not great at seduction," I say, walking over to the bed. "Maybe I should add that to our little syllabus, just for practice."

"To be honest, I thought your pajamas were part of it." He pulls back the blankets for me.

"These?" I glance down at myself. "I wear pajamas like this every night. And just to hang out at home."

He blinks, his eyes roaming over my body. "You do?"

"Yes." I slide into the bed.

"I'm glad to know that, but now I'm going to be thinking about that all the fucking time." He wraps an arm around me and drags me toward him.

"This is the tamest stuff I have." I press myself against

him. He's so perfectly big against me, broad and strong like he could envelop me entirely.

"Fuck, Bianca." Waylon skims his hand down my back and to my ass, gently squeezing. "Can I add stuff to your bucket list? Namely seeing your entire collection?"

I laugh. "We can figure that out later."

"Good," he says.

He puts two fingers under my chin and kisses me, his hand sliding into the back of my shorts. I melt against him — I can't help it. This isn't even a real relationship but I've never been kissed like this before, by anyone. Like he's actually into *me*, not just into the fact that he's going to get laid by someone.

I shove that feeling into the back of my head and focus on what we're doing -- his hands exploring my body underneath my tank top and shorts, and my fingers threading through his soft hair.

"So what item are we checking off this list?" Waylon asks, pulling my leg over his hip.

"Just sex where I actually come." My voice is already a bit breathy. "Not super exciting, sorry."

"Trust me, I'm extremely excited." He grinds his cock against me. "Every single time you fuck doesn't have to be over the top with bondage and role-play. It's all just as good to me."

He presses his lips against my neck, then my collarbone. The hand that's down the back of my shorts grips my ass.

"Promise to tell me what you need if I'm not giving it to you?" he asks.

"Yes." I gasp as his fingers slip against my entrance from behind. I'm already a little bit wet.

Waylon guides us so I'm on my back and his body is hovering over mine. Even though he hasn't put his weight on me, I still love feeling him over me, just kissing me all over, peeling off my tank top. He works his way down to my breasts, teasing my nipples, while his hands wander over my hips. An electric current runs from each nipple and down to my clit.

His soft groans as he worships each of my breasts makes me heat all over. I've never thought they were anything special, and my exes hadn't paid much attention to them either. They aren't particularly big. But Waylon genuinely loves them like they're perfect.

My hips start to move of their own accord, trying to get some friction against my clit. I find some against his body and whimper. Do I want him to keep playing with my nipples, or do I want his mouth on me again? I can't bear to let him stop touching me, but I'm being selfish — he's so hard but I'm not pleasuring him the way I want to.

"Wait," I say. He lifts his head immediately, his glasses fogged. "I never got to suck your cock last time."

"You want to?" He rolls onto his back, his cock literally twitching in his pajama pants. Unfortunately, he takes off his glasses and puts them on the side table.

I nod, biting my lip and climbing between his legs. He helps me pull off his pajama pants and boxers. It looks even bigger than it did on our video call, thick and long, stretching up toward his bellybutton.

He sucks in a little breath when I grasp him at the base of his cock. The pulsing of his heartbeat taps against my hand.

"Will you tell me what you like too?" I ask, my own heart beating hard and fast.

The only other time I've asked a guy what he liked, he scoffed at me and said I should just know. I stopped asking the question at all after that. But Waylon is different.

Instead of getting annoyed, he says, "of course."

I take a deep breath and lean down, running my tongue up his cock from the base to the tip. His cock is so thick that I'm worried I won't be able to fit it in my mouth. But I try, taking as much of him as I can without accidentally grazing him with my teeth. His hip twitches underneath my hand, so I keep going.

The more his body reacts to each of my little changes and strokes, the more confident and wet I become. It's a rush knowing I'm making him feel good. Now I understand why he was completely fine with going down on me for so long. It's like getting off without having to touch myself at all.

"Fuck, yes, princess," he says, gasping when I get my hand and my mouth in sync. "Your mouth feels like heaven. Make it wetter."

I pop off and try to do as he says. He threads his fingers through my hair, not pushing my head down but keeping it steady. His thumb gently rubs my temple, almost tenderly. Goosebumps erupt across his skin and he moans when I let the tip of his cock reach as far back as I can get it.

"God, I can't wait to fuck your mouth," he says, his voice raspy. "Not today, but soon."

"Not today?" I ask, my lips popping off his cock.

"I think we should save that for later," he says, guiding me back onto his cock. "Because I won't be gentle. When I fuck your mouth, you won't be able to think."

My pussy clenches at his words alone. I want him to fuck me, hard. Control me completely and make me lose my mind. I pick up my pace as I start sucking him off again, my hand pumping up to meet my mouth so I can stroke the part of his cock that I can't reach with my mouth. I could listen to his moans and grunts all day and all night.

"Bianca," he grunts. "Wait. I don't want to come in your pretty mouth. At least not now. Get on your hands and knees."

I sit up and take him in. He's flushed from his chest up to his hairline, his eyes dark with lust I never would have imagined he was capable of when we first met. I have to lean in and kiss him. I can't help it and luckily, he doesn't ask me what the hell I'm doing. He slips his tongue into my mouth, his hand digging into my hair almost a little too hard.

When we break apart, I do as he says, getting on my hands and knees with my cheek on the pillows. He hops off the bed and grabs a condom from his bag, putting it on the bed.

I'm plenty wet, but he's not going to fuck me yet, is he? He hasn't even put on the condom.

I let out a squeak when I feel his tongue on me from behind, licking from my clit to my entrance and back. His big hands are on my ass, spreading me so he can get to what he wants. He feasts on me, making my legs shake as I cry out into the pillow. This shouldn't feel this good, like he's rearranging my DNA.

"You need more? Do you need my cock?" he asks, only stopping for a second.

I legitimately don't know — I can barely think with his lips lightly suctioning around my clit. He gently pushes a finger into me and I clench around it. *Yes.* I need more inside of me. His finger is good, but not enough. I want to feel full the way I've only felt full with my toys.

"Please," I whimper. "Please fuck me."

He pulls away, making me sag against the pillows. I hear him unwrap the condom and put it on.

I tense unconsciously and he slides a hand down my back, soft and soothing.

"You okay?" he asks, his voice the gentle one that he uses every day.

"Yeah." I turn my head and look at him. His cock looks even more intimidating from this angle. "You're just a whole lot bigger than what I'm used to."

He grins, because what guy wouldn't when being complimented on his cock?

"I'll go slow. Tell me if it's too much," he says, still in his everyday voice. "Okay?"

I nod. He puts his tip against my entrance and gently presses inside. Just the tip feels like a lot, and he keeps pressing forward. I'm being split in half, the fullness almost too much. Finally, he stops when he's fully in.

"Don't move," he says to me.

"You don't want *me* to move?" I ask, my voice breathy.

"No, because your pussy feels like..." He pauses, his breathing audible. "It feels really fucking good."

We sit there for several beats, adjusting to each other. The fullness of his cock inside me turns into pleasure rather than tension. He starts moving, slowly sliding in and out of me. His pace is gentle and steady, and feels good. But just good. I let him fuck me, savoring the feeling of his hands on my hips and ass.

"Talk to me," he says, reaching around to touch my clit. He feels where we're joined, and slides that wetness up to my clit. "So we can make you come."

"I-I don't know," I admit. "It feels good, though."

He lets out a sound that tells me he heard me and adjusts the height of my hips. Eventually he slides some pillows underneath my stomach and pushes me forward, staying inside of me. When he thrusts again, I see stars. He's hitting my g-spot over and over again, which I can usually only do with my best dildo, some contortion, and well-rested arms.

"*Yes*," I cry out, trying to press back against him.

He tries out a few paces before he finds the one that makes me let out the roughest sound into a pillow — hard and steady, not too fast or slow. My butt is popped up high enough for me to reach around and rub my own clit. The combination makes me start to shake all over. I'm reaching that long plateau right before I come, the one that's so pleasurable but not quite *there*.

I whine, digging my fingers into the pillow and rubbing my clit. So *close*. Everything feels so fucking good but how do I get over this hurdle? Rub my clit differently? Change the angle of my hips?

"Don't think," he says, his hips slapping against my ass. "Just feel."

I let out a shaky breath and try to wipe my mind clean. Everything in the world shrinks down to just his cock hitting the best spot, over and over again, my fingers on my clit, and his body against mine.

My orgasm hits me like a train, making me cry out so loudly that I should be embarrassed. But I'm not. I'm just rolling across the feelings, clenching around his thick length and shuddering through the pleasure.

I finish coming, my whole body sagging into the bed. At some point, Waylon must have come too, because he's bracing himself above me, panting. He pulls out to dispose of the condom, leaving me in a puddle on the bed.

He comes back to the bed and slides in next to me, rubbing his hand across my back. My skin is so sensitized that every little touch makes me shiver. I roll over toward him and he keeps rubbing his hand up and down my back.

The little touch is everything, bringing me back down to reality.

"You good?" he asks. I nod. "Good."

We aren't quite cuddling, but we're not *not* cuddling. He has his arm extended across the pillows behind me, and with a little shift from either of us, he could be cradling me.

I close my eyes for a second, sinking into the pillows. Being next to him is way too comfortable, especially now that I'm not completely wiped out from drinks and socializing all night. I've known I'm an introvert for most of my life, so it's rare that I feel like this after such a long day — relaxed.

Well, mostly.

"Did I do okay today?" I ask.

"What do you mean?" He lifts his head.

"Like when your mom was asking me questions, do you think she suspected anything? Men might have post-nut clarity, but I have post-nut anxiety, I guess."

He rolls onto his side, facing me.

"I don't think she suspected anything," he says. "But either way, sorry she was grilling you."

"It's not your fault at all." I turn on my side too. "I was bracing myself for it at some point."

"Good." He blows out a breath through his nose. "At least everything else was good. It's been a while since I've actually won one of Wes's bets."

I smile. "I can't believe that's an ongoing bet."

"It's a little trashy but sometimes it's nice to let go." He smiles. "My mom's sisters — aunt Nadine aside — are a lot less proper. I guess they get it from Nana."

"She sounds fun," I say.

"Maybe we'll run into her. She's usually pretty busy since all her grandkids are here." He shifts, his leg touching mine, but he doesn't move it. "You'll like her."

He phrases it like we're going to meet. Like he *wants* me to meet her. My heart flutters despite myself, like this is real and he wants me to be a bigger part of his life.

My heart shouldn't be fluttering. This is just supposed to be him helping me check things off my bucket list so I can move on in New York and have better sex with whoever I click with. To actually *date* people who want something serious, at least eventually.

But after this, I want to experience all of that with him.

SIXTEEN

WAYLON

I WAKE up before Bianca the next morning, still naked from the night before. She's sprawled across me like a rag doll, her breath soft and warm on my chest. My dick is already hard just because it's the morning, but it twitches as I take in her. She's a model — and as much as she says she wasn't a good one, I don't believe her — but she's absurdly gorgeous in a way that goes beyond just finding a woman on a billboard pretty.

Especially seeing her underneath me, writhing against me and finally losing herself to pleasure.

I sigh through my nose and grip my cock at the base. I could easily go for another round right now, but we don't have a bucket list thing to check off. Unless she wants to see if she can come more than once in one go, which I'm more than happy to try.

Bianca shifts in her sleep, rubbing her leg against mine and curling up closer to my chest. The little sigh she lets out tugs at my heart in ways it shouldn't. It's like she's exactly where she wants to be. Where she *should* be.

No, we shouldn't go out of bounds. We're sticking to the bucket list, period. Not making it any more complicated than that.

But I hope we can check off more things soon, because I'm addicted to how she feels. To how she shivers all over right before she comes. To her pert little ass that feels just right in my hands.

Bianca yawns and stretches, her eyes fluttering open.

"Hi," she says, her voice rough with sleep.

"Hey." I sit up on one elbow. "Sleep well?"

"Very." She bites her lip like she's trying not to smile. "A little sore, though."

"Sorry." I let myself squeeze her hip. "But it felt good at the time, right?"

"Oh, definitely." She finally smiles. "I still have so many things I want to try from my bucket list."

"Let me know when you want to try them and I'll be there." I bite the inside of my cheek. Does that sound too desperate?

Duke stands up and stretches, walking over to the bed and resting his chin on it. He wags his tail, looking so damn cute that I have to get up and pet him.

"Want a walk, buddy?" I ask. Sadie pops up from where she was sleeping and lets out a tiny *arf*. "You too, Sadie?"

"I can walk her." Bianca yawns again and starts to get up.

"Nah, it's fine. I'll take them both and check on breakfast." And I need some fucking air. She smells too good, and I can smell her all over the sheets.

I throw on some clothes and get the dogs ready to go out.

Since it's still early, the resort is pretty quiet, giving me space to think. The dogs sniff everything they pass, exploring the edges of the path.

We need to crank through this bucket list just for the sake of my ability to keep my hands to myself. Now that we've fucked, it's like I've popped a seal. All the lust I've been harboring since the moment I saw her, plus a dry spell, and then some lackluster sex before that are coming to a head. I need to fuck her until I hit that point where I'm used to it again.

But maybe that's exactly what I need — putting the bucket list in the forefront of my head instead of faking the relationship, just to put some distance between us. People are already convinced that we're real, even after the hiccup last night. We don't have to try all that hard.

And maybe people are just saying we work because it's been a while since they've seen me with anyone who isn't Catherine. Thinking back to how often we bickered still makes me want to cringe. Literally everyone I knew saw how bad things had gotten but I was somehow blind to it.

Duke barks, pulling on his leash as JD and Big Bubba come into view around the bend of the trail. Big Bubba does the cute, tippy taps dance he always does when he's excited and lightly pulls on the leash JD is holding.

"Morning," JD says with a nod once we're within earshot of each other.

"Morning." I loosen the dogs' leashes so they can all sniff each other.

JD is quiet and rarely starts a conversation on the best of days, so I expect him to stand there in silence. But instead, he surprises me.

"Your new girlfriend is nice," he finally says, completely unprompted.

"You think so?" I raise both eyebrows in shock.

"Mmhm." He tucks his hand into the pocket of his sweats. "You two complement each other. And she's doing well with the company's social media. It's hard to attribute sales directly to that, but she's helping us move in the direction I think the company should go in. Dad's a little stuck in the past."

I swallow, then nod. "Good. Glad you like her."

He grunts in response, signaling the end of the conversation. I give Big Bubba a pat on the side as they continue on their walk.

I can't believe JD actually said something about us. He tied the compliment to her work for the business, which makes sense, but he's never had much of a personal opinion on anyone that I've dated.

Maybe it's because he and Bianca are similar — quiet and icy on the outside, but nice when you get to know them. That has to be it. Otherwise, I'm worried he got kidnapped and replaced with a clone.

Then again, the consensus among my family members seems to be that she's great. And she is. But I didn't anticipate my family members liking her this much.

That was the whole point of the fake relationship, so why am I worrying about when we have to "break up"?

SEVENTEEN
BIANCA

I SHOULDN'T BE SWEATING over a nail appointment, but I am. Jada and I are meeting in fifteen minutes at the nail salon, aptly called Jepsen Nails, and I'm so nervous I feel a bit sick.

It's been so long since I've done anything social like this — with someone who I genuinely like and want to get to know. What if she talks to me and realizes she doesn't actually like me?

I feel like the awkward girl I was for most of high school, with Kaitlyn as my only friend, and I hate it.

I check my outfit for the hundredth time before tucking Sadie into her crate. Since she's used to going with me everywhere, I assumed she'd hate the crate for the short stretches where I have to leave her home. But she naps in there like it's no big deal. Then again, she mostly just takes naps and eats treats between being petted all the other hours of the day.

I drive into town, finding the nail salon. It's small, tucked between a boot shop and a knickknack store, and I see Jada sitting in the waiting area.

"Hey!" she says when I walk in. I wave, holding onto my purse like a lifeline. "You ready? You just want a gel manicure, right?"

"Yeah, that sounds good." I haven't had a gel manicure in ages.

"With nail art?" A woman with a pink apron around her hips and a name tag that says Daisy appears in front of us.

"Get nail art!" Jada says, perking up. "I'm getting some."

"Uh, okay, sure." I've never gotten nail art that I've chosen myself, so why not now?

The woman in the apron waves us to the back and introduces me to my nail tech, Annie. They hand me a big sample wheel of colors and I busy myself with it.

"I have some pics too, if you're on Instagram," Annie says, tapping a card with her details on it. "If you want inspiration."

I murmur a thank you and check out her page. It's a slow day, but I still feel pressure to pick something fast.

"Do you know what you want, Jada?" Daisy examines Jada's nails. "Or do you want me to surprise you?"

"Surprise me." Jada scoots up in her seat.

"Yeah, surprise me too," I say to Annie before I can stop myself. It's not a bucket list item, but it's not something I'd normally do — why not?

"Yessss, thank you." Annie takes my hands and runs her thumbs over my nail beds. "You have such nice nail beds. I can do so many things. But I'll try to match your vibe."

The nail techs mask up and start on our nails.

"How was the family reunion?" Jada asks me.

I almost give the knee-jerk reaction of "fine", but what's the point of lying? "It was...interesting."

Jada snorts. "I bet. The Stryker family is huge so I suspect there's a bunch of weirdness in there."

"Yeah. I met a whole bunch of them." I shrug. "But they seem like they love each other, even if they're wrestling each other."

"Oh, Brett and Darren?" Jada asks. I nod. "Yeah, they just do that. They were a year or two behind us in school. It's all dumb brother shit."

"Waylon did win a bet, though," I say. "That they'd end up wrestling before and after dinner."

"One of Wes's little bets? Yeah, those are impossible to not buy into. It's never stuff that's too serious so it's fun."

A little tinge of jealousy pops up — I almost wish I'd known people that long or had those kinds of connections. But then again, everyone I've met (aside from Waylon's shitty aunt Nadine) has embraced me.

Maybe a little too hard.

"Can I ask something about Waylon's mom?" I ask, my voice low. "Is she always kind of extra?"

"Assuming this conversation stays in this room, god, yes." Jada heaves a sigh. "She's so extra. Sometimes it's kind of fun. Like in high school she was involved in all the stuff where the parents helped us plan and things were always over the top. But she also puts a ton of that energy into pushing Waylon to succeed."

"I definitely noticed that." Even though he's had enough accomplishments for a lifetime already.

"Yeah. Back in high school, I kind of got it — he was able to get into a bunch of good colleges because he was doing everything, all the time with her guidance. But now she wants him to be involved in all these things around town."

"Which he doesn't really want to do," I say. Jada makes a sound of acknowledgment. "But it seems like she wants *me* to do those things now."

"Ah, shit." Jada shakes her head. "Once she has you in her crosshairs, I doubt she'll let up."

"Awesome." I watch Annie start shaping my nails.

"Not to be a bummer," Jada says. She pauses, nibbling her bottom lip. "She was really like this with Catherine, but Catherine was more than happy to jump through all the hoops in the world to stay on Delia's good side. Probably because she knew she was trash."

I chuckle. "I'm not unique in that way?"

"Nope. But I don't think Delia notices how much all that pressure really affects someone." She pauses. "I think she just wants everything to look picture perfect. And so far, Waylon is the best chance for her to get that since he's always been a natural overachiever."

I swallow. "That must wear on him. Always feeling like he could be doing more. And what if you fail? Everyone fails."

"Yeah." Jada puts one hand into the curing light. "Waylon and failure aren't friends."

The seriousness of her tone, such a contrast from her usual light one, gives me pause. I try to imagine him even failing at all and can't. He gives off an aura of competence, which is pretty hot, but I never thought about the flip side. Dealing with failure when you aren't used to it.

My heart sinks a little. If I don't live up to his mom's expectations, will he feel like this whole fake relationship is failure? I just thought this would be me going on a few dates with him and me being done with it.

"We tried to get him to not think of the whole situation with his ex as a failure," Jada says, her tone somber again. "But I think he's kind of internalized it like that. I'm not a psychologist or whatever, but I think that's why it's taken him a bit to get back out there. But then he met you, so I'm assuming he's getting over it."

I bite the inside of my lip, just nodding. He's *so* not over it. And getting rid of the pain from a breakup on top of internalized feelings of failure, one of his biggest fears? That's not something people can just shake off.

EIGHTEEN
BIANCA

I RUB my eyes and lean back in my seat. I've been staring at my screen all morning, trying to force information on business operations into my head. Kaitlyn and I plan to bring someone else on to manage operations for the spa, but what's the point in me being involved if I don't know everything in and out? Or at the very least, the basics of business so I don't make an ass out of myself?

The problem is actually learning all of this. I was a mediocre student in high school, so this is the most studying I've done since graduating. I assumed getting back into learning, especially learning something actually important, would come easily to me, but that couldn't be further from the truth.

I scratch Sadie between her front legs. She's been a nice little warm weight on my lap — just what I need since I'm on my period. Who needs a hot water bottle when you have a little dog who loves napping on you?

Plus, my nails look amazing even after a week, which

makes typing feel fancy. Hanging out with Jada gave me a little burst of energy too. I forgot how much I like hanging out with people I actually like.

But reality came back in not long after. Will we still stay friends when I move to New York and "break up" with Waylon? I doubt Waylon would talk badly about me after, but it would still be a little bit awkward for her, wouldn't it? And it's not like I could come back to visit Jepsen without much of a reason.

I'll figure that out once I get to that point, but thinking about it now isn't helping me at all.

My phone lights up with a text from Waylon, saying he's outside if I'm still free to have him help me with the house. I'd gotten so wrapped up in my studying that I forgot he was coming today. We've been texting off and on, mostly jokes and dog pictures, but the one thing that's actually important slipped my mind.

I scoop up Sadie and head to the door, trying to find some chill within me. I forgot how awkward crushes are — I'm aware of everything about myself and don't know how to look like a regular person. It's like my arms and legs just decided to do their own thing and not communicate with each other. My period doesn't help me feel my best either. I'm puffy and bloated. I didn't even bother to cover my hair or use a satin pillowcase last night so my curls are all over the place.

"Hey," I say, checking him out as subtly as I can. He's just in what he usually wears when he comes to work on the house — old jeans and a t-shirt, but he still looks so good.

"Hey." He smiles, holding up his tool bag. "I figured I could do some stuff outside today."

"Yeah, sure." I can't keep the disappointment that he won't be near me out of my voice, but he doesn't seem to pick up on it. "Just let me know if you need anything or want some water or a snack. I'll just be in the breakfast nook."

"Sounds good." He hesitates for a second. "I was also thinking of installing a few security cameras and a security light for you since it's so dark at night. It's fine if you don't want them — I just figured it'd be a good idea."

At least he leaves off the obvious part — that Kyler's being a dickhead and a creep. But if he went through the trouble and already bought the cameras, why not?

"I'd like that." I'm so glad my skin tone is deep enough to hide blushes, or at least make them much less obvious. "Thank you."

"No problem." He puts out a finger for Sadie to sniff and I hold her out so he can pet her. "I'll start in the back, if you hear a bunch of banging around back there."

He heads to the back and I go back to the breakfast nook. My laptop went to sleep and I don't want to wake it up quite yet. But I told myself I'd make it through a few chapters of this book.

I sigh and call Kaitlyn just to take a break. She answers in a few rings.

"Hey, doll," Kaitlyn says. "What's up? Everything okay down there?"

"Yeah, it's good." I put Sadie on one of the other chairs and get up so I can pace around. "I was just doing some reading on business operations and needed a break."

"That's good. Any news on the house?" Kaitlyn asks. "You think you'll be able to put it on the market soon?"

"It's still a work in progress." I wander over to the

window. Waylon is down the side of the house, fixing the outside of a window. "But Waylon's working on it."

"Speaking of Dr. Hottie, Animal Savior..." I can hear the smirk in Kaitlyn's voice. "How's the bucket list stuff going? Let me live through you vicariously to escape my routine existence."

"Yeah." I walk back over to the pantry. "It's...going."

"Oh?" Kaitlyn pauses. "Is it bad?"

"No, it's just really, really good. Like absurdly good." I resist the urge to peek at Waylon through the window again. His ass looks way too good in his jeans. "A little too good. And he's a little too sweet and likable."

"Bianca..."

"I know." I grab a bag of popcorn from the pantry. "But it's just a dumb crush. I've never been in a situation where I'm banging a guy I have a crush on."

"That wasn't part of your plan, was it?" Kaitlyn asks.

"Of course not. But it doesn't really matter." I push down the ache in my chest and dump some popcorn into a bowl so I don't slam the whole bag in one go. I don't want to go back to the store. "I'm moving to New York and he has some baggage with his ex. He's not interested in any relationships, ever again."

"What's the deal with that?"

"I'm still not completely sure, but I know enough to piece things together. His ex is super shitty and it clearly ended very badly. I don't want to press him about it." I hate the way the light in his eyes goes out any time his ex is even vaguely mentioned. "So everything kind of works out. I have to leave and he doesn't even want a relationship. It's just sex and friendship."

"Okay. As long as you can keep that shit compartmentalized." Kaitlyn doesn't even try to hide her skepticism. "Speaking of relationships, some of our mutual friends told me Kyler keeps being all mopey over you, apparently."

I roll my eyes. "I know. He's still trying to text and DM me. I wish he'd just get over me or at least put that energy toward actually getting somewhere with his career on his own. I know my dad has a lot of sway in the industry but he's not the *only* producer out there."

"To be honest, your dad is kind of it. Doesn't he know everyone? Especially for his kind of pop," Kaitlyn points out. "And your dad will absolutely go to bat for you. He might get him blacklisted."

I lean my hip against the counter, vaguely close to where I've been keeping dog treats. Sadie walks up to me, her tail whipping back and forth, so I give her a little peanut butter treat just for being cute.

"I mean, you're not wrong. But maybe it'll just be harder for him to get off the ground." I stuff a handful of popcorn into my mouth. Some of it tumbles from my hand and Sadie clears up the bits I drop.

"With his music?" Kaitlyn scoffs. "Bianca, be real. He was fucking awful and I'm so glad I can finally say it out loud."

"He wasn't *that* bad." I suppress a smile.

"He was so bad. If he didn't have such a pretty face, he'd be playing in his bedroom in the basement of his mom's house," she says.

"Okay, fine, he wasn't that great." I laugh. "But he has to get over me at some point whenever he finds another producer."

"Just be careful, okay?" Kaitlyn says softly. "I know he's not particularly intimidating or scary, but desperation does weird things to people."

"I know. I will be." If I tell her about Waylon installing cameras of his own volition, she'll start down a whole rabbit hole of theories about what it might mean.

"I gotta run, but keep me posted on the house sale, okay?" Kaitlyn says. "We can do something fun to celebrate your move when you get here."

"I will."

We end the call and I go back to my seat, Sadie trotting behind me. I put her on my lap again and munch on my popcorn as I wake my laptop up again. I have to focus. I refuse to come across as an idiot when we start ramping up the business.

I wolf down more popcorn and hold Sadie to my lower stomach to ease my cramps, working through the dry textbook. Eventually a tap on the back door startles me out of it — it's just Waylon, his hat pulled low on his forehead.

I let him in. His sweat smells clean, mingling with the masculine scent of his deodorant.

"Want some water? It's pretty hot out," I say. "Sit down."

"That sounds perfect, thank you," he says, sitting at the table. Sadie squirms out of my arms and goes over to Waylon. "I just needed a little break — the sun is pretty intense."

I pour him a glass of water and hand it to him. He throws it back and I refill it again.

"Thanks," he says after taking the second glass.

"It's no problem." I sit down at the table too. Sadie looks so comfortable on his lap, looking up at him with her cute little fox eyes. My cramps are killing me and I want her back.

"Am I interrupting your studying?" he asks, gesturing to my laptop.

"No, you're saving me." I sigh. "I didn't love school when I was in it so having to study and actually give a shit about the information all of a sudden is a bit much."

"Do you want any help?" He shifts closer to me. "I minored in business, but I can't guarantee that I've seen whatever you're working on."

"You're already out there fixing the house. You don't have to help." Self-consciousness makes me shift in my seat. I'm not nearly as educated as he is. I don't want to embarrass myself.

He lifts a dark eyebrow, a small smile coming onto his face. "Believe it or not, I want to help just because we're friends."

"Can you first help me out by giving me Sadie back?" I ask. "She's my hot water bottle."

"Hm? Sure?" He hands me the dog.

"Period cramps," I add, sliding down in my seat a little and placing her in the right spot. "Which is also why I haven't really done anything about the bucket list in a few days."

"Oh," he says, not at all freaked out that I dare to have a period. Thank god. Kyler was always squeamish about it, as if it's not natural. "And it's fine. I'm following your lead on the bucket list. I don't want to pressure you into anything."

"You wouldn't be. I'd be down with you initiating," I say. I *want* him to. This whole thing is fake, but I like being pursued.

"Then I'll try something when you're up to it." His voice takes on that low heat that I'm becoming addicted to. "Anyway, did you want help with the business stuff? Because I'm happy to."

I swallow my pride and say, "sure."

I wake up my laptop again and show him what I'm studying. He scans the document, his rich brown eyes flicking back and forth.

"Okay, I remember this. What are you getting tripped up on?" He sits back in his seat.

He doesn't sound judgmental. Then again, I doubt he would seem that way. I know him by now. I explain the problem I'm having and he listens intently before explaining it back to me in a way I actually understand.

I'm supposed to keep this relationship compartmentalized, but how can I if Waylon is so fucking irresistible doing the most mundane things?

"Thank you," I say once I wrap my head around the concept. "I just want to get good enough at business stuff to not embarrass myself at meetings."

"I'm sure you'll do great." He takes off his hat and rakes a hand through his hair. "In my experience it's easier to remember stuff when it's relevant to what I'm actually interested in. It might be the same for you. And there's probably some app or program that can do all the number stuff for you."

"Maybe, yeah." I try to think of applying the concepts to the spa. "I haven't felt this enthusiastic about something before, but mostly it's just anxiety. Most businesses fail, don't they? And if I fail, then what do I do? I don't want to go back to modeling and I don't want to move home. It has to work."

I swallow the knot in my throat. My damn period. I'd

rather die than break down in front of someone, especially Waylon, but my body might make the decision for me.

"Then you figure something else out." He shrugs, resting a forearm on the table. We're sitting close enough to each other that his body heat is softly radiating against my thigh. "Which is the worst answer in the world, but it's kind of true."

I shoot him a look. "Easy for you to say. You actually have skills you can fall back on."

"So do you. Or at least you're trying to build them." He nods toward my laptop. "You can always learn something new and try something else."

This man's optimism is almost infectious. Almost.

"I wish you didn't make sense sometimes." I sigh, and he just smiles.

"I just see that you're underestimating yourself." He leans back in his seat and stretches, his arm coming to rest on the back of my seat. His arm isn't quite touching me, but it's close enough that I want more. "You left everything you knew after a breakup and moved to Jepsen of all places. And on top of that, you're actively trying new things that aren't entirely comfortable. An average person doesn't do that."

"Because those "new things" are shit that most normal people have already done with their lives?"

"Bianca." He gives me a look, then gently touches my shoulder. "Be honest — would any of the people you used to hang with back in LA do anything like this? Voluntarily with no other reward than wanting to grow as a person?"

I bite my bottom lip and shake my head.

"So, there you go. It's a big deal to you. Doesn't matter

whether it's a 'big deal' in the big scheme of things." He shrugs. "You're taking a leap."

"You should add motivational speaker to your resume." I can't help but crack a smile.

"Not hard to motivate someone when they're already doing good stuff." He pushes back from the table. "I should get back to it. Thanks for the water."

"Thanks for the pep talk."

He squeezes my shoulder, and the light gesture makes me flush from head to toe. I watch him leave, my eyes drifting down his back. Once he's out of the room I sag further into my seat.

Is there any point to me trying to compartmentalize this? It almost feels like building a wall with paper and expecting it to hold back a flood.

NINETEEN

WAYLON

> Ash: Sup nerds, how many strippers are we getting for Wes's bachelor party?

WHY IS Ash texting me and JD about this at eleven in the morning? Then again, I have no idea what time zone he's in. But also, I wouldn't put it past him to be thinking about strippers at eleven in the morning on a Tuesday.

> Me: Wes said no strippers

I go back to looking at the records for a cat I'll be seeing in the next forty minutes. He just needs a tooth removed, and since he's otherwise healthy, it shouldn't be a major procedure. Plus, it's a slow day, so I won't have much going on after that.

> JD: It'll be at the bar, end of discussion. Absolutely no strippers. And no exotic dancers or any performer who takes their clothes off.
>
> Ash: Y'all are fucking boring

My phone lights up again and I sigh — this time it's Mom. I don't have to read the message to know it's more bullshit about the shelter board or whatever other thing she wants me to be a part of.

The more she pushes, the more her disappointment starts to creep through. And the more disappointment comes through, the more I feel the need to cave. I wish I didn't. I *should* be able to tell her to stop and leave it at that. I'm not in high school anymore — I don't have to fill my schedule with a thousand different activities. But old habits die hard, and the rush of approval and (her version of) success still calls out to me just a little.

I'm about to put my phone on 'do not disturb' when a text from Bianca pops up. My heart does an idiotic flutter and I check it. It's a picture of Sadie, eyes closed close to a fan, her fur blowing back.

> Bianca: From last night. She was having a supermodel moment

I grin. As much as I miss having Sadie around the house, I'm glad she and Bianca are bonding.

> Me: Cute. Are y'all staying cool at the house?

> Bianca: Mostly. The AC is definitely being taxed during the day.

I jiggle my leg. The HVAC system is probably ancient and will probably cost a lot to fix. It's definitely outside of my bubble of expertise. But it's been unseasonably hot lately.

> Me: Come by later so you can stay cool. I should be out of here by 5:30

I pause, wishing I could unsend it. I don't want them to be hot, but I don't want to seem too pushy.

> Bianca: I think we will, thanks

I blow a breath out through my nose and finally put my phone on do not disturb. That's future Waylon's problem.

I focus again, familiarizing myself with my afternoon patients before moving onto the cat's tooth removal. Everything is relatively routine, so I call her humans and tell them it all went fine.

The rest of the day is more of the same, borderline boring. Same when I get home — I take Duke on his walk and let him play with Murphy until they're both tuckered out. Bianca texts me, asking if she can come over to cool off, and I give her the okay.

She arrives a few minutes later, a tote bag on her shoulder and Sadie in one arm. She looks like she's going to a yoga class in her leggings and fitted top, both the same shade of deep red. I don't know how many of these matching sets she has, but I hope she has them in every color. They look like they were made for her.

"I figured I'd bring wine or something?" She shrugs and pulls a bottle out. "As a thank you for letting us hang here until it cools down. But I don't even know if you drink wine, so if you don't, I can just take it back."

"I like wine. I don't know much about it but it's good with steaks or Italian food," I say, taking the bottle. "Thanks."

"Good. I don't know anything about wine either." She puts Sadie down, and the dog strolls deeper into the house toward the living room. "I should have brought food, though. I guess I can run back and grab something."

"It's fine. I was going to cook some pasta, actually." Since today was pretty slow, I feel like cooking for once. "Do you like pasta?"

"I do. Haven't had it all that often recently, so it'd be a nice change of pace," she says. "I can only eat so many grain bowls before I go insane and takeout's mostly a rip off."

I laugh, walking toward the kitchen. Sadie is sitting at the back sliding door between the kitchen and the back porch, nose to the glass with her tail wagging. I let Duke and Murphy inside and they all greet each other.

Murphy trots into the middle of the kitchen, right where we need to walk, and stretches out with a heavy sigh.

"Tired, buddy?" I ask. "Scoot over there, Murph."

Murphy lifts his head an inch, then flops back down. Sadie joins him, but Duke sits where I've trained him to sit while I'm cooking — out of the way.

"I guess he is." Bianca smiles. "Maybe he's just choosing a strategic position to get the most dropped food."

"That would mean that he's capable of masterminding anything." I give him a scratch above his tail. "I like dogs that are just happy to be here even though they have absolutely no idea what's going on."

"Kind of like Sadie?" She follows me deeper into the kitchen, which is open and attached to the living room.

"Yeah. They just like being with their people no matter what. Even if you're in a shitty mood, they're there to cheer you up." I gently slide Murphy across the floor with my foot and move Sadie over near where Duke is sitting.

"It's nice. If I'd known dogs were like that, I might have gotten one a long time ago," she says, looking over at Sadie with a soft smile in her eyes. "I had a lot of days where I needed that."

I wash my hands and open my fridge to double check I have what I need. My grocery shopping strategy is just grabbing whatever looks good and figuring it out later.

"The pasta sauce is just a Bolognese. I can easily make it without dairy," I say, pulling out some Italian sausage and beef. I grab an onion and garlic bulb next. "It'll go well with the wine."

"That sounds amazing." She rests her hands on the counter. "I can only cook about four things, and even then I rely on pre-chopped veggies."

"Do you want to learn how to cook this?" I ask, pulling out the cutting board and pots. "It's really easy."

"Sure, yeah. And I'd feel bad for not helping." She comes around to the side of the island where I am. "How can I help?"

"You fine with touching raw meat? You could mix the seasoning in the ground beef and sausage while I start making the sauce." I grab a bowl from the cabinet and put it down, then dig through my spice rack to find the right seasonings.

"Yeah, I can handle the meat. You're making the sauce from scratch?" she asks.

"Yeah. It's not that hard." I shrug and chop up an onion.

"Says you. I'm impressed."

A stupid flush of masculine pride appears in my chest. I busy myself, trying to get a hold of my knee-jerk reaction. But what guy wouldn't be psyched that he impressed a beautiful woman?

A guy who had some sense to keep women, especially women I explicitly set out to not date, in the back of his head.

I ask her about her day as she starts mixing in the seasoning into the meat and she fills me in on how everything is going at work and with her prep for running the business. It sounds like she's hit a good stride. Even if she's not staying here for long after she sells the house, I'm glad she's adjusting to Jepsen more.

Dinner comes together as quickly after the pasta cooks, and I fill two bowls with pasta, topping it with a little chopped parsley to make it look fancy. I grab some parmesan for myself, and the wine.

"This looks super good." she says.

I watch her take the first bites as I put cheese on my pasta. She takes a small bite, then nods.

"Like it?" I ask.

"So good." She digs in again. "I should add learning to cook more stuff to my list. I can make whatever looks trendy. I still don't get the point of a smoothie bowl, though. Just drink the damn thing."

I laugh. "I can teach you a few things. Or we could go to

Nana's and she'd be happy to help. Though she might just sit in a chair and roast you while she barks orders."

"That would be fun." She smiles and my heart flutters despite myself. She smiles so much more when we're alone and it makes her even prettier. "I'm assuming you're speaking from experience?"

"Yeah." I take a swig of the wine. "Nana's my mom's mom, but they couldn't be more different. Nana doesn't give a single shit of what people think about her and she's always willing to give you her opinion, even if it's hard to hear. She's taught all of my brothers how to cook, at least a little. Wes is the best at it."

"Yeah, Rose brings leftovers to lunch and they always smell so good." She takes a dainty sip of wine, whatever gloss she has on her lips leaving an imprint on her glass. "This is going to sound terrible, but the closest I've gotten to a home cooked meal that tasted good is something our family's private chef made."

"A home cooked meal that tasted good," I point out. "So there have been ones that tasted bad?"

"Yeah, sometimes my parents' friends have double dates with them to cooking classes at wineries. They'll come home thinking they're hot shit with what they learned. Then my dad will overcook stuff, and my mom will overseason everything." She swirls her wine in the glass, warmth in her eyes. "Mom always claims that she grew up knowing how to cook, but I really doubt it. No one can regress *that* hard."

"Sounds like you miss them."

"I do." She pushes some noodles around on her plate. "Being around them is really relaxing and always has been. I guess it's because they're into the actual music rather than all the shit that comes with being famous, so things feel more normal. Dad notoriously hates doing press and once the hype from her biggest hit songs died down, Mom mostly focused on working behind the scenes or doing normal mom stuff."

"That would go a long way in making things feel more normal," I say.

"Yeah. They're kind of like me — they like stuff like trying a new restaurant or staying in like this with dinner and a movie." She shrugs. "Some people say it's boring, but sometimes the little spots of boring are just what we need in between rushing around."

"Yeah. I'm starting to appreciate it more."

Especially here with her. Sure, we could go out every other night just to go out, or make elaborate plans. But just being able to fully relax with someone and get the same pleasure out of it as spending time alone isn't an everyday occurrence for me.

It's almost terrifyingly easy to slide Bianca into place in all the regular things I do, like she's supposed to be here.

But friendship can feel the same way, can't it? It has to. The friendship side and the sex side of our relationship need to stay as far apart as possible, even if she looks really fucking pretty sitting across the table from me.

TWENTY
BIANCA

THIS CONVERSATION WAS SUPPOSED to be a casual dinner chat, not a revelation that hanging out with Waylon feels as easy and natural as hanging around by myself.

I shouldn't want him the way I want him right now. I want more dinners and comfortable silences. More of this calmness that I've only ever felt around him or the people closest to me. More of his warm, genuine smiles.

I swig down some of my wine to soothe my dry mouth. Wanting him physically is the least complicated way I could want him. He wants to fuck me, I want to fuck him. I want to (continue to) learn what good sex is actually like.

I need to focus on that. I *need to*. Because imagining more is the worst thing I can do. Staying in Jepsen is temporary. And even if it wasn't, Waylon told me he flat out didn't want anything serious.

After I finish eating, I stretch, and his eyes go to my (admittedly modest) cleavage.

"I've got it," he says to me when I stand up to put my dish in the sink.

"Thanks. But aren't I supposed to do the dishes or something because you did most of the cooking?" I ask. "It's like four things and you have a dishwasher."

"You really don't have to." He takes my dish and pops it into the dishwasher. "You helped."

"Fine, let me get the pot and cutting board, at least." I nudge my way in front of him to the sink and start washing the big things.

"Thanks." He rests his hip against the counter and watches me.

His body language is relaxed but I'm definitely not relaxed. I'm wound tight, aching between my thighs already just from the way he's looking at me. It's like my body knows what comes after that look.

He snags one of my curls and gently tugs it, winding it around his finger. He isn't even touching my skin and electricity makes its way all the way through my body.

His hand travels down the side of my neck to cup the back, his skin slightly rough against mine. The little circles he makes with his thumbs give me chills as I finish cleaning the last pot.

The contrast between the friendly, polite version of him in public, and this version, who looks like he wants to devour me, sends a bolt of warmth down my spine.

"All done," I say, looking up at him. "Though to be honest, you distracted me."

"A good distraction?" He pulls me closer to him.

"Very good." I glance at his lips. I want him to kiss me, but now I'm rethinking it. Does he think it's too intimate to just do that? There's a big difference between a kiss to start and kissing me in the heat of the moment.

He kisses the side of my neck instead, his hands roaming all over me. Adjusting to my post-modeling body — even though it's not that different — has been hard, but the way he can tell me he's into me without saying a word eases some of my fears. His hands skim down my hips and around to my ass, giving it a squeeze.

"Any ideas about what you want to learn today?" he asks, his lips on my collarbone.

"I brought some toys," I say, letting my hands inch up his chest. "Just in case."

"That's perfect." He grins, his fingers threading in mine. "C'mon."

I let him lead me upstairs, scooping up my tote bag on the way. We pass by what looks like his home office before we reach his bedroom. It's very him — tidy but not so tidy that it feels like no one actually lives there. He gently nudges me to sit down on the bed and he shuts the door behind us.

"So the dogs don't bother us," he says, putting out his hand for the bag. I hand it over.

He nods as he looks inside — it's just a small dildo and a wand vibrator. How is he planning to use them? He gently pushes me onto my back, covering my body with his and boxing me in. The heat and size of him over me is about to make my heart beat out of my chest.

It nearly does when he leans down and kisses me, deep and dirty from the start. Nothing at all like the kiss we would have shared in the kitchen. I thread my fingers through his soft, dark hair and throw my leg over his hip. I want to feel every moment of this — just us, his arm behind my back to hold me closer.

His lips trail down the side of my neck, then he peels off my top. The top is lined, so I didn't bother with a bra.

He murmurs something I don't catch, but it sounds like he likes what he sees. I arch my back when he sucks one of my nipples into his mouth, hard. It's right at the line of pain and pleasure, which we haven't explored yet.

"More," I say. Telling him what I like is second nature at this point.

"More?" He briefly lifts his head before doing the same to my other nipple. "Like that?"

"Yes." I gasp, sliding my fingers under the neckline of his t-shirt. His skin is warm, almost feverish. "Just like that."

"You like a little pain, then?" he asks before doing it again. I nod, gripping his hair. "Good to know."

He makes me squirm for so long that I'm seconds away from shoving down my leggings and touching myself for relief. Thankfully he pulls away, taking his shirt off before pulling down my bottoms.

"All I need you to do is not come," he says.

I sit up on my elbows, checking to see if he's kidding. He's not.

"We've spent a whole lot of time trying to get me to come, and now you don't want me to?" I ask, my eyes skimming over his shoulders and chest. He's muscular but not chiseled. I prefer him this way.

"Oh, you're going to." He kneels between my legs, parting them, his thumbs rubbing over the lace of my panties. "You're going to be begging to. But you're going to learn how to hold back."

I bite my lip as he presses his thumb against my clit through my panties.

"You're sure?" I ask. Now that I've come every time we've fooled around, I can't go without it. And now I don't know if I can hold back.

It's a better problem than not being able to come at all, though.

"You trust me?" he asks. I nod. I trust him a terrifying amount. "Then you don't have to worry."

He tugs my panties to the side and dips one finger into my pussy. His fingers hit just deep enough to make my toes curl.

"Do you want me to take these off?" I ask, my fingers going to the waistband of my panties.

"Not yet. I like them too much," he says. "I love all the panties you wear."

I start to make a mental list of the lingerie sets I could wear around him but my mind goes blank as soon as he presses his tongue to my clit. He can work me up so fast now, one hand holding my panties to the side and the other working in my pussy. I lose myself in the feeling, relaxing the way I only can with him.

Time doesn't exist — only the feelings he's pulling out of me. I inch up that hill to the plateau I always linger on before I come, my pussy clenching around his finger. Everything starts to get fuzzy and my chest heaves.

Then, he stops.

"What's wrong?" I ask, popping my head up.

"I told you not to come. But I didn't tell you I'd do my best to make you try." He grins. "I'm going to keep you on edge until you're begging me to let you come."

"Oh." I blink. "*Oh.*"

He runs his hands up and down my thighs. "Just tell me if you're close. I think I know, but just to be safe."

"What if I don't?" I ask with a smirk. He picks up that I'm just being cheeky and his smile widens even more.

"I wasn't planning on adding punishment to today's lesson, but I'm more than happy to teach you how to be a good girl."

"I'll be good." I lift my hips so he can tug my panties off.

"I know you will." He picks up the wand vibrator and turns it on, cycling through the settings before settling on one of the lower ones.

He tests the toy on my outer lips, just gauging my reaction, before circling my clit. I press my thighs apart further so he can put it where I want it. It's so good, but so maddening to not have control over where he puts it. Every time I move my hips to get it in one spot, he puts it somewhere else.

But I climb closer and closer to coming until I can barely take it.

"I'm close," I choke out. He pulls the toy away immediately. "Shit. That's...a lot."

My pussy is still tingling from the vibrator, and my whole body tingles when he kisses my inner thighs. Once he sees I've come down, he starts again.

I start to lose count of how many times he brings me *right* to the edge before pulling back. He cycles between the vibrator, his fingers, his mouth, and the dildo in different combinations that drive me nuts in different ways. I'm dizzy with need, my pussy so soaked that I'm sure there's a damp spot on the bed beneath me.

At some point I start trembling from head to toe, like all

the sensations inside me are threatening to burst out of my skin. I've never felt like this before, like I'm just a bunch of nerve endings arranged like a human being. How did I go through life without knowing feelings like this existed?

And how did I go through life not seeing Waylon from between my legs, his entire focus on me and my pleasure?

"P-please," I gasp when he stops on me again. "Please. I need to come. I'm going insane."

He sits up, his cock making a bulge in his shorts. My pussy aches just looking at him. I want him inside me.

"You want to come on my cock?" he asks, hopping up and shedding his shorts and boxers. His cock has a pearl of precum on the tip, which glides down the underside of his shaft.

"Please."

He reaches over to the side table and grabs a condom, suiting up in seconds.

"I'll give you what you asked for since you asked nicely. Hold your legs back, princess," he says, picking up the wand toy. "I'm not going to be gentle."

"Don't hold back." I do as he says, my eyes on him.

Instead of plunging inside of me right away, he puts the wand against my clit again. I'm so close that I cry out, breathing deep so I don't come before he's buried deep. He brings me up and up until I'm nearly at the edge before he pushes inside me.

The sudden fullness brings tears to my eyes and steals my ability to breathe. And when he starts to fuck me hard while keeping the toy on me?

I'm done. I can't stop myself from coming. His thick cock pounding me, grazing my g-spot again and again, is too much to process. My brain shuts down all activity besides the ones that control how I feel. The pleasure literally makes me cry, tears streaming down my face.

I manage to pull it together long enough to look up at Waylon, who's equally as lost in me as I am in my own pleasure. The eye contact is electric. Not too much. Not too intimate.

"Fuck, I can't anymore," he says, tossing my toy to the side.

He presses my legs back even further and fucks me so hard that his bed slams against the wall over and over again. I manage to pull him down into a kiss that's barely a kiss, it's just us touching in any way we can. Getting as close as we can. He buries his face into my neck as he comes, his entire body shuddering.

He manages not to squish me when he relaxes, not that I would have done anything. I've merged with this bed and couldn't move a muscle if I tried. He pulls out and goes to throw out the condom before laying back down next to me.

"Holy fuck," I say, once I catch my breath. "That…I…"

"You okay?" He swipes a tear off my face with his thumb. It's so tender that I almost cry again, but I hold my shit together and nod.

"It was just…it was really intense," I say, my heart still racing.

"You want to take a shower?" he asks. "To decompress a little."

"Yeah, that sounds good." I need something to bring me down a bit.

We head to the bathroom, which is tidy and surprisingly spacious. I wind my hair up into a bun on the top of my head while he starts the water for us. He gestures for me to go in first. The hot water feels like a balm on my skin.

"Temperature good?" he asks, stepping inside behind me and hanging up a fresh washcloth, before closing the curtain.

"It's perfect." I let my chin fall to my chest and let the water fall down my back for a little too long. "Sorry, I'm hogging the water, aren't I?"

"A little bit." He gives me a half-smile and we switch places. "But I understand. It's a good shower."

"I've never really done this before," I admit. "Showering with anyone."

He wets his hair, then looks at me, not judging. "Not even an ex?"

"No. But now that I think about it, we had some awesome showers where we could have." The master bath in the apartment I shared with Kyler had a gorgeous, deep tub and a bathroom with multiple shower heads. But still, the idea of showering together never seriously crossed my mind. "It felt too...I don't know. Never mind. It's stupid."

"Why would it be stupid?" He grabs a bottle of body wash.

"I was just self-conscious. Physically, I mean." I sigh. "As if I hadn't been mostly naked in front of cameras and plastered all over the internet."

And as if I hadn't taken a few spicy pictures of myself early in our relationship. I still wish I could unsend those, especially now. He claims he deleted them but his track record with the truth is pretty iffy.

"Being naked at work is different than being naked at home." he says, pausing. "That's not something I ever thought I'd say."

I laugh. "Yeah, but it makes sense. Being naked or mostly naked on set is so clinical and unsexy. Like I'm freezing my tits off in an uncomfortable pose and some photographer is yelling stuff like, 'unclench, Bianca! You look like you're taking a shit waiting for the bus!"

Waylon bursts out laughing. "That's a little too specific to be something you thought of off the top of your head."

"Yeah, I have a whole list of wild stuff photographers have said," I say. "But yeah, that kind of energy makes me feel less nervous about being so exposed. Plus I got photoshopped to hell and back. Showering with my exes would have made me feel too exposed. Even though it wasn't like they hadn't seen me naked in bed. The more I talk about it, the more it sounds absurd."

"No, I get it, I think. In bed, you're moving and you're in a certain headspace. But in the shower you're just casually naked." He leans against the wall. "And in the light."

"Exactly." I slip under the water again.

Being casually naked with Waylon feels way too natural — like I hadn't even thought to be self-conscious about it.

"I get what it's like to be self-conscious around the people who you shouldn't be self-conscious around," he says after a comfortable pause. "Not physically, but just in general."

He's talking about his awful ex, I'm guessing, and now I dislike her even more.

"That too," I say. "It's not even something conscious."

"You just wake up one day and you realize that you're holding shit in." His tone is soft and filled with understanding.

All I can do is nod, or I'll say something that breaks this

little bubble we're in and lets in all the ugly stuff from the past come through.

My stomach twists in knots even though the water is soothing. I know Waylon isn't like my exes at all, but the more I open up, the more I worry about the other shoe dropping. Or worse — I worry about him being just right for me, but him not feeling the same way.

TWENTY-ONE
BIANCA

THE NEXT FEW weeks go by in a blur — a good blur, not the kind where I feel like I'm being thrown from one place to another. So far, I haven't had any more bad news from the press or from Kyler.

I go to work (and actually enjoy it), get prepared to open the business, then have Waylon come by to fix parts of the house. And then we fool around and he gives me lessons on almost everything I've ever wanted to know.

I like that part the most, but in the same way I like food I know will give me a stomachache. But I do it anyway then try to shove down the absurd crush I have on him. What if I'm just blinded by these feelings and he turns out to be a dick in the long run? Then again, where can whatever this is even go? Whatever trauma he has from his past relationship isn't the kind of thing you can get over in however long I have left in town.

I bite my bottom lip, watching Sadie sniff around the grass outside of the Stryker Liquor offices for her pee break. I found a list of realtors in the area who could help sell my house but I haven't made a move yet. At the rate we're going, we could have the house done not long after the wedding.

Kaitlyn is thrilled because me moving to New York means we can really make strides on the spa. But the closer that date gets, the more uneasy I get.

Sadie looks up at me, wagging her tail, so I scoop her up and head back inside. Will Sadie be happy in New York? She generally likes to be in my lap or on the closest soft surface, but she's never been to a place like the city as far as I know.

I sit back down at my desk, placing Sadie in my lap. Rose isn't there, but she comes back in with a light sigh.

"I know the wedding will be amazing the day of, but I'm fucking tired of all the little bullshit that keeps getting thrown my way," she says, flopping down into her chair. "Today it's ribbons. For what? I don't even know."

"I'm sorry," I say. "But the wedding is soon, at least."

"Yeah. By the way, want to come to my bachelorette party? It's going to be pretty casual with just a few of us — just going to the bar for a drink with the guys, then going back to our place for a sleepover."

"Oh." I get a ridiculous rush of happiness. She wants me to go? We're friendly but I wasn't sure if she cared enough to invite me to something. "Sure, I'd love that."

"Awesome, I'll text you the details." She grabs her phone and starts tapping out a text. "I'm heading to the bar after work too, if you want to grab a drink. Waylon can come too."

'Yeah, I'd love to."

I shoot him a text to ask. We've been texting back and forth more, just day-to-day chat and funny animal memes.

Even though his responses are sporadic because of his work, I still like talking. Thankfully he responds with a yes right away so I don't have to overthink it.

I look forward to drinks throughout the rest of the day, then follow Rose to the bar. It's not too busy, so we sit closer to the front, near the big floor to ceiling windows.

"I've got the first round. What do you want to drink?" Rose asks, putting her purse in her seat. "I can put in an order for some food next door too."

"Anything as long as it's not too strong. And fries would be amazing."

"Gotcha."

I watch her head to the bar. Wes spots her immediately, his face lighting up. Rose goes on her tiptoes and he leans over the bar to give her a deep kiss. The brightness in his eyes makes my heart ache, and I'm sure Rose's expression is the same. They're so cute together.

Duke gets to the table a few moments before Waylon, and I put Sadie down so they can hang out.

"Hey," Waylon says with a soft smile. My heart flips in my chest and I give him a little wave.

He's wearing his glasses again, and a dark green t-shirt of a similar color. His hair is damp, a dark curl falling into his forehead.

"Hey," I finally say. He kisses me on the temple, just for show, and slips into the seat next to me. "Want me to grab us drinks?"

"Rose has the first round." I nod in her direction.

Waylon stands and catches Wes's attention over Rose's shoulder. Wes just nods in understanding and grabs another glass.

"Was your day okay?" he asks.

"Yeah, why?"

"Just wondering. We've never grabbed drinks after work so I was worried it was a 'I need a drink' kind of day." He presses his knee to mine, and just that tiny point of contact makes me stupidly giddy.

"Has it been a day like that for you?" I ask.

"It hasn't been the best day, but it hasn't been the worst day either." He rakes his fingers through his hair. "I'm looking forward to the weekend."

He glances over his shoulder. Wes and Rose are clearly still flirting it up while Wes makes us a pitcher of something.

"I was thinking of going up to this good stargazing spot. If you want to come for your bucket list," he says. "We'd be camping overnight, though. Wes and Rose can watch Sadie."

"I'd love that." Curling up with Waylon in a tent, stargazing, feels romantic as hell, though.

I guess I can delude myself into thinking it's real, even for a night.

"Okay, we've got mango moonshine margaritas," Rose says, putting a pitcher and glasses on the table. "And food'll be ready in fifteen-ish."

"Thanks." Waylon pours a drink for each of us, sliding one to me first.

I lift the glass to my lips to take a sip, glancing out the window, and nearly choke. Kyler is standing outside, looking around and at his phone. How did he find me here? Then again, Jepsen's not very big. But one of the few times I come into town, we run into each other?

I freeze, hoping he doesn't look inside.

"What?" Waylon asks, following my gaze.

"My ex," I say softly. "Don't look."

Waylon turns his head back right as Kyler does. Of course, today is the day we sit right near the window.

"If you need me to scare him off, I will," Waylon says, resting a hand on my leg.

"Maybe." I blow out a breath and put my hand on top of Waylon's. My heart is racing so fast, mostly out of shock, and I need to stay upright.

"Bianca. I found you," Kyler says, as if we've just gotten separated in a crowd.

I finally let myself take him in all the way. He looks so wildly out of place here, so airbrushed even in person. He's good-looking but I'm not at all attracted to him anymore, especially with Waylon right there. Seeing them in the same space feels like it should break some kind of law of the universe.

"Why are you here?" I ask. Waylon's hand squeezes mine and I squeeze it back.

"Because I was in Nashville for a few days trying to..." He pauses. "Just having some meetings. And I pulled a few strings to find out where you were so we could talk. You've been ignoring my calls."

"Typically when someone ignores your calls, they don't want to talk to you," I say. "What could you possibly have to say?"

Kyler finally acknowledges Waylon and Rose, his eyes flicking over them.

"Can't we talk in private?" Kyler says. "It won't take long."

Kyler isn't threatening whatsoever, but I don't want to be alone with him.

"No," I say. "Whatever you can say, you can say here."

Kyler sighs heavily, glancing at the spot where Waylon and I's hands are joined. His eyes narrow.

"C'mon. Literally two minutes of privacy." His tone is a borderline whine. I forgot how much I hated that. He's a grown ass man.

"I'll go if Waylon can come," I say with a swallow.

"No, of course not." Kyler laughs. "This is about our relationship. Not whoever he is."

"Our relationship that doesn't exist anymore. And Waylon is my boyfriend," I say. Irritation is making the volume of my voice climb, so I swallow to cool myself down.

"You can't be serious," Kyler says.

"She is," Waylon says. "Get to the point or leave."

Kyler's eyes narrow again. "Fine, this is fucking annoying. Bianca, let's go home. Please. We can sort things out."

"We absolutely cannot sort things out when you *cheated* on me then had the balls to plan a proposal like nothing was wrong," I say, my brows shooting up. I feel Waylon flinch a tiny bit — not so much that others would notice, but I felt it. "Are you kidding me? Get out of here."

Kyler runs both hands through his hair, his tell for frustration. Which usually happened when I pushed back against him with anything.

"You can't *live* here." Kyler gestures vaguely around here. "You're really going to stay here with this guy in this random fucking town?"

I press down on Waylon's thigh when he shifts to get up.

"I can." I'm absolutely not telling him what my future plans are.

"Bee." He looks at me with that *look*, the one that used to get me every time. But now it just pisses me off. What did I ever see in this man?

"Y'know what, come here," I say, standing up. If I'm going to bitch him out, I don't want to do it in front of everyone. I don't need more eyes on us.

"Do you need me?" Waylon asks, gently grabbing my wrist. His deep brown eyes are filled with concern.

"I've got it." I lean in and give him a soft kiss on the cheek. He reluctantly lets me go. "But thank you. We'll be out front so you can see us."

I follow Kyler outside and stop in front of the big window. He looks left and right, like he doesn't want to be noticed.

"We're 100% done, Kyler. You cheated on me and made it extremely clear that you're only interested in me because of who my father is," I say, crossing my arms over my chest.

"No, I didn't!" He pauses. "I mean, yes to the cheating part, but that was only physical, babe. It didn't mean anything."

I roll my eyes. "Okay, sure."

"Be honest though, B." Kyler sighs. "You never came. You always acted like sex was a chore. It just wasn't your thing. I have needs. And as for your dad…I don't know. Like, if the cheating was just a physical thing, why does your dad have to blackball me?"

I can't stop the laugh from bursting from my mouth. He looks genuinely confused. Like he didn't put in the bare minimum amount of effort into sex. Like going out and banging some other models wasn't a huge ass deal, regardless of whether there were any emotions involved. Like my protective father wouldn't want to murder him for what he did. Blackballing is the least of his worries.

"You saying that just shows me how little you know me and how dead our relationship is." I scoff. I nearly tell him that sex definitely *is* my thing, especially with Waylon, but I don't want him to go off on another streak of excuses. I turn to go back inside.

"Bianca, please," he says, gently grabbing my shoulder. I shake him off. "I'll do anything. I'll give you extra money to invest in that spa thing you wanted to do."

That spa thing. Even the way he phrases it makes it sound dismissive.

"Money won't fix it," I say. "Just go home, Kyler. There's nothing you can say to fix this."

"Bianca." He tries to grab my hand again, right as Waylon steps outside.

"Don't touch her," Waylon says, taking my hand and gently tugging me back. "I don't have to hear her say anything to understand she doesn't want to talk to you."

"You're really her boyfriend?" Kyler looks Waylon up and down. As if he can even vaguely compare to Waylon.

"Yes." Waylon steps up to Kyler, making Kyler take a few steps back. Waylon is usually so gentle that I forget how physically imposing he is. "So you have no reason to talk to her anymore. Leave, or I can make sure you do. Don't touch my girl, ever."

"If you touch me, I'll call my lawyer." Kyler takes a few more steps back.

Waylon laughs. "I don't think I'd have to lay a finger on you to get you to leave, man."

"I'm tired of this shit," Kyler finally says. "I'm leaving. Voluntarily. You'll regret this, Bianca."

"Okay, sure," Waylon says with a scoff. "Bye."

Waylon keeps an eye on him until he disappears around the corner.

"I'm sorry," he says, his body language softening with Kyler out of his sight. "I know you were handling it but when he touched you, I kind of lost it."

I smile at Waylon's version of 'losing it'. Yeah, he was clearly pissed and he definitely isn't the kind of guy that people mess with, but he stayed as levelheaded as he could possibly be. I liked that — I'd seen Kyler fly off the handle before, mostly at people he assumed were lesser.

God, what did I ever see in Kyler? And how could I think that Waylon would ever turn out to be a dick like he was? Kyler was flinging out little red flags for so long, and I ignored them until they were hitting me in the face. Waylon's been green flag after green flag.

"It's fine. Thank you. He wasn't really leaving me alone so I needed some backup." I sigh, resisting the urge to lean into him. But he steps forward and I end up leaning against him anyway.

He smells nice and clean, but as always, he isn't wearing any overpowering scents. His arm goes around my back in a hug and we just stand there for several seconds.

"You want to sit out here and get some air for a while longer?" Waylon asks, gesturing to a bench along the outer wall of the bar.

"Sure, yeah." I don't know if I can go back inside and act like everything's fine with Rose just yet.

We sit down, our thighs pressed against each other, and I

lean back into the bench with a sigh. The more distance I get from the incident, the more surreal it feels. How did Kyler find me? I'm sure he still has the means at this point, not that he will forever with the trajectory his career is on. But still, it's terrifying. Imagine if he were actually threatening? Then what would I do?

I take a deep breath and let it out. It doesn't really matter - I doubt he'll come back after seeing Waylon and I together. He's not the brightest but he's fully aware he'd get his ass kicked if it came down to it.

"He cheated on you?" Waylon asks, his voice soft.

"Mmhm." I brush at a bit of dust on my jeans. "Honestly, when I found out, I stayed quiet about it for a long time. I just could not believe he'd do it and barely cover his tracks. It was almost insulting but mostly it just hurt."

Waylon nods, looking at an undefined point in front of him.

"I know the feeling," he finally says. "It makes you question everything about yourself."

"Exactly." Like how did I even let this happen, and mostly, was there something wrong with me to make him do that?

Now I can see that there wasn't — Kyler is a douchebag who barely wanted to put in effort in our relationship. But still, at the time, I sobbed my eyes out until I could confront him.

"Did you get...?" I let him fill in the blank, and he nods again. "I'm so sorry, Waylon."

"It's in the past," he says. But he doesn't say it's okay now. "I'm over her completely, but the mindfuck of catching her cheating *twice* still has me questioning my own memories. Like I knew her but there was this whole other her underneath. We've known each other for so long but only started dating in college. Then that imploded around the time we graduated because she cheated. My biggest mistake is taking her back years later because she said she'd grown up. The whole second leg of our relationship was a disaster."

"I can't imagine how awful that is," I say, leaning against him. "And it's not dumb to take her back if she sounded like she was genuinely sorry. It's on her for being a shitty person and betraying your trust."

He doesn't respond, he just puts his hand on my thigh and lightly squeezes it. I rest my hand on top of his. All the little bits and pieces I know about him start to click into place — his insistence on keeping things casual, the icy tension between him and his ex.

I felt like my whole world had been flipped upside down when I found out Kyler was cheating and we had only dated for two years. I can't imagine the level of betrayal I would feel if I'd known him my whole life *and* if I'd given him a second chance.

"Sorry, it's not about my own bullshit," he finally says, shaking his head. "Ready to head back inside?"

"Sure, yeah." I stand up and he takes my hand, just as naturally as ever. But after everything he told me, I doubt we'll ever be more than what we are now.

TWENTY-TWO
WAYLON

"I SHOULD HAVE CHECKED the weather, sorry," I say to Bianca, looking out the window. It's pouring out, thunder rolling in the distance. "We'll have to try camping another weekend."

"It's cool," Bianca says. "To be honest, I just got a shipment of a bunch of my favorite snacks that I can't find around here so I was going to lay around all day and watch TV."

"That sounds really nice. And I'll probably end up doing that too." I lean down to pet Duke when he leans against me.

I rarely ever get days when I can just sit around and do nothing, especially when the weather is perfect for just that. I'm still working on not feeling guilty about it, a remnant of my years and years of constantly doing stuff.

"Would you want to hang out together?" she asks after a little pause. "I was thinking I'd rewatch Breaking Bad or something."

My heart flips up into my chest. I've wanted to hang out

with her one-on-one for longer than I want to admit, but I haven't had the chance to bring that up organically. At least when I go help with the house, I have a reason to talk with her. Inviting her to just hang out felt like I was crossing some imaginary line.

"Yeah, that sounds great." I try to keep my voice neutral, but I probably sound excited. "What time were you thinking?"

"Maybe in half an hour? Can we do it at your place? Your TV is probably bigger."

I take a glance around my place. It's clean enough, but thirty minutes will make it 'clean enough for a guest" clean.

"Sure, yeah." I grab a t-shirt I threw onto the couch after coming in from a run with Duke yesterday. "See you in a bit."

I end the call and start throwing shit into the spare bedroom. My robot vacuum can't do the whole living room in one go, so there'll just have to be dog hair everywhere. Not that I can ever be completely free of all animal hair. By the time Bianca arrives, my house looks cleaner than it has in ages.

I wish I didn't care so damn much. That isn't part of the plan.

"Hey," she says. She's in a crop top, zip-up hoodie, and soft-looking leggings. Just the tiny bit of exposed skin across her stomach makes me want to touch her.

"Hey, come in," I step back and pull her in from the rain. "Hope you didn't get too wet."

"Nope, we're good." She moves her arm to reveal Sadie in her bag. "And the snacks are good too."

She follows me to the living room, where she places

Sadie down on the armchair next to Duke. The two dogs cuddle up, with Sadie curling up against Duke's belly.

"So what are these snacks?" I ask, blatantly taking in the view of Bianca from behind.

"You might think they're gross," she says, putting her bag on the coffee table and sitting down. "There's a lot of fake cheese in here."

"I'll try them if you're down to share." I sit down next to her, my thigh against hers. "I have some food but it's all boring stuff. We can trade."

"I have this popcorn with vegan cheese, these faux-cheese kale chips, some dark chocolate covered pretzels, dark chocolate covered fruit..." She puts the snacks out on the table. "Then some basic stuff like potato chips."

"Faux-cheese kale chips?" I grab the bag and take a look, frowning. "But why?"

"What do you mean?"

"Why would anyone voluntarily create that and why would anyone want to eat it?" I ask.

"They're not bad!" She takes them back and tears open the bag. The scent inside makes me wrinkle my nose. "Okay, they're an acquired taste."

I reach into the bag and take one, examining it before popping it into my mouth. It tastes like toes. Just toes, distilled into their most potent form.

"That's...a flavor." I choke it down and cough. Bianca laughs, smacking my back.

"Then there are more for me." She grins.

"You and all two of your taste buds can have them." I hop up. "You want a drink? A seltzer or something?"

"Sure, please."

I go into the kitchen to grab us some drinks, glancing over at Bianca. Seeing her curled up on the couch, the dogs relaxing together like they do this all the time, settles something inside me. Like she's supposed to be here all the time, already comfortable in my space.

By the time I return with some additional snacks, Bianca is settled even further into the couch, her legs curled up under herself. She's eating the popcorn, which thankfully doesn't smell like a gym bag.

"You're ready to rewatch Breaking Bad?" she asks, reaching for her popcorn.

"Yeah, if you are." I put our drinks and snacks on the table. Something there has caught Duke's attention, and he sniffs the air. "None of this is for you, Duke."

Duke grumbles and rests his head right on top of Sadie's. I pull up Breaking Bad and hit play on the first episode on the first season. I've seen it at least four times, so my mind starts to wander, mostly to Bianca's warmth next to me. I put my arm across the back of the couch and take a peek at her.

There's no way I'll be able to make it through this day without touching her at least once. The longer the episode goes on, the closer Bianca gets. Soon she's curled up against me, her head against my shoulder. I'm not sure how she manages to smell so good all the time, but it's driving me nuts.

I swallow. This shouldn't be as big of a deal as it feels. We're hooking up — I'm giving her sex lessons, for fuck's sake. But any cuddling is usually incidental, just our bodies finding each other's warmth if we fall asleep after we have sex. This feels like something I'd do with a girlfriend.

Or a thing I'd *want* to do because Catherine never

wanted to just sit around and do nothing at any point. Nothing but the rain falling outside, our bodies warm next to each other, both of us being okay with a little silence.

I snag one of the dark chocolate covered pretzels, and lean back against the couch again. Bianca settles back into her position. I close my eyes and take a subtle breath out of my nose. I need to disconnect this from cuddling, girlfriend-ish shit.

"Bianca," I say.

"Hm?" She looks up at me, then at my lips.

I take the remote and pause the show before taking her lips in a kiss. She melts into me right away, letting me press her onto her back. I hold her close, deepening the kiss, making it harsher. I want her, yeah, but I'm not going to let tenderness be a part of this.

I help her tug her hoodie off and toss it to the side, then work on her snug top. She's not wearing a bra, and her perky tits bounce free. They're perfect, just like the rest of her — the size, the shape, the feeling of her nipples in my mouth.

I kiss my way down her neck before sucking one of her nipples into my mouth a little harder than I usually do. She sucks in a breath, her body arching toward me. I slow down, waiting for more of her cues, but she just presses against me, wanting more.

I worship her breasts until she's whimpering, her nails harsh against my scalp. My cock is so hard that it hurts, and I need release.

"Come here," I say, hopping off her and tugging her leggings down just below her ass so she can't part her legs. I shove my shorts down, my cock springing free.

She squeals when I press her knees back to her chest.

Her pussy is already slick, peeping from between her bound legs. My cock twitches at the thought of her I'm moments from just plunging inside of her before I stop.

"Shit, condom," I say. How did I almost forget? Trying to block out feelings doesn't mean I need to block out sense.

"I have an IUD," she says, breathless. She loops an arm around the back of her knees. "And everything came back negative when I got tested. I mean, if you want to."

I've gone bare in the past with my ex, but that was different. I always pulled out anyway because she didn't like to deal with cum after. I wasn't going to be an asshole and ask if I could come inside her just once because the idea was so hot.

"I've been tested too, and everything was good," I say, swallowing. "You're fine with me...?"

If I even say the words, I'll bring myself moments from losing it.

"I want you to cum inside me," she says. "Please."

"*Fuck*," I mutter. She doesn't have to tell me twice. And she doesn't have to say please.

I push inside her tight, wet heat, sucking in a breath. The positioning of her legs makes it an even more snug fit, so snug that I have to pause for a second. Once I get control again, I fuck her hard and slow, grabbing her hips to get leverage. Her head falls back and she moans with every stroke.

I brace my hand on the back of the couch so I can look down at her. I still can't believe she's even real — so painfully beautiful, especially like this. Her bottom lip between her teeth, long, elegant neck exposed. The hot rush of affection at seeing her like this, in contrast to when we first started hooking up, slams into me like a truck.

I close my eyes, trying to shove the emotions out of this, but it barely helps.

I pull out and flip her onto her stomach, lifting her hips just enough to slide in. I press her down so she's flat on her stomach, her favorite position. And one of mine, too. I love feeling her smaller body underneath me, and the way she tightens up just right.

"Waylon," she whines, kicking against the couch when I slam into her.

"You can kick all you want. You're not moving from this spot," I say into her ear, my hand around the back of her neck firmly enough for her to feel it, but not enough to hurt her. "But you don't want to move, do you? You want every hard stroke."

She buries her face into the cushion and nods with a whimper. Her pussy is clenching around me so tightly that I think she might come, but I want to guarantee it.

I pull out and yank her hips back, burying my face into her pussy. She cries out, pushing back. Her taste is so good that I have to grip my cock to keep myself under control. I don't stop until she shudders from head to toe, coming with a muffled cry.

I'm back inside her before her orgasm fully subsides, making her so much tighter than she was. I'm a goner, instantly, and lose myself inside her. It's so intense that I lose every sense except for touch for a moment. I've never come so hard in my entire life.

Once my ears stop ringing, I slowly pull out. Seeing my cum drip out along her glistening wetness makes me groan. My cock throbs even though I just came.

I get my senses back and roll off the couch to get her a

damp washcloth. But she ends up following me. I give her privacy to clean up, then she opens the door again. I catch my reflection in the mirror next to hers.

I look both sated and wound up, scratch marks on my shoulders, and she's glowing, completely relaxed. Completely comfortable standing there naked, like we do this every day. Not trying to look a certain way or put on an act. Like a couple would.

"Your neck," I murmur, brushing the mark I left when I held her down by the back of the neck. It'll probably fade in a few hours. "I'm sorry — I didn't know I was holding you that hard."

"I liked it. And I would have told you otherwise if I didn't," she says, looking at the spot in the mirror. "I liked how rough you were in general."

"Yeah?" I tuck some of her curls over her shoulder.

"Yeah. It was different." She glances at the spot again, running her fingers over it. "And I don't mind the mark."

The mark makes me feel like she's mine, even though she isn't and she won't be. Thinking I could keep her as a friend and not more was a fucking joke. Why did I let it go this far when I know better than to fall for anyone?

I let out a breath and push those thoughts into the back of my head. Maybe I can enjoy this for today and think about how to solve it later.

TWENTY-THREE
BIANCA

I GOT PSYCHED about Rose's bachelorette party when she told me we were going to spend more time getting dressed than we would at the bar.

Not that I don't want to go to the bar, but getting ready to go out has always been my favorite part. Once I feel like an outfit and makeup look have been seen enough, I'm done.

And to be honest, most of the clubs and parties I went to weren't actually fun. People didn't dance that much and we had to "make appearances" for whoever called the paparazzi on themselves that night.

I grab my dress, heels, gigantic bag of makeup, and overnight bag before heading over to Rose and Wes's side of the duplex.

Rose answers the door, her braids up in a scarf. Music is blasting somewhere deep into the house.

"Hey! Come in!" Rose steps aside to let me in. "Let me get you a drink."

We walk through the house, which has the same layout

as Waylon's, but in reverse. Their kitchen is much more decked out than Waylon's, with different appliances dotting the counter and a full bar cart. A whole array of snacks are spread across the middle island. Jada's there, along with two girls I vaguely recognize but have never officially met.

"Bianca, I don't think you've officially met Sabrina. She's a bartender at the bar." Rose gestures to the Latina girl, who has cute dimples and some of the shiniest dark hair I've ever seen. "This is my cousin, Natasha and my best friend Jo."

Natasha nods a hello. She's petite like Rose, and her hair is also wrapped in a scarf, but more for fashion than function. Jo is around my height, her skin a shade or two lighter than mine and her hair back in a chic bun.

Shyness takes over me for a second, but I manage to say hello. Since I've been paraded around Jepsen, I've gotten over most of my initial social anxiety. Weird how that didn't happen in LA when I was meeting people just as often, if not more.

"What do you want to drink, Bianca?" Rose asks, looking over their full bar car. "I can make a cocktail, but we have champagne too."

"A cocktail would be great. Anything is fine as long as it's not whiskey." I've seen the drink called *Just Trust Me* on the menu at the Copper Moon, which only Wes and Rose make on the fly based on whatever the customer likes. I've never had it, but if it's popular enough to go on the menu, I'm guessing it's okay.

"Is that all makeup?" Sabrina asks with a pleased gasp when I shift my bag around and everything clicks together.

"Yeah. I got a lot of PR gifts that I can't use." I hold up the bag a little higher. "I didn't get the chance to donate it before I left. It's a lot of weird stuff, to be honest, like crazy colors and glitter. Stuff I wouldn't use every day."

"So, perfect for us dressing up an absurd amount to go to the local bar we go to all the time." Jada grins. "I'm going to go so extra."

"I don't think you could do anything less," Rose says, shaking a cocktail shaker and pouring my drink. "Here you go, Bianca. Let me know if you want something different."

I thank her and take a sip. It's perfect, light and lemony with a bit of lavender.

"This is amazing. How did you know I'd like it? This is something I'd totally order," I say.

"I just read someone's vibe. You seem like a tasty cocktail on a patio in the summer kind of person." Rose shrugs.

I am, and the fact that she picked up on it after we've only known each other for about two months makes me feel warm inside. Or it's the drink. Maybe both.

Wes comes down the stairs in jeans and a t-shirt, Murphy and their big orange cat Dennis trailing behind him. Murphy wanders up to us, tail wagging, but Dennis peels off into the living room, ignoring us completely.

"You're still not getting dressed?" Wes asks, putting his arm around Rose's waist.

"No, but we're about to." Rose looks up at him, her body pressed to his side. "Aren't you supposed to be at the bar already?"

"Nope, but I'm about to leave. I'm mostly waiting for my brothers to get settled before I go," he says. "I'm sure Ash and JD have gotten the first part of their bickering done with."

"Mm, I hope so." Rose tilts her head back and Wes kisses her forehead. "We'll see you there."

"Okay." Wes leans down and says something in Rose's ear that makes her laugh and smack him lightly with the back of her hand.

"You creep. Get out of here and let us have fun," Rose says.

She and Wes kiss one more time before Wes leaves.

"Ugh, y'all are lucky you're cute," Natasha says once Wes is gone, grabbing a pretzel and dunking it into some chocolate dip.

"Seriously. I'd be exhausted of you otherwise," Jo adds as she pets Murphy. She has the accent of someone who grew up living in a lot of places in and out of the US.

"Same. My love life is dead and my sex life is even more dead. If my vagina stays abandoned any longer they're going to throw a Spirit Halloween in there." Jada laughs and throws back the rest of her drink.

I snort so hard that I nearly choke on my pretzel.

"It's true. They're just waiting for the right season," Jada says, still smiling from her own joke while whacking me on the back. "Trying to date here is the worst. I've either known them since kindergarten or they're creeps. Whatever, I don't want to be a bummer on a night like this. Let's go get overdressed."

We take some snacks and head upstairs to the master bedroom. It's cozy and lived-in with a desk that looks like it's been cleared just for tonight. Rose has extra mirrors set up, along with some extra seats. I put down my gigantic makeup bag on the desk next to the other smaller makeup bags.

"Natasha is amazing at doing hair, if you want your hair done," Rose says, tapping around on her phone until music comes out of a little Bluetooth speaker in the corner.

"Assuming you aren't indecisive as hell, then yeah." Natasha gives Rose a pointed look.

"It came out great, though," Rose says, untying the scarf around her braids. They look really good — neat and tight but not so tight that they'll tear her edges to pieces.

"Okay, true." Natasha suppresses a smile and starts unzipping a silver makeup bag. "I have a bunch of makeup that's good for cosplay nerd shit but not doing normal person stuff."

"Don't worry, I just have the basics plus about ten thousand shades of lipstick," Rose says. "Not super helpful."

"Same. And some shadows I bought and never used," Jo says.

"Holy shit," Sabrina says when I open my bag. "It's like a Sephora in a bag."

"Yeah. I got a crazy amount of free stuff. In lots of shades too." I start pulling palettes I haven't even taken out of the box yet and stack them next to me. "There's something that could work for all of us."

"I know being even vaguely famous probably sucks ass, but I'd love random places to send me a bunch of free shit." Sabrina picks up a palette and examines it.

"It is pretty nice," I admit.

"Too bad I do eyeshadow like a toddler." Sabrina puts the palette down.

"I can help. It'll be kind of basic but we can use some interesting colors." I haven't done this kind of thing with girl friends in ages so I forgot the etiquette. I once offered to help this other model I'd barely met and she acted like I'd asked to help her cross the street.

"That would be amazing." Sabrina plops down in the seat at the vanity and I pull a chair over.

"Can you do me next?" Jo asks. "I always end up making it all look a bit muddy."

"Sure, yeah. No guarantees it'll look professional."

"Still, it's def a step up for me." Jo sits down on the bed, stretching her legs.

Getting ready with everyone is so *nice* — no edge of competition between us, no petty little swipes that could be brushed off with some mental gymnastics. Just music, drinks, and hanging out. Like I fit in even though they've known each other a lot longer than they've known me.

As we get dressed, Dennis meanders into the room, weaving between our ankles and meowing.

"What, little buddy?" Rose asks. Dennis meows again. "We already fed you. You can't have human snacks."

Hearing 'human snacks' Murphy pops his head up from his spot on the bed, his tail thumping against the comforter.

"No human snacks for you either," Rose says. "Waylon said you were getting a little chunky at your last visit. Both of you."

Dennis chirps and leaves the room again, tail high. Murphy still looks like he's waiting for treats.

"Speaking of Waylon, how are things with you guys?" Jada asks. "Is he behaving himself?"

I snort, thinking back to the other night when he pinned me down and fucked me like his life depended on it. The vanity where I'm sitting has the best light, but the marks he left are long gone. I wish they'd lingered a little longer.

"Pretty much," I finally say, packing a little bit of glittery shadow onto my eyelid.

"So I'm guessing he's behaving in all the right ways, and misbehaving in all the ways I'd rather not think about because Waylon is basically my bonus brother?" Jada says. I nod. "Well, that's good. I was worried he'd stayed all weird and distant. Or at least that's the impression he gave off."

"I don't think that's changed all that much." I tap the side of my brush against the edge of the container.

Something between us feels closer, more intimate. But I can feel him holding back. If you asked me for something specific, I couldn't give an answer, but I can sense it somewhere in my heart.

"Damn it." Jada sighs.

"Wait, what's the problem?" Rose asks.

"Waylon's being..." Jada makes a vague gesture, nearly hitting a lamp on the side table next to the bed, and doesn't finish her sentence.

"Okay...?" Rose looks between us in confusion. Jo shrugs from her seat across from me while Natasha starts on her hair.

My gut rarely has strong feelings, but I have a feeling that I can open up to them without being judged. But how do I talk about this without giving away that our relationship is supposed to be fake?

"When I came to Jepsen, our relationship was supposed to be sort of a fling, and Waylon said he was only interested in something casual," I say after I gather my thoughts. "But now I want it to be something more serious and I'm not sure if he does. The only problem is that I was sort of planning to move to New York after I get the house fixed up and maybe sold. Now I don't know what to do."

"Do you like living in Jepsen?" Natasha asks, gently

parting Jo's hair to section off the front. "Like would you want to stay here for him if it got serious?"

"I do like it here, actually," I say right away. "I thought I'd hate it because it's so small and I assumed there wasn't a ton to do, but I've never been truly bored since I've gotten here. And it's beautiful and the people are nice. It's cozy. But I don't know if Waylon would want me to stay if it meant being serious."

"That dumbass." Jada shakes her head. "Like don't get me wrong — he's one of the smartest people I've ever known, but he keeps getting in his own way because he got all traumatized from being in a serious relationship with that sentient piece of garbage he calls an ex."

"What did he see in her?" Natasha asks, raising an eyebrow.

"I don't know. But my theory is it was because she was also an overachiever and she had her moments of not being the absolute worst. Rare moments." Jada rolls her eyes and leans back, propping herself up on her hands behind her on the bed. "But anyway, I'm glad he found you, Bianca. You're chill and he needs that. Someone to keep him from burning out."

I swallow and focus on finishing up my eyeshadow so I can move onto my base.

"You can see that, but I know he doesn't want it to be serious." I grab a cotton circle and put some makeup remover on it. A ton of the glitter from my shadow has ended up on my cheeks.

"Are you sure, though?" Jo asks, her tone gentle. "Like have you asked directly, any time recently?"

"Well, not really. But I can pick up on the vibe. I think." I grab my foundation and a fresh sponge.

"Being direct will take away a lot of that uncertainty." Jo reaches for some gel.

"Even though it's kind of scary," Rose adds. "And to be honest, hearing the flat out truth is scary too."

"Sounds like both options kind of suck," I say with a soft laugh.

"But spinning your wheels over and over, trying to read his mind is even suckier," Rose says.

The others nod and unfortunately, they're right. Why am I torturing myself assuming that he still feels the same as he did before? Maybe he's still wary, but maybe our connection is enough for him to take the leap.

Now I just have to figure out how to gather the nerve to bring it up to him.

TWENTY-FOUR

WAYLON

"YOU'RE HAVING A SHOT NOW?" I ask John David. The Copper Moon is closed for Wes's bachelor party, which isn't even set to start for another half hour. It's going to be a half bachelor, half bachelorette party since Rose and her friends are coming by for a drink or two before going back home for a sleepover.

"I need a shot before Ash gets here." He throws back the shot of moonshine he poured for himself and winces.

"It'll be okay," I say, as if things have ever been okay between them. "He's not bringing strippers."

That I know of.

A cab dropped him off at my house late last night, and he promptly passed out in my guest bedroom. This morning I woke up and he was just eating straight up coffee grounds and chasing them with water instead of making coffee like a normal person, wearing a red, tiger printed silk robe. I have no idea what he's doing at the house right now, but I'm honestly a little worried.

Wes is somewhat chaotic, but in a lighthearted way. Ash is chaotic in a way where we worry he'll end up dead or butt naked on a boat going down the Amazon River.

"Then where is he?" JD asks, going behind the bar and pouring himself a soda.

"He said he'd be here." I shrug and check my phone. Nothing from Bianca, and I'm not sure how I feel about that.

I take a deep breath and pour myself a shot too. I know I can't pretend that I don't have feelings for her anymore, especially after our day in together. Everything just clicked once I stopped getting in my head too much about it.

But now I have to think about what we are. And that thought is making my stomach churn.

I toss back the shot right as the door swings open. Ash strolls in. He's impossible to miss — he's wearing a bright red silk shirt, jeans, and boots, sunglasses on even though the sun has almost set. His tattoos peek out from his rolled up sleeves and the open neck of his shirt.

"Sup, nerds?" Ash asks, taking off his sunglasses. "Ready to party?"

"As long as we keep it reasonable," JD says with a sigh.

"You look fucking tired already." Ash grabs an entire bottle of vodka from behind the bar. "Lighten up. It's a bachelor party.

"Don't drink straight out of the bottle." JD slides him a shot glass. Of course, Ash swigs directly out of the bottle. "You owe us fifty bucks."

"Fifty dollars for this bottom shelf shit?" Ash looks at the bottle like it's offended him.

"Surcharge for being a pain in my ass," JD says.

"Oh, get fucked, JD. I've been here thirty seconds."

"You can get on my nerves in half a second, easy."

"Can we just relax?" I ask. I don't know how I ended up as the peacemaker of us all, but it's been my default position since we were kids. "We should just have a good time."

Ash and I exchange a look. He listens to me about 50% of the time, and hopefully today is one of those days.

Ash sighs and leans against the bar. "Whatever. I'm still not paying for this bottle."

"Yeah, you fucking will." JD wipes down the counter, almost compulsively.

"Who'll do what?" Wes asks, coming into the bar.

"Nothing," I say. "You want a drink before people start arriving?"

"Yep."

JD pours Wes, then all of us a drink.

"Who's making a toast?" Wes asks, looking to me.

"To your last days with your dick free," Ash says before I can get a word in otherwise.

I raise an eyebrow. "Try again."

"To your past life and everything it taught you, and to the new life you'll have with Rose in the future," JD says after a long pause.

We tap our glasses together and take a drink.

"Surprisingly deeper than I thought you'd go," Wes says.

"Still waters and all that," JD adds, deadpan.

"It was hardly poetry," Ash snorts and takes a sip of his drink.

From the way he and JD are glaring daggers at each other, it's only a matter of time before they start at each others' throats again, but thankfully, Jasper, one of our good friends who works at the bar, comes in with a few other people carrying bags of food.

Thankfully the food keeps JD and Ash apart, and the party slowly starts to rev up. Ash takes control of the music and JD makes drinks. I always forget how many friends Wes has. It feels like half the guys in our town have descended on the bar.

"I can't believe you're getting married," Jasper says, clapping Wes on the shoulder. "You. Of all people."

Wes laughs. "Thanks?"

"Not that you and Rose aren't good for each other — if you two didn't get together after I choked through all that tension for months, I'd be pissed," he says. "But if you told the version of you from four or five years ago about this, would you believe him?"

"Oh, fuck no," Wes says with a snort. "I definitely wouldn't believe I'm getting married period, much less marrying Rose."

"See? There you go." Jasper takes a hefty sip of his cocktail. "A lot of shit can change in five years."

I hum in agreement. I wouldn't have guessed Wes would be the first of us to get married at all. He really *was* completely different five years ago — he was still my twin and best friend, but he wasn't nearly as mature and put together.

He was sleeping around, keeping things casual. He wasn't unhappy, but he wasn't nearly as happy as he is now.

A pang of jealousy pokes through my buzz. Part of me wants what he has — someone to come home to. But letting go of all my fucking baggage isn't as easy as shaking off a lifelong rivalry. Then again, the tension between wanting

Bianca and fearing I'm going to end up fucking myself over again is going to drive me crazy.

Having drinks and talking to friends is helping some, but I can't help but feel like I seem off. Even when more people arrive and the party picks up over the next hour, I feel like I'm only 75% present.

"Oh, there's Rose," Wes says, his eyes lighting up.

He murmurs a goodbye and weaves through the crowd to his fiancée. I scan the room for Bianca since she's supposed to be here too. I spot her next to the bar, facing away from me, and Ash facing her. The lazy, warm smile on his face while he talks to her says everything I need to know.

The jealousy and anger that rush up in me nearly make me dizzy. I know Ash has no idea who Bianca is, but seeing him flirting with her makes me want to do something I'd possibly regret. *Possibly*. Ash and I get along well and almost always have, but if I had to, I could beat him in a fight.

I storm over, locking eyes with Ash for a second. He looks bewildered, an eyebrow going up, and Bianca turns to look at me too. She smiles, and I manage to smile back a little.

I slide an arm around her waist and kiss her the moment I can get a hand on her. She smells even better than she usually does, and I want to press my face into her neck. Is it her hair? Or just her lotion? I don't know, but it's making me even more feral.

"Ash, this is Bianca. My girlfriend. Bianca, this is my brother Ash," I say, cutting off whatever conversation they were having. I don't even care that I'm being rude. My pulse is still racing, but having Bianca close is slowing my heart down.

"*Oh*. The girlfriend I've heard whispers of. So that's why he looked like that," Ash says with a grin, shaking her hand and giving her a little more space. "I've never seen him look like that in his whole life."

My face flushes with heat, especially when Bianca looks at me, curious.

"Look like what?" she asks.

"Like he wants me dead for even daring to look your way." Ash notices that my face is probably beet red, but thankfully ignores it and says, "When'd you roll into town, Bianca?"

"A few months ago," she says. "How'd you know I was new here? Or did Waylon tell you?"

"I can tell by looking at you. I haven't lived here since I was eighteen but I can still tell when someone's not from around here." He sips his drink. "And I've spent enough time other places. I'm in a band."

"Oh." An inscrutable look crosses her face before disappearing. "Where are you based?"

A dark look crosses over Ash's face for a moment before he pulls himself together. "Yep. And right now...kind of all over the place. The band tours a lot."

There's definitely more to what Ash is saying, but if I ask, he'll never tell me.

"To be honest, I'm surprised Waylon's seeing someone." Ash recovers with a smirk and elbows me. "Especially someone half-way interesting."

He's not completely serious, but I still glare at him. He grins in response, not a care in the world.

"Being from out of town doesn't automatically make me

interesting," she says. Her tone is the same, but I can see the shyness in her eyes.

"More interesting than a lot of people who never leave this place." Ash glances at me. "Waylon doesn't count, though. And neither does Wes."

Bianca just nods, completely unaware of the dig at John David. He went straight from high school to under Dad's wing at the company, taking remote college classes instead of leaving for school. Ash was fully moved out of the house the day after high school graduation, and has only come back for Thanksgiving and Christmas when he's felt like it.

"How'd you meet, then?" Ash asks. He'd never admit that he's just as nosy as Mom is, but he is.

"Just luck, mostly. Everything just fell into place." Bianca looks at me with such warmth and affection that I can't help but feel that in return – even if it's fake. "We connected because he was taking care of my great aunt's dog after she passed. He's really helped me feel more at home here and helped me get used to being a dog owner."

"Waylon the dog whisperer." Ash scans Bianca's face, more out of curiosity than flirtation like he was earlier. "I'm glad to hear y'all found each other, then. It's been a while since Waylon's looked at home with someone."

Ash saying something like he means it is rare, so the compliment hits differently. Our relationship isn't real, but are we really pulling it off that well? Ash's bullshit detector is pretty good, but he's convinced.

"Y'all want a shot?" He asks, grabbing his bottle off the bar.

"No, I think I need something to eat to balance this." Bianca holds up her can of moonshine margarita.

"Let's get food, then." I lace my fingers through hers and nod goodbye to Ash.

The food is just from the tavern next door, so nothing special. But Bianca fills up a little plate with chips and guacamole, plus a single lemon pepper wing.

Now that I'm not focused on keeping Ash away from Bianca, I can take her in. Out of everyone, Ash is the only guy I know who'd have the balls to approach someone as gorgeous as Bianca. She's wearing more makeup today, something glittery around her eyes that's not too over the top and a lipstick in a shade of red-orange. I don't know anything about makeup, but she must have done something else, too, without looking like she's trying to be someone else.

And her dress. It's red, form-fitting and a little short. She looks way too good in it.

"I didn't tell you how beautiful you look," I say, taking a chip from her plate when she holds it out to me.

She smiles, warm and familiar. "You don't have to tell me that every time, you know."

"If it's true, I'll say it." I look around at the party. "Things with Rose and the others are good?"

"Yeah, really good." She holds her hand in front of her mouth while she chews. "I like that we spent two hours getting dressed and we're only staying for less than an hour. Not sarcasm, by the way. I always wanted to get dressed up but going to sit in a loud club after everyone already saw my outfit was really exhausting."

"Isn't the club the whole point of the night?" I ask.

"Technically, yes, but it's not the most fun. Clubs are just a weird, fancy way to judge people. You'd be horrified if I told you all the weird stories I have." She shakes her head.

"It was just a thing for social media anyway. Going out in Jepsen suits me better. Especially since it's not deafening in here."

I bite back the question I want to ask — does she want to stay, since it seems to suit her more?

I try to think of what life would be like if she did. Would we keep this charade going? I can only see this tension between fearing the mess a relationship can bring and wanting her getting worse the more time goes on. If that's tearing me apart now, it'll only get worse later on as we grow more attached.

And if we get attached...that didn't work out well at all the last time, as much as I was into Catherine.

I'll talk to her about it after the wedding. We weren't supposed to "last" much longer than that, so it's a place to end this. A short term hurt to save us both a lot of heartache. I'll savor the illusion until then.

TWENTY-FIVE
BIANCA

WHY AM I so nervous for someone else's wedding? It's not like I haven't interacted with a lot of the guests before. Maybe it's the fact that this is supposed to be the big main event, the main reason why Waylon and I even started fake dating. Now we're here and this relationship has gotten way more complicated than either of us planned for.

I resist the urge to jiggle my leg as I sit and wait for the ceremony to start. I'm seated near the front since Waylon is the best man, near some of his family. People are slowly drifting to their seats, but so far I'm alone.

I study the floral arch at the end of the aisle, biting the inside of my cheek so I don't mess up my lipstick. I need to push anything outside of the bubble of this wedding out of my head. It's a gorgeous day and the venue is equally beautiful — we're outside and the reception will be in the fully updated and renovated barn not far from us.

Thankfully Jada and Jeremiah sit down near me and distract me with some small talk. Fifteen minutes later, the officiant comes down the aisle and people settle in their seats.

The only other wedding I've been to was Kaitlyn and her husband's, and hers was on the beach in Thailand with just a few people. Waylon and Jo, Rose's maid of honor, come down the aisle together and take their places on either side of the officiant. I saw Waylon in his tux earlier, but seeing him again still makes my heart jump in my chest.

He smiles at me once he turns around, making my heart flutter even worse.

Wes comes down the aisle next, and finally, Rose. She showed me pictures of her dress a long time ago, but seeing it in photos didn't do the dress justice. It's off the shoulder and hugs her body just enough, the intricate beading catching the light. And the look that Wes gives her, like he can't believe she's real, chokes me up a little.

Waylon and I lock eyes every once in a while, but we always break contact after a few seconds. His looks are warm, but I'm not sure if it's directed at me or if it's just a general good vibe. His attention drifts back to the happy couple every time.

The ceremony is short and sweet, ending with a kiss that makes some of the older guests tut in disapproval. Rose and Wes leave, followed by Waylon and Jo. Waylon smiles at me again as he passes, and mouths *see you in a bit*.

Some attendants usher all of the guests to an outdoor area for cocktail hour. The drinks start flowing immediately, along with small bites of food. Jada and Jeremiah keep me company while I wait for Waylon. I'm itching to touch him, just to feel his warmth and get a better look at him in his tux.

Finally he comes around the corner of the barn with John David, chatting.

"My face hurts from smiling for so long," he says when he approaches me.

"Don't smile, then," JD says as he passes by. Waylon laughs, but JD is dead serious.

"I've never had to get so many photos taken in my life," Waylon continues to me. "I don't think I could cut it as a model, aside from the obvious reasons."

"You'd actually be good at it," I say, pulling a hair off his sleeve. "You're really photogenic."

"I am?" He looks genuinely surprised.

"You've never looked at yourself in a photo?"

"I mean, not very hard." He shrugs. "I just kind of assumed I looked decent enough most of the time."

"That's a very guy answer." I smile and put my drink down on one of the high-top tables.

"Sorry, didn't mean to eavesdrop," a photographer says. "But I'd love to get a photo of you two if you're up to it."

"Sure." Waylon slides an arm around my waist and pulls me close. My immediate urge is to pose and not smile, but I decide to be a normal person and just...smile. My normal smile instead of the one I've perfected for photoshoots.

"Excellent, thank you so much." The photographer leaves us alone.

Waylon grabs a drink off a tray as a waiter passes by. The DJ starts up some music and a few people start dancing already.

"Just a warning, I'm a terrible dancer," he says as he looks around at his family.

"Like how bad? Funny bad, or just tragic?" I ask.

"Depends on who you ask and when." He scans the crowd. "It'll probably be funny later tonight."

"I'm looking forward to it." And it's been so long since I've actually danced at an event rather than sitting around, looking at everyone else.

We don't have much time to linger, though — the attendants whisk us over into the barn for dinner. Circular tables span half of the space, with the other half being a dance floor with the DJ booth.

We find our names on one of the first tables, alongside John David, Ash, and his parents. I swallow and sit down in between Ash and Waylon. Ash already looks a little drunk, and I can't tell if John David was or not — his face is just as stoic as always.

"Such a lovely ceremony, wasn't it?" Delia says when we sit down. She looks pretty in a light blue dress, her dark hair in a chignon.

"It was," I say. Each plate has a menu on top with various courses, and my spot has a little circle indicating I'm dairy free. I completely forgot to tell Rose, so I'm guessing Waylon is the one who did it.

"I love weddings. This turned out so well too. All the planning Rose and I did really paid off." Delia smooths her napkin into her lap.

Mr. Stryker just grunts in agreement, throwing back his drink. Ash sighs through his nose.

"What's wrong already?" Mr. Stryker asks Ash, his tone sharp.

"It's nothing. Why does it always have to be something?" Ash asks. "I just sighed, for fuck's sake."

"We have a guest, Ashley," Delia says, glancing at me.

"Watch your language."

"You're an adult, aren't you?" Ash asks me. I just nod. "She'll live with me saying a few four letter words, Mom."

"It's still impolite." Delia sips her drink, leaving a light lipstick print on the rim. "Anyway, hopefully we can plan another wedding soon."

She gives us a not-so-subtle look.

"Mom, do we have to do this?" Waylon asks, clearly uncomfortable rather than flat out annoyed. "We should just focus on Rose and Wes."

"Fine, fine. Later." Delia smiles at me. "Plus, you haven't properly been brought into Jepsen. There are so many ways to get involved. You can fill up all your time and then some."

I nod, even though the idea of stuffing every minute of my day with activities sounds like a nightmare, especially social stuff. I can sense Waylon's slight annoyance but he doesn't speak. But Delia picks up on it anyway.

"What's wrong with that, Waylon?" Delia asks, exasperated. She looks surprisingly like Ash right now. "Volunteering in town isn't that big of a deal."

"It's nothing," Waylon says, sipping his water. "It's fine."

Waylon and his mom exchange a long, silent glance, and eventually we're all left with air thick with tension. Did something happen with them that I'm not aware of, or is Waylon just tired of being prodded?

"Let's welcome the new Mr. and Mrs. Stryker!" The DJ yells into the mic, snapping us out of it.

Everyone cheers as Wes and Rose come out and sit at the head table, smiling and holding hands. The meal starts being served, saving us from awkwardness. Delia switches over to talking about other things like everything it took to plan the wedding, and now I understand why Rose was crumbling under stress. Delia never does anything halfway, and I can see how that could wear on someone if they were constantly pushed to do more.

Waylon's hand finds my leg closer to the end of the meal, his thumb making little circles just inside of them. My dress hits just above the knee, so his skin is warm on mine, stirring some feelings that I probably shouldn't be having right in front of his family.

But it does give me an idea to fulfill a bucket list item.

"C'mon," I say once the last course is over.

"Where?" He takes my hand when I extend it to him. "Hopefully not dancing yet."

"Just somewhere private."

The hall looks much more clinical than the rest of the barn, so I'm guessing it's where catering and other vendors do everything. The space is much quieter than the main hall, but the sounds of partying and music drift toward us.

"Bianca..." His tone is a playful warning.

"Yes...?" I glance at the doors as we walk down the hall. One's clearly where the food is being made, and the others seem to be in use.

"Are you planning to check something off your bucket list right now?" he asks.

"Maybe." I squeeze his hand.

I absolutely am. He's done most of the initiating, and I want to be bold for once. I feel safe enough with him to take risk, even if he's had his moments of being closed off.

I try the handle of a door labeled "storage". It opens easily, revealing a supply closet, with shelves of paper towels and toilet paper along one wall. It's a bit dingy but it's mostly private and clean.

He pulls me to him and kisses me before I can kiss him, and I press myself against him as much as I can. The heat of his body is addictive, as is the feeling of his lips on mine. It doesn't even matter that we're in a closet. It might even be better because of where we are — we're out of sight but someone could walk in. My heart is racing, the fear and adrenaline rush mingling.

He scoops me up and sits down in the one little seat in the room, resting me on his lap.

"Show me your panties," he says, pushing the bottom of my dress up.

I help him pull the dress up all the way, showing him the blue sheer panties I chose. He lets out a hum of appreciation and pulls the panties to the side, his fingers finding my clit. I rest my forehead against his as he teases me, our breath mingling.

"I wanted to do this the moment I saw you in this dress," he says, kissing my exposed shoulder. "It's like you were made to tempt me."

I tilt my head back so he can kiss my neck more. I want to be naked, to have him touch my bare skin everywhere, but getting butt naked in a place where I might need to quickly dress is a bit further than I'd like to go.

I reach down between us and start to undo his pants. His cock is already straining the fabric so much that it looks like it's leaping into my hand when he's finally free. He lets out a soft breath when I grip his cock at the base.

"So hard," I say softly, stroking his cock up and down. "All for me?"

"Always for you." He cups the back of my neck, avoiding the elaborate bun my hair is in, and pulls me into a hot kiss.

My toes curl between the kiss and how he's playing with my clit. I have to bury my face into his neck, biting my tongue so I don't moan too loudly. I don't know if people are wandering the halls, but letting myself get as loud when we're alone probably isn't the best idea.

I lift up and guide his fingers toward my entrance. They slip right in, making a slick sound.

"Greedy girl," he says with a smile. My eyes flutter closed when he strokes the upper wall of my pussy, making me clench around him.

I spread the bead of precum over the tip of his cock and it twitches in my hand. I've gotten to know his body just as much as he's gotten to know mine, and I can tell when he's getting close to the edge. But I need him inside of me.

"I need to ride you," I say, coming off his lap and pushing his pants and boxers all the way down.

I take whatever words he was about to say when I slide down onto his cock to the hilt. The fullness still rocks me just as much as it did the first time, like he's reaching every part of me from the inside.

"Fuck." He lets his head fall back, thumping against the wall. "So perfect."

I roll my hips, taking time to find a rhythm that hits my G-spot just right. He holds me close, his hands on my hips and his body pressed to mine. Being chest to chest, his breathing in my ear and my breathing in his, feels so perfectly intimate. We're in rhythm and I never want to fall out of sync.

He grips my hips and starts thrusting upward, our bodies

making enough sound that I hope the music playing can drown it out. I reach down and rub my clit, building up higher and higher. I rest my forehead against his, feeling him tense the way he does before he comes.

I fall over the edge, losing myself in the moment. He murmurs that he's close and I slide off of him, taking his cock into my mouth. He comes moments later, deep into my throat, and lets out a choked groan.

He slumps in the seat for a moment before helping me up to my feet. I help him up too, a few moments later. His cheeks are flushed and he has a smile in his eyes. My heart is pounding a thousand beats per minute, and the rush of feelings is almost too much for me to take.

Both of us jump when two voices come down the hall, having what's either an argument or a spirited conversation. Waylon peers out the door before pushing it all the way open. Jada and Ash of all people are walking down the hall, passing us while Jada wildly gesticulates.

They round the corner without seeing us, leaving us alone again.

"I wonder what they're talking about," I say.

"Don't know." Waylon shrugs. "Knowing both of them, they're probably trying to one-up each other in one way or another."

We wander down the hall in the opposite direction, toward a door to outside. Thankfully once we get out there, we have some level of privacy. I don't know if it's part of the post-sex high or how close we just felt, but I'm feeling the burst of courage I've been needing.

"Do you ever think about us becoming something more?" I ask.

My words leave my mouth right along with the some of the courage I had built up, especially when I feel him shift next to me.

"Like a real relationship?" Waylon asks. His tone is depleting the last of my courage reserves.

"Yeah. I mean..." I swallow. My mouth is suddenly bone dry. "I was just trying to figure out whether I should stay in Jepsen or not."

"Don't stay here for me, Bianca. You have bigger things waiting for you," he says, pushing off the wall. "I don't know if starting a relationship is something we should do."

My chest tightens, but I keep my composure. "But why? I know there's something here that's worth giving a shot."

Waylon doesn't speak for the longest time, but I can't bring myself to look at him. If I look at him, I'll crack, and if I crack, I'll fall apart completely.

"I just can't right now," he says softly. "It's just safer if we end it now."

"Safer?" I blink, everything inside of me turning to a slow-burning irritation. "*Safer?* Not better because you don't feel the same way?"

"No, I..."

I finally look at him as he runs his fingers through his hair. There's a war going on in his head, clearly, but to me, it shouldn't be that hard of a decision. We both know there's something between us, and flat out denying it for whatever reason is ridiculous. There's no 'yes, let's take it slow', or anything like that.

The realization is like a knife to the chest. He'd rather choose his fear over me.

I must not be as important to him as I thought.

"Safer for you, maybe. And your feelings," I continue, my voice wavering. "Even though I thought we had something. And I thought you felt something too based on what we just did. But I guess I was wrong."

"Bianca, this was never a real relationship. We fooled my mom, and now we can part ways as friends," he says, his tone almost anxious. "We explicitly said that early on."

We stop at the intersection of two hallways and come face-to-face with Delia. Her eyes are wide.

She definitely heard him. That was never part of the plan.

"Go handle things with your mom," I say. "I already know exactly how you feel."

I heard him say my name one more time as I turn the opposite way and head back inside.

TWENTY-SIX

WAYLON

I DON'T FUCK up a lot, but apparently when I do, I fuck up in multiple ways, as hard as possible. Do I chase after Bianca and try to put things back together, even though she (justifiably) hates my guts, or do I go after my mom?

I press the heels of my hands to my forehead for a second before decided to go for my mom.

"Mom, wait," I say, catching up with her.

"I don't want to hear it, Waylon," she says, not even looking at me or stopping. "I can't believe you'd *lie* to me and fake something with that poor, sweet girl. She likes you. And I thought you liked her too, but you had me fooled. I suppose that's what your goal was."

Her words rub salt into my wounds. I thought I'd made her disappointed in me in the past — when I didn't get an A or when I turned down an opportunity to do an extra activity that would suck up my free time but make me look good.

But those moments are completely insignificant compared to now, and it's a punch to the gut.

"I can explain," I say.

But can I, really? The words about breaking up because it's safer felt wrong coming out of my mouth when I spoke to Bianca. Even though we've technically been lying to everyone this whole time, saying that I didn't think we should start a relationship was the only thing that truly felt like it was false.

Mom stops, and I almost run right into her.

"Waylon, I never thought you'd ever lie to me in general, much less lie to me to pull one over on me for some reason," Mom says. "I'm not ready to speak to you and I don't want Wes and Rose's day to be ruined. Let's not talk for the rest of the evening."

Mom walks away, sniffing, and I lean against the wall. She's right. We don't need to taint the wedding because of my fuck-ups.

Being inside is making me feel itchy, so I take off my suit jacket and walk outside. A few people are mingling, talking and having drinks. I spot Ash sitting alone on a bench, slumped and looking at the sky.

"Hey," I say to him.

He looks up at me. "Hey. Who shit in your cereal?"

"I did."

"In your own cereal?" He sits up, frowning. He didn't bother shaving or even getting a haircut before this. Between that and his bloodshot eyes, he looks like he's just crash landed from Vegas. "Don't shit where you eat."

"I fucked up bad." I sink down on the bench next to him with a heavy sigh.

"You look like you did." He leans back on the bench

again, closing his eyes. "What'd you do? Accidentally came in second place?"

I know he's joking, but it still burns.

"I fucked up by lying to Mom," I say, keeping my voice low.

"And?" Ash sits up, raking his fingers through his hair. "I lie to Mom all the time about shit. Not that I'm proud of it, but it's just a fact. I love her, but she's a lot, and sometimes a little white lie is preferable to being smothered. I don't know how you've managed to live your whole life doing what she says instead of telling her to fuck off like you should have ages ago."

"That's exactly how I got into this. She was being too much and I got fed up with just dropping hints and flat out saying no. So I lied about something kind of big and she found out. And on top of that, I fucked things up with Bianca even worse than I fucked things up with Mom."

"Oof. Sorry." He pushes up his sleeves. His colorful tattoos are a sharp contrast to the white of his shirt. "She dump you?"

"It's a lot more complicated than that," I say. "But I did the wrong thing even though it feels like it should have been the right thing at the time."

Ash raises an eyebrow at me. "I have no idea what you're talking about."

I rake both hands over my face. "Long story, but she wanted something more serious. And I said no because I got fucked over hard by my last relationship. But now that I told her, I know I made a mistake. A huge mistake."

"So you're into her?"

"Yes." I'm falling in love with her, but saying that out

loud right after I absolutely tanked everything will only make me painfully emotional out here in the open.

"Oh, so you fucked up *super* hard," Ash says. "Yikes."

"Thanks, Ash."

"Well, would you ever come to me for advice in most circumstances?" He plays with the silver ring on his thumb.

"No, to be honest." Ash will always be blunt and honest, but his ideas are always a bit off the wall. He's always done his own thing.

"Today's not any different because Wes's getting married." He chuckles.

We sit in silence, my chest burning from the inside out with the swirl of feelings inside me. I want to talk to Wes or Jeremiah or Jada (though I think Jada might kick my ass for hurting Bianca), but I don't want to start different rumors by bringing it up in person.

"Have you ever been in a serious relationship?" I ask, mostly out of curiosity.

"Fuck no," he says with a laugh. "Maybe some six month long flings, but it works for me."

"You never want anything serious? Even though you've never been hurt before?" I ask. "By a long-term girlfriend, I mean."

"Nope." He shrugs, rubbing one of his eyes. I assumed his eyes were red for more nefarious reasons, but the longer I look at him, the more I realize he's just exhausted. The dark circles under his eyes look terrible when his face catches the setting sun. "Seriously, if you *ever* see me with a long-term girlfriend or even worse, see me get married? Assume I've been bodysnatched."

I laugh, but it comes out weird. "Okay, I'll remember that."

"But for real," he says. "Serious relationships seem like they fucking suck. They give someone else the power to do this to you."

I shrug because I don't know what to say. I used to agree with him on that, but now I feel like shit for turning one down.

"Here's some advice that doesn't suck. Probably." Ash stands up and stretches. "With the thing with Mom, just let her calm down a bit. She's been pissed off at me plenty of times — a new thing for you, I know — and she'll soften up as long as you give her space."

"Good to know." I sigh. "But how long does that take?"

"Fuck if I know. I pissed her off all the time so she probably recovered faster. But with you? Her precious golden boy?" The sarcasm in his voice stings a bit, but again, he's not lying. "I'd give her a lot of time."

"Yeah." I sigh. I've never seen my mom look that hurt before and I hate myself for being the one to make her feel that way.

"By the way, what's the deal with your hot friend?" Ash asks. I stare at him blankly. "Yellow dress, long locs, glasses?"

"Oh, *Jada*?" I blurt. I recognize that Jada is pretty and all, but she's practically my sister so I never think of her like that. "What about Jada?"

"Wait, *that's* Jada? History club Jada? Salutatorian Jada?" He looks genuinely shocked, and Ash is never surprised by anything.

How the hell did he remember she was salutatorian? I

didn't think he paid attention to me or my friends at all, especially after he graduated.

"You didn't ask her name when you were talking in the hallway?" I ask.

He waves his hand. "Not the point. Never mind. Forget I said anything."

I narrow my eyes at him. "Ash."

"Relax, Waylon. I'm not going to do anything dumb now that I know." He yawns. "I'm going to get some cake or something. I doubt this conversation helped you at all."

I have to laugh. "Thanks for having it with me, then."

"You came to me," he says with a grin. But he quickly turns serious. "Seriously though. Take it from a guy who's a fuck-up — don't linger on the mistakes too long. Just try to move forward and get out of the situation."

Ash is rarely this serious, so I take his words to heart.

"I'll try," I say.

He nods and heads back inside, but I stay on the bench and try to pull myself together.

I'm on that bench for a long, long time.

TWENTY-SEVEN
BIANCA

"ALRIGHT. Just a little more paperwork and this house will be good to go for the next owners," the realtor says to me.

"Great," I say with a little fake pep, even though I'm crumbling inside.

I've been crumbling for the whole week since the wedding and Waylon's rejection. Sadie definitely notices, because she won't leave my lap if I'm sitting and insists on snuggling all the time. At least she makes me feel a tiny bit better.

But she can't stop the constant loop in my thoughts — that no one will ever choose me for me. That I need to offer them something else to make me worthwhile. With Kyler, he obviously wanted my connections. And with my exes and friends before that, they wanted clout or something equally stupid.

Waylon hurts the most, though. He doesn't want any industry connections or clout. So the more he got to know me, the more he probably realized that I don't have much to offer him. Or at least I don't have enough to offer for him to stay.

I sign a bunch of paperwork and head out to my car. I sit there, zoned out, for a few minutes. It's Friday, and I'm done with work. But I want to be alone, but I don't want to go home yet. Even seeing Waylon's house or hearing Duke and Murphy playing in the yard makes my heart ache.

But sitting in the parking lot, staring off into space, probably looks weird. I start up and drive home. Or to the house, I guess, because home isn't a definite spot anymore.

When I get home, I let Sadie out before laying down on the couch. When I broke up with Kyler, I had a good, long moping period, but it didn't feel like this. Like I've been excavated and left open in the hot sun.

I look just as rough as I feel too. I've been too exhausted to wrap my hair at night or even get my satin pillowcase out, so my curls are a little all over the place. And I have dark circles underneath my eyes that I haphazardly covered with a little concealer.

My phone rings — it's my mom. The urge to cry suddenly takes over me, but I tamp it way down. If Mom senses that I'm upset, she'll get my dad, then Dad will also be upset.

"Hi, B," Mom says when I answer the phone.

"Hey." I scoop up Sadie and rest her on my stomach.

"What's up? You sound tired."

I squeeze the bridge of my nose. Of course Mom picked up on something right away.

"Just a long week," I say. "But I just sold the house, so I won't be here too much longer."

"You did? That's great." I hear Mom muffle the phone, as

if muting doesn't exist, and calls out to my dad, "Bianca sold the house."

"She did what?" Dad yells back.

"She sold the house!" Mom says louder. "Anyway, since you sold the house, when are you moving to New York? We can meet up with each other whenever you get settled. Or if you want help with your move, we can do that too."

I take in a deep breath and let it out. "Yeah, maybe."

"You don't sound very excited," Mom says. "Do you like it down there?"

I pet Sadie. "It's complicated."

"Complicated?"

"I do like it, but it's..." I try to search for a word that distills the dread I feel at the thought of leaving while also having the urge to flee despite having friends here who I'll miss. "Complicated."

"Mmhm. I'm guessing you'll tell me whenever you're ready," she says. I breathe out a sigh of relief. "Just know that we're here and we love you. No matter what happens."

I stare up at the ceiling, tears stinging my eyes. My social life might be a confusing shit show, but I can always count on my parents to have my back. And a lot of people don't even have that.

"Love you too," I say.

Mom shifts gears and starts telling me about their latest vacation and some event that she went to that had a bunch of drama. It's nice to just listen to her talk about something that isn't related to Jepsen or my life at all.

"We've got dinner reservations, so I have to go get ready," Mom says eventually. "But tell us when you're moving. We have a few things planned and we want to make sure we're there when you need us."

I don't need the pressure to figure out when I'm leaving, but I know Mom means well. "Okay, I will."

We say our goodbyes and I hang up. Sadie is lightly snoring on my chest, which soothes the bits of nerves left over. I'm not sure what kind of magic my mom does to make everything seem like it's going to be okay, but I *almost* feel like I'll be able to sort all of this out and mend my shattered heart.

I turn on the TV and let it play some show I don't have to pay too much attention to. It's a good distraction until Mom's PR company's name pops up on my phone. My stomach leaps up into my chest.

"Hi, Bianca?" Flo says. Her grave tone makes my stomach flip upside down.

"Yes, hi."

"Do you have a second?" Flo asks.

"Yep. I'm guessing it's bad, so feel free to just drop it on me," I say.

"Some personal photos of you and less than flattering texts have been leaked online. The source isn't clear, yet, though."

I close my eyes and take a deep breath through my nose. I expect a rush of tears coming to my eyes, but I just feel empty.

"Can you send them over?" I ask, even though there's only one person who could have leaked them. "I can pin down the source based on that."

"Sure, just a second." I hear her typing on her end. "Check your inbox. The photos aren't more than what you'd wear on a swimsuit shoot, to be honest. The texts are more damning.

I grab my laptop and open my email. The photos attached are exactly the ones that I knew they'd be — the ones I'd sent to Kyler and wished I'd never sent, even though they aren't too racy. Somewhere deep in my gut I knew that he'd probably try to use this against me, no matter how tame they are in comparison to my normal modeling photos.

The texts, which I sent right after those pics, are a whole lot worse, though.

I remember the day I sent them — Kyler had texted yet another girl that I "didn't need to worry about," some up and coming model. In a jet-lagged, crabby state, I let it rip on her, dragging her and calling her everything I could think of before laying into Kyler. I don't even want to read them.

It wasn't my finest moment, but knowing the context at least makes it make some sense. But still. It's not a good look, and attaching the photos with the texts make it hard to deny it's me.

"I jinxed it, Sadie. Of course Kyler wouldn't leave me alone." I blow out a breath and she puts her paws on my chest, licking my chin. "He literally said that he'd fuck me over, didn't he?"

Sadie just curls up against me and sighs, like she's tired too.

Maybe this is something that could blow over, but if Kyler is on a revenge kick, he could blow it up more. It's not the way I wanted to start my time in New York, but it might have to be.

TWENTY-EIGHT
WAYLON

THE ONE UPSIDE TO work being slammed is that I barely have time to think about Bianca. I still do, of course, but I need to focus most of the time.

Shit gets darker whenever I go home. There's only so much working out and organizing and studying I can do. I've slept like shit since then because my thoughts keep spinning until I just pass out.

Today has been a little slower, with routine appointments and treatments all day. It's given me more time to think than I'd like. But my last two appointments seem more involved than the ones I've had all day without the issues the pets are facing being life-threatening. At least there's that to look forward to.

"Your last two appointments rescheduled," Marisol says about fifteen minutes before my second to last appointment.

"Oh." Great. I run my hands through my hair and check my watch. I don't want to spend even more time at home. "I can stay until close for emergency walk-ins, if you need me to."

"Okay, sure." Marisol shrugs and doesn't ask anymore questions.

I work on my paperwork and prepare for tomorrow, snagging one of the rescue kittens to cuddle while I do. I'm just twenty minutes away from wrapping up when Marisol pops her head into the back.

"Dr. Stryker, we have a last minute appointment," she says, glancing between me and the lobby down the hall. "It's Catherine and Buttons."

I blow out a breath. I usually don't handle Buttons, Catherine's mixed breed dog, because of our history, but I'm the only vet left here for the day. I hate being around her but I'd never refuse any animal that needed help.

"I'll be there in a second." I stand up and put the foster kitten back.

Catherine is sitting in the lobby, Buttons on her lap. Her hair is in the messy bun it's always in when she's stressed, plus leggings and a t-shirt. I have no idea what's going on in her life aside from whatever's going on with Buttons, but she's not as put together as she usually is.

"Hey," I say. Her eyes snap up to mine. "What's going on with Buttons?"

"Dr. Healey saw him the other week for this rash he has and it looks like it's getting worse," she says putting Buttons down.

She got Buttons toward the end of when we were dating, so Buttons knows me. He wags his tail and sniffs my leg before I guide us into one of the exam rooms. I shut the door behind us and sit down on the floor. Buttons isn't big enough to be considered a big dog, but he's not small either. His black and white fur looks healthy and fluffy, aside from one spot near his back left leg.

I check over his rash and she fills me in on what Dr. Healey said. Buttons tries to climb in my lap to cuddle and a pang rings in my chest. We agreed that he was Catherine's dog when she adopted him, but I always assumed he'd be ours. Splitting up and not having him was another punch to the gut on top of everything else.

"We'll try some anti-fungals next," I say. "And if that doesn't work, come back to the office and we can try a different approach."

Buttons turns in a circle on my lap, nearly stepping on my balls, and flops down, completely content. The rush of memories is like being hit by a train. I thought we were in the happiest days of our relationship when we first adopted him — I thought we'd healed from the first time she cheated, but she was out there hooking up with other guys.

"Is it a pill? You know he doesn't like pills," she says, eyeing her dog on my lap.

"It's a shampoo. Give him a bath weekly with it, and apply a soothing cream. We'll get you both of them," I say, trying to ignore her *you should have known that* tone. Other people — particularly Jada — picked up on it when we were together, but I missed it. Now it's so damn obvious that I can't believe I didn't notice it until someone pointed it out. What was my problem?

"Okay." She gets up and picks Buttons off my lap. Snatches, almost.

"I'll go write his prescriptions. They should be ready to pick up by tomorrow afternoon."

"Fine."

No thank you, apparently. Not that I'm surprised. She lost her polite sparkle once we broke up, almost as if she'd been this way all along. I hold in a sigh so I don't start anything with her and get out of the room as soon as possible to write Buttons' prescriptions.

Someday I won't feel completely thrown off by having a normal interaction with her, but today isn't that day.

It's not that I'm wrestling with lingering feelings of betrayal — I've accepted the fact that she was two-faced for our second shot at a relationship. I just can't get past the fact that I thought I knew her so well but I was so fucking wrong. Her condescending attitude, her judgment of shit that really isn't all that weird. Now it all looks obvious. Though maybe she just got a whole lot worse the more time went on.

I can't believe I was so blinded by love. Or by the person I assume she was.

I wrap up the day, still playing irritating memories on loop that make my brain ache like a bruise. Jeremiah's text asking if I want to get drinks comes at just the right time — I need to decompress.

I head home, shower, then take Duke to the bar. Jeremiah and Jada are in the back at our normal table. The look Jada is giving me has some venom in it, so I'm assuming Bianca told her that we "broke up". Or maybe Bianca even told her everything about this fake relationship and she hates me for lying.

"The only reason why I'm not going to rip you in half is because you were my friend first," Jada says. "But it sounds like you really fucked with Bianca's heart, so I'm still kind of pissed at you."

I sigh and slide onto a stool. "I understand."

"So? Explain," Jada says.

"Let the man breathe and get a drink." Jeremiah pushes an empty glass and the pitcher toward me. Usually we do the pitcher because it's cheaper, but I almost want something a little stronger.

I pour myself a drink and down half of it. I'm tired of lying — I lied to Mom and it's hurt our relationship. I don't want my best friends finding out the same way Mom did.

"There's more to Bianca and I's relationship than I told you both," I say.

I tell them everything — from our awkward first meeting in person, to the fake date that spiraled into our arrangement, to what happened at the wedding. They listen intently, eyebrows going up higher and higher.

"That's fucking crazy, man," Jeremiah says.

"Which part?" I ask.

"The whole thing. Especially the fact that you let a woman go who you have feelings for and vice versa because of fucking Catherine." He leans back, drumming his fingers on the table. "You know she was the worst. Bianca is very clearly not the worst. So what are you doing?"

"For real. And Bianca seemed really torn up about it, by the way," Jada says. "Or at least over text."

"Have you seen her in person?" I ask. I know I hurt her, but the thought of her being alone and hurt is even worse.

"No. I'm not going to crowd her unless she asks for company."

I rest my elbows on the table and run my hands down my face. Duke lifts his head and rests it on my foot.

"But again, what are you even doing?" Jeremiah asks. "I

get being gun shy, but there's a difference between gun shy and completely illogical."

I bristle. "I'm not completely illogical."

"You kind of are." Jeremiah sits back in his seat. "Bianca's not Catherine. We knew Catherine, and to be honest, she always had her issues way back in college."

"But you guys didn't say anything when I took her back?" I pour myself another drink, then a glass of water.

"We did, dumb-dumb," Jada says. Jeremiah shoots her a look "Sorry for being harsh, but we did. As gently as possible because you were making heart eyes at each other for some reason. We didn't want to shit all over your parade, especially since you knew her better than we ever did."

I blow a breath out of my nose. I *was* a little too into her — Catherine was smart, funny, and charming a lot of the time. And we were seen as similar by everyone else. The overachievers who "did everything right".

God, I was so stupid.

"Seriously, just think about it since we're here to keep you on track," Jeremiah says, leveling me with a look that's more serious than I've ever seen him. "Think about the last time you saw Catherine. I know things are tainted because hindsight is 20/20, but just do it. Is she anything like Bianca whatsoever?"

"I saw her today," I say. "And...she was pretty fucking terrible. She wasn't *that* bad when we dated, but to be honest, I saw little glimpses of those traits today when we dated. And I've been pissed off at myself ever since."

Now the constant churn of memories from earlier starts to shift. Catherine isn't a great person, especially not for me. But just because she was doesn't mean that I have to beat myself up over it. I can just take what I learned and fully move on.

"Don't be pissed at yourself for how you felt in the past," Jeremiah says. "That's some bullshit. Because your feelings were involved and you made some mistakes. We all fuck up. But what's even more messed up is letting all the bad thoughts you've had about how things went with Catherine keep you from something good."

"Seriously. And based on the way you and Bianca are together, there's a lot of good there," Jada adds.

I hear what they're saying, but being able to shut off those old thoughts isn't as easy as hearing and agreeing with a good argument.

But the more I let it sink in, the more what they've said makes sense. Being with Bianca always feels easy — I don't have to live up to absurd expectations. I just have to be myself. I never felt like that with a romantic partner. It was a feeling I assumed I had to go to my friends for. But I can have that feeling with the person I love.

Except I've clearly hurt Bianca and I have no idea how to fix things. She's been rejected and fucked over by too many people in her life to easily forgive — not that I deserve her forgiveness just because I'm falling for her. But I want it more than anything.

TWENTY-NINE
BIANCA

GOING over to Jada's for one last girls' night is bittersweet. When I told them I was moving this soon, they were shocked, but accepted it. I didn't go into detail as to how I got things wrapped up so fast and they didn't ask. My stuff is mostly packed and my flights to New York are booked for the day after tomorrow.

Soon Jepsen will just be a part of my past. Something I look back on five or ten years from now and feel too many things about. Or maybe it'll just be those weird few months I had by then because my life ends up being amazing. But somehow, I doubt it. This place, of all places, has burrowed into me for good.

I pull up to Jada's apartment, which is next door to her family's hotel.

"Hey!" Jada opens the door wearing leggings and a big Crescent Hill University sweatshirt. "Come in."

I've never been here, but it's very her — bold and fun. Everything should clash and feel too loud, but somehow, it feels just right. Something in the oven smells amazing, like sugar. Bookcases are all over the place, with books stuffed in without much rhyme or reason.

"You look…" Jada looks me up and down as I pass her.

"Not great?" I catch sight of myself in a big, ornate mirror in the short hall between the entryway and living room. I look more alive than I did before and I put some effort into my hair today. But I still look colorless and tired.

"Well, I was trying not to say it. But it's written all over your face." Jada squeezes my arm. "But that's what we're here for."

"Sorry. This was supposed to be a fun last night together," I say with a wince.

"We can get the feels out and have fun after."

Rose is curled up on the couch when we get to the living room. I let Sadie out of her tote and she runs over to Rose, leaping up into her lap to say hello.

"Hey!" Rose says, petting Sadie. "How are you feeling?"

Her eyes are soft and sympathetic, which makes me want to burst into tears. It's nice to know that people have my back, even when I'm miserable and less-than-fun to be around.

"Not great," I admit, sitting down on the other end of the couch.

"I'm sorry." Rose puts Sadie down between us. "Here, take Sadie."

"I think Sadie is tired of me squishing her and listening to me cry." I take her anyway and she sits in my lap with a yawn. "But I'll be leaving soon to New York and I'll have a packed schedule."

The idea of all the crap I have to do to when I get there,

then all the stuff we'll have to do for the business fills me with dread and preemptive exhaustion.

"You just sounded like you're moving straight to hell to be beaten," Jada says, disappearing into the kitchen.

"Yeah, I kind of feel like that." I pause. "That's way too dramatic, sorry."

"You just got dumped. You can feel like shit." Rose snags the chips, catching Sadie's attention. "And moving sucks."

I sink further into the couch, holding Sadie back from leaping on Rose's chips.

"It's kind of tiring, but I can't just turn the feelings off." I sniff. "It's more complicated than I want it to be."

"Yeah, Waylon told me what he did. What you both did." Jada returns and stretches out on the floor like what she said is no big deal and Sadie hops down to join her.

"He did?" I freeze.

"Yep." Jada pats her stomach so Sadie climbs onto her. "And he feels like shit about it all. Especially for fucking things up with you."

"Oh." At least I don't have to go into the full story with them, then. "You aren't shocked? By what we did?"

"Wait, wait, what are you talking about?" Rose asks, offering a chip to us.

After eating a few chips, I give her a super brief summary of my fake-turned-sort-of-real relationship with Waylon, including the spa and my plans to leave for New York. Jada lays on the floor, Sadie resting on her stomach, taking it all in.

"Holy shit." Rose is sitting up now, cross-legged. "I can't believe it."

"I'm sorry." I scratch Sadie's back, right before her bald

patch starts. "It was sort of a thrown together plan. We shouldn't have lied."

"No, not that. I just can't believe you two were fake the whole time and we didn't even realize it. Even Wes was fooled. Then again, it did turn real."

"Mostly. Except I wasn't enough to go full-on serious with." I let Sadie have one chip, which she inhales in an instant.

"Nope, no blaming yourself on this. This is on Waylon for being an idiot. You're more than enough," Jada says, sitting up. She brought out the sugar cookies she made while I was recapping the story to Rose. The shape is a little spread out because she used vegan butter, but they're still good. "And I think he knows that. He just has to make a move."

"He hasn't even texted me." And meanwhile, I've typed and deleted about a million texts to him.

"He'll do it. I know he will," Jada says with her usual confidence.

"I'm moving, though. And he's definitely staying." The sadness spiral I've been caught up in for days comes back. "So why would he bother?"

"Because he should know y'all have something special." Jada accidentally drops a chip and Sadie lunges for it. "I've known Waylon for a long ass time and I've never, ever seen him look more relaxed and at home with someone. And if anyone needs to chill the fuck out and take it easy, it's him."

I mull over what she said for a second, grabbing a cookie. Sure, he feels that way, but how can I not be upset that he has feelings for me and still chose to ignore them? It wasn't even like he gave the excuse of us doing long distance or anything like that.

"But I'm still pissed off at him as much as I want him," I say. "And then there's the whole issue of long distance. The spa will be in New York and as much as I've been able to work on it here, I don't think I can live here full time. At least for a while."

"The long-distance thing is surmountable," Jada says. "It's not like he's living on Mars."

"It is harder, though," Rose adds. "But yeah, not impossible. And even if it doesn't work, you can at least try."

"Exactly," Jada says.

I murmur in agreement. They're making sense, but it doesn't change the fact that I'm moving and he hasn't said anything.

"I'm not going to be telling you to forgive him, as much as I love Waylon," Jada adds when I stay silent. "He has to earn you back. You're more than enough."

"You are," Rose echoes.

"Thank you." I swallow the lump in my throat.

I'm going to miss them so much more than I ever thought I would. I'm used to getting support from Kaitlyn and my parents, but having Rose and Jada on my side, even though Waylon is their friend too, hits different.

"Sorry, I'm still bringing down the energy. Weren't we going to watch a movie?"

"Yes!" Jada pops up and grabs some Blu-ray boxes from a stack next to her TV. "We have some options."

"I still can't believe you own the physical copies instead of just streaming everything." Rose grabs one of the boxes.

"Hey, I actually own these. Streaming can snatch my faves away at any point." Jada spreads a few more Blu-rays on the table for us to choose from. "I have more where that came from."

We rifle through her extensive collection and finally choose a dumb romcom that only Jada has seen. It's light and funny enough to distract me, at least for the most part. But instead of thoughts of Waylon distracting me, the things Jada said ring in my head – that I'm enough as I am and that Waylon will have to do more than throw a few gifts at me or send a text to win me back.

THIRTY

WAYLON

LIKE ASH SUGGESTED, I give Mom space. And even more space. And then some.

It's killing me, but I don't want to mess things up by talking to her too soon. I think I've already fucked it up with Bianca again. She left for New York before I could go talk to her, and she hasn't responded to any of my texts.

Jada refuses to give me any hints as to how to crack her code, but that's fair. I need to figure this out on my own.

Whenever I get a text these days, I nearly jump out of my skin. Usually it's Wes or work or some spam. But this morning, it's Mom.

Mom: Let's get lunch today.

I'll take it. I reply with a yes and wait for a break in my appointments. My stomach turns in knots the moment I'm done seeing a puppy who'd eaten (and thankfully passed) a whole toy. This is my mom. I know she loves me, but I don't know how I'll be able to face her disappointment again. At least I've had time to process it and accept how deeply I messed up.

I walk down to the café that Mom picked out, which we rarely ever go to. Maybe it feels like more neutral ground to her.

She's sitting outside with Lady again, and waves to me when she spots me. Her expression is hard to read, a far cry from the usual smile she has when greeting me. Lady's thrilled that I'm there, of course. She'll always be happy to see me.

"Hi, Mom," I say, sitting down with a sigh. "I'm sorry. For everything."

"I can tell you are." She crosses one leg over the other and looks at the menu on the table in front of her instead of at me.

"I really am," I add. "I shouldn't have lied to you about anything, much less put on a whole ruse to trick you. It was a dumb idea, and I should have just dealt with the issue head on."

Mom's eyes finally soften and relief floods me.

"I know, sweetheart," she says. "And I'm glad you gave me time to cool off."

"Ash told me that would be a good idea." I down half the cup of water that was at the table when I arrived.

"Ash would know." She chuckles. "My only question is why? You've never done anything like this before."

I take a deep breath, then let it out. I've been thinking of ways to explain myself this whole time, but now that I have to tell her, the words aren't flowing. Thankfully a waiter comes to take our orders. I just get what Mom gets so I don't have to think.

When the waiter leaves, Mom looks at me expectantly.

"I just..." I rake a hand through my hair. "The pressure, Mom."

"What pressure?" She sips her water, looking genuinely confused. Despite my relief, I feel a tinge of irritation too. How does she not know?

"The pressure you put on me to be everything." I sit back in my seat. "When I was a kid, it was about grades and getting into the best schools, which helped me. But now the pressure to be involved in everything in town even though I've said no. And the pressure to settle down with the perfect person...it's a lot. It feels like the goal post always moves."

Mom frowns, taken aback.

"I just..." Mom is at a loss for words for once. "I had no idea. I just assumed because you did a lot in the past that you'd want that kind of life."

"I don't. I'd like to be involved in the board, but in my own way. And I'd like to not run myself ragged like I did when I was younger. I want to enjoy some down time instead of always chasing success, as good as it feels."

Mom studies my face, like she's trying to understand me – *really* understand me -- for the first time.

"My pressure on you to date is what led you to put together this plan with Bianca?" Mom finally asks.

I nod. "It was all me. Bianca had her own reasons for this, but it wasn't her idea. Don't put any blame on her."

"I wasn't going to." Mom looks down at her hands for a moment. "But I'm so sorry, sweetheart. I made a lot of assumptions, and they hurt you. I just know that you're so helpful and kind and I just wanted you to share that. In the way I saw fit rather than how you'd naturally do it, I'm now seeing."

The apology soothes the raw part of me that's been getting worse and worse for years. Now Mom sees – actually sees. I doubt everything will magically change overnight, but it's a step in the right direction.

"But Bianca was a sweet girl and seemed good for you, so at least something positive came from this. And she very much liked you." A tinge of disappointment colors her last sentence. This time, I accept it. "It looked like you liked her too."

"I do. But I let my past problems get in the way of letting myself be with her." I swallow.

'Because of Catherine?'

I nod. Lady wedges herself between me and Mom, putting her head on my leg. Her warmth is comforting.

"I don't know how to fix it. I *want* to fix it. But now she's going to New York," I say.

"It's easier to stay in touch with people than ever," Mom points out. "You could do long distance and figure something out. If it's meant to be, it'll work out."

That sounds surprisingly romantic coming from Mom. Her relationship with my dad seems to be based on him finding her beautiful and her liking that he mostly leaves her be to do whatever stuff she likes to do. Plus, money.

"I'm not sure what to text her." I rest my hand on Lady's head.

"Texts? Oh, honey." Mom sighs. "You can't make a declaration of love over text. What is this young people nonsense?"

"Then what should I do? How do I actually get through

to her and fix this?" I don't want to be like her ex and constantly bother her.

Mom drums her nails on the table. "I don't know her the way you do, so I don't know. But what would be meaningful to her?"

The waiter returns with our food and quickly leaves us.

"A lot of things," I say, taking a fry off my plate "But knowing which meaningful thing to do is the hard part."

"I know you'll figure it out, hun." Mom unfolds the napkin in her lap. "I have a good feeling about you two."

That's the other side of my mom that I appreciate the most. She'll always support me with everything she has. I'll need all the support I can get.

THIRTY-ONE
BIANCA

EVERY SINGLE DAY that I've been in New York, I've gotten a little gift from Waylon. Dark chocolates. Flowers I'd mentioned to him offhand. Some snacks I loved from Tennessee. Even a special pie Gladys made for me without dairy.

The gifts are sweet and thoughtful, but they aren't quite *right*. Anyone can buy me gifts, but I need more so I know he's serious. I refuse to crack until I'm absolutely sure he's willing to meet me where I want to be. I owe myself that after all of this.

But the gifts do make me miss him. Even with all the exhausting things I have going on – the move, the spa, the PR mess that's come from Kyler's attempt at slandering me – Waylon still pops into my head. Whenever I see a dog on the street or a meme he'd like, the ache for him returns with a vengeance.

"Hey, do you want lunch?" Kaitlyn asks. "We have that

meeting soon. There's that new bowl place down the street that sounds pretty good."

"What?" I look up from my laptop and blink, scratching Sadie between her ears. As always, she's on my lap. We're in the office space we rented since Kaitlyn doesn't work well from home. "Sure? And what's this meeting again?"

"With an investor," she says.

I wait for her to say more, but she doesn't.

"Okay...? That's a little vague."

"He's great. I promise." She taps around on her phone and hands it to me. "Here's the menu."

I pick out what I want in the bowl and give her the phone back. The spa is the bright spot in my life right now. It'll still be about a year until we can officially open since we need to get a few more investors involved, like this mystery guy we're meeting with today. But that means I have a whole year to throw myself into something I care about and let the media mess around me fade.

Time flies and Kaitlyn goes to grab the food from the front desk. When she returns, I hear her voice mixing with a very familiar one.

Sadie leaps off my lap and sprints down the hallway, barking. Only one person could get that reaction from her. My heart starts pounding out of my chest and I look around like I can grab onto something that keeps me stable.

But nothing could keep me stable when I see Waylon again, Sadie content in his arms. He's in jeans and a button-down, glasses on. Of course, he looks great, but that doesn't matter as much as his presence. He fills up the space and all the air in it, taking my breath away.

"Hey," Waylon says softly.

"Hi." I swallow, fiddling with my necklace.

"Sorry, I had to say he was an investor so you'd see him," Kaitlyn says, putting down my lunch. "I'll let you two sort everything out."

Waylon and I look at each other, not speaking, until the door shuts behind Kaitlyn.

"Am I crossing a line by dropping in like this?" he asks, still standing closer to the door.

I open my mouth, then close it. If it were anyone else but him, it'd feel like that. But I've been aching to see him again since I moved. *He's* the gift that I wanted, not any of the nice things he sent. Living proof that he's serious about us and not just trying to pacify me with gifts.

"Good." He takes a step closer, looking down at his shoes for a moment before looking up at me. "I debated with Jada for days about just coming up here and saying what I should have said before you left. Or at the wedding. Or even before the wedding when I knew I was falling in love with you. But I don't think sending gifts is enough."

My heart leaps into my throat. He's falling in love with me?

"I'm sorry I let the past get in the way of what was right in front of me." He finally closes the gap between us. My legs are too weak to stand, so he extends that hand that isn't holding Sadie and pulls me up to my feet. "I knew deep in my gut that you're different and that we fit together in a way I shouldn't ignore.

I nod, my stomach doing somersaults. My mouth and brain have disconnected from each other, so I still can't say anything.

"I want you for you, Bianca. When we're together, it just

feels easy in a way I've never felt with anyone else. I have no idea how our relationship would work since you're here and I'm back in Jepsen, but I want to make it work," he says. Then, he pauses. "If you want to."

"Sorry, I...I'm just a little tongue-tied," I finally say, shaking my head. My whole body is flushed with heat and I want to think coherently, but can't.

"It's okay." He squeezes my hand. "I'm just hoping you'll say yes."

"Yes," I blurt. "I want this. Us. I want to make it work. I'll live in Jepsen and fly up here if I have to. As long as we're together."

"Really?" Relief washes over him, his shoulders lowering, and he beams.

"Really."

He pulls me in for a kiss, squishing Sadie between us. It hasn't been that long since we've kissed, but I soak him in like we've been apart for years. We fit together just right, and feeling him against me is like coming home after a long, exhausting day.

Sadie interrupts the moment, licking both of us under our chins.

"Sadie," I say with a laugh.

"She's just giving her blessing, I guess." Waylon pets her.

"Good, because I wouldn't want to date someone she didn't like." I give him a cheeky smile.

"Good thing Sadie loves me then," he says. "She'll be excited to see Duke and Murphy again when you get back to Jepsen."

"I'll just have to tell Kaitlyn that I'm moving back," I say, smoothing his collar even though it's not rumpled. "How did you get in touch with her anyway?"

"Jada. She follows Kaitlyn on Instagram and connected us." Waylon runs his thumb along my cheek, looking at me with so much warmth that it almost makes me tear up. "I didn't want to pull a move the way your ex did, so I figured I'd ask if you'd be open to this."

"What if we never mention each other's shitty exes ever again?" I squeeze his shoulder, then his upper arm. "And just think about us in the future?"

Waylon's smile brightens even more, which I didn't even realize was possible. I want to imprint the memory of it into a safe part of my brain.

"That sounds like a really good idea," he says, leaning down to kiss me again.

EPILOGUE
BIANCA

ONE YEAR *later*

The lobby of the spa is already packed with people and the opening party has barely begun. Kaitlyn and I have been meeting on video calls in between to get all the details right, and in between when I fly up from Jepsen.

My stomach churns. What if it all fails? I'm still doing freelance social media work for Stryker Liquors, but —

"It'll be great," Waylon says, coming up behind me. Do I really look that tense? He rests a hand on my lower back and kisses my temple. "Look at all these people."

"But —"

"Shh." Waylon kisses me on the lips to quiet me. "Even if it doesn't work — which it will — you can at least celebrate all the hard work you've done to get this place open. It looks great and you're going to help a lot of people."

I smile and step closer to him, letting myself get wrapped up in his arms.

"Thank you." I run my hands up and down his arms. "And are you ready to meet my parents?"

Waylon goes a little pale this time. "Um...yes."

"You sound so sure," I tease.

"I'm terrified but can you blame me? I want them to like me," he says.

"They'll love you because I do," I say, kissing him. "I need to go greet a few people, but I'll find you, okay?"

"Okay. Good luck." He kisses me again and lets me go into the crowd.

I saved up all the mental energy to network tonight, and I work the crowd as the event starts, saying hello to so many people that I get dizzy.

"Hold on, now," my mom says, catching me by the arm. "We've been trying to catch you all night but you've been so busy."

I throw my arms around her, then my dad, who's standing behind her. I've seen them a few times since I moved to Jepsen, but seeing them in person always lifts my mood.

"I'm so glad to finally see you," I say.

"We're so proud of you, honey," Mom says, cupping my cheeks. "I still can't believe you live in *Tennessee*."

I laugh. "It's not Mars."

"But it's so different and so far. And you're making it," Mom says. "And we met your boyfriend, by the way."

"I wanted to introduce you all formally," I say, my shoulders slumping. I hope Waylon was okay.

"It's fine. We just bumped into each other, and I recognized him from your Instagram. We had a very nice chat." Mom squeezes my shoulders.

I started posting Waylon's face once we got back together. The shitstorm that Kyler caused by leaking my texts and photos took a while to die down because of the photos of Waylon, but the chatter eventually stopped. Did my reputation among a certain subset of people take a hit? Maybe. But I've stopped caring about what random people on social media think. The only things that matter are my friends and family.

"Very nice," Dad says, echoing Mom.

"Okay...?" My parents are a little weird, but they're being extra weird.

"We'll let you go. Find us later, okay?" Mom gives me one more kiss on the cheek and Dad hugs me, leaving me back to the crowd.

The event goes beautifully — people are interested in booking services and love the brands we're going to carry. The more I sift through the crowd, the more I see people from Jepsen. Rose and Wes made it up, as did Jada. Even Waylon's parents came.

Delia's been lowering the pressure on Waylon, and by extension, the pressure on me, ever since they talked. Waylon has been a part of the shelter's board in his own way, focusing mostly on the animals and how they can best allocate the money to pay for treatments.

The event runs late, until we literally need to usher people out the door. Only our families remain, mingling outside.

"I'm so wiped," I say to Waylon, leaning against a wall.

"I'd be concerned if you weren't." He takes my hand. "C'mon, let me show you something."

"What? Where?" I let him guide me toward the back in

one of the rooms of the spa — one of my favorite spots. It's much more spa-like than the rest of the space, with calming colors and bamboo. Someone's lit a bunch of candles in here, giving it a romantic air.

"Mm, what are we getting up to in here?" I ask, pressing myself against him. "Our families are literally around the corner."

"I know." Waylon looks pale, even in the candlelight. "Because as much as I want to do that now, I need to do this before I lose the nerve."

Waylon gets on one knee. Symbolically, I know what this means. But my brain can't wrap itself around the fact that Waylon is *on one knee in front of me and holding a small velvet box*. Right in front of me.

"Bianca, I know we started off in a weird way. I never thought I'd ever fake a relationship," he says, opening the box. I just see a sparkly blur because I'm already starting to cry. He hasn't even finished talking yet, god. "But I never thought I'd end up with someone as incredible as you. Someone who I click with and can just sit there next to because we're that comfortable with each other. Will you marry me?"

I nod because I can't speak, and yank him to his feet so we can kiss. I can feel him smiling through it.

"Here, let me put this on," he says. "Rose said it was your size based on what she saw in your room."

"What a little spy," I say, sniffing and putting my hand out. He slides the ring on my finger and it's a perfect fit. It's gorgeous too, cut in a way that makes it glitter like crazy no matter what angle I look at it from. "I love it."

"C'mon, let's go to part two of the party," he says with a grin as he guides me outside.

"Wait, did you tell my parents you were proposing?" I ask. "Because they were acting really weird."

"Yep." He kisses the side of my neck. "But you weren't expecting this, were you?"

"Not tonight, no." I stop before we round the corner. "I'm so overwhelmed and excited and happy that I need a second."

"Okay, let's take it, then." He just holds me for a second, and I relax. His arms are my comfort spot every time.

I get over feeling overwhelmed, but the excitement and happiness? That's definitely here to stay.

THANKS FOR READING! Want a protective, brother's best friend novella set in the same universe as *Just the Tipsy*? Sign up for my newsletter at https://BookHip.com/RSGVPPZ and download it free! You'll also get updates on my upcoming books, looks behind the scenes, and some A+ memes.

Want to read Wes and Rose's story too? Check out *Sips About to Go Down*, a spicy rivals-to-lovers, forced proximity story! Keep reading for the blurb!

SIPS ABOUT TO GO DOWN

The only thing worse than being roommates with my rival?
Falling for him.

Returning to my small hometown after I crash and burn in the city is bad enough. Having my lifelong rival, Wes Stryker rub it in my face doesn't make it easier.

Even worse, I'm hired to help him pull his family's distillery out of a rough patch. Oh, and I'm forced to be his roommate. And that means dealing with his annoying flirting and one-upping all day, every day.

He's unbearably cocky, and his dimpled smile charms everyone with a pulse – except for me.

At least until he starts to make me ugly laugh and I see glimpses of his big heart under the side he shows everyone else. Resisting him when he wanders around the house in nothing but sweatpants, undressing me with his eyes? Not possible.

But I've sworn off charmers like him and the last man I let into my heart destroyed my confidence and my career. I won't make that mistake again.

Read Sips About to Go Down here!

ABOUT THE AUTHOR

Audrey Vaughn is a spicy small town romcom author who will show you all the memes and dog photos on her camera roll. She lives with her husband in Florida despite hating to sweat.

You can follow her on Instagram at @audreyvaughnbooks for some of these memes, plus updates on her upcoming books.

Printed in Dunstable, United Kingdom